Acclaim for Joan Wolf

"Wolf holds our interest by skillfully conjuring up a fascinating version of Rahab's story, successfully persuading us that the story is far more complex than merely a 'scarlet cord.'"

— *Publishers Weekly* review of
This Scarlet Cord

"Esther and the king make an appealing couple, and the supporting characters, even the one who comes to play the role of the villain, are three-dimensional and sympathetic. With a fast-paced plot and details that bring color to the story but don't weigh it down, this is an excellent start to Wolf's projected series of biblical romances."

— *Historical Novels Review,*
regarding *A Reluctant Queen*

"Wolf's latest gives readers a wonderful glimpse into the life of Queen Esther. Readers will enjoy getting to know her as a woman beset with political ambition and family rivalries . . . [R]eaders will . . . enjoy this Cinderella tale come to life."

— *Romantic Times* review of
A Reluctant Queen

"In *A Reluctant Queen* author Joan Wolf's creativity and excellent writing skills bring to life this powerful, timeless story of love, faith, and how God works His plans through ordinary people. She convincingly fills in the gaps of the biblical account with beautiful enhancements of the romance as well as the drama. While learning proper royal protocol and amid entanglement in palace intrigues, the unlikely happens: Queen Esther falls deeply in love with her husband. When she discovers the diabolical scheme of an evil high-ranking official against the Jewish nation, she has to make a decision that threatens her marriage and her life to save her people . . . With romance, wonderful characterizations, historically based accounts of the ancient Jewish and Persian cultures, and an amazing ending, this excellent read will be a hard-to-put-down winner for historical romance fans."

— *CBA Retailers + Resources*

This Scarlet Cord

Joan Wolf

THOMAS NELSON

Since 1798

NASHVILLE   DALLAS   MEXICO CITY   RIO DE JANEIRO

Published in Nashville, Tennessee, by Thomas Nelson. Thomas Nelson is a
registered trademark of Thomas Nelson, Inc.

Thomas Nelson, Inc., titles may be purchased in bulk for educational,
business, fund-raising, or sales promotional use. For information, please
e-mail SpecialMarkets@ThomasNelson.com.

Published in association with Natasha Kern Literary Agency, P.O. Box 1069,
White Salmon, WA 98672.

Library of Congress Cataloging-in-Publication Data

Wolf, Joan.
  This scarlet cord / Joan Wolf.
    p. cm.
  ISBN 978-1-59554-877-1 (trade paper)
  I. Title.
  PS3573.O486S27 2012
  813'.54—dc23   2012010908

Printed in the United States of America

12 13 14 15 16 QG 5 4 3 2 1

For my beloved sister, Patricia Demarest

A Note from the Author

THE NAME OF RAHAB'S HUSBAND APPEARS AT THE beginning of Matthew's gospel, where he is referred to as Salmon. His name also appears in Luke's genealogy, where he is called Sala.* Since Salmon has a rather unfortunate fishy connotation for the modern reader, I have chosen to go with Sala.

In regard to the language of the novel: the languages that would have been spoken by the characters in this book are Hebrew and Canaanite. These languages were closely related and were both part of the language group known as Western Semitic. What you will be reading is a "translation" into modern English.

---

* New Revised Standard Version, 1989.

PART ONE

First Meeting

One

THE CARAVAN WAS HALFWAY TO JOPPA WHEN IT WAS attacked. Roaming groups of bandits were not uncommon in Canaan, but usually a large group of people traveling together was safe. These were not ordinary bandits, though; they were riding horses and wielding flashing bronze swords. The caravan was from a small farming village near Jericho and was composed of forty donkeys loaded down with the goods they hoped to ship from Joppa into Egypt. The villagers were virtually helpless before the onslaught.

Rahab was at the back of the caravan with her mother and two of her brothers. Her father and her other brothers were toward the front, walking with the donkeys that carried their casks of precious wine. The boys and men had only sticks, but they shouted at the women to get behind them and bravely prepared to defend their own.

At first, Rahab had been too startled to be afraid. Then, as one of her brothers pushed her behind him and she looked up to see an enormous horse bearing down upon them both, she screamed. The horse came on in a cloud of dust and Rahab felt her mother grab her cloak and pull her backward.

Her brother raised his stick and held it braced right at the height of the oncoming horse's chest. The horse swerved at the thrust and the horseman missed her brother with his thrusting sword. Rahab pulled herself from her mother's grasp so she could drag her brother away from the plunging horse. As she grasped his tunic, she spared one fierce glare of hatred for the man who had managed to right his seat on the horse and was coming on again.

There was chaos in the caravan. People were shouting and screaming and some of the loaded donkeys were being driven away by the bandits. The deadly swords cut down anyone who tried to go after the donkeys. Then before Rahab knew what was happening, the horseman plucked her away from her brother and lifted her to lie on her stomach before him on the horse.

Rahab fought. She kicked at the horse's legs, screamed, and squirmed to get away. The animal reared and she almost managed to slide down to safety. But cruel hands gripped her and the horse was swung around.

Rahab heard her mother shouting her name. "Mama! Mama!" she screamed back. She kicked at the horse again and the man holding her muttered something, then raised his fist and hit her hard on the chin.

Everything went dark.

When Rahab came to, she was lying flat on her back. Her head was pounding, her jaw felt as if it were on fire, and her mouth was dry as sand. She lay still and looked around. What had happened? Where was she? How had she gotten here? Why did she hurt so much?

She lifted her eyes and saw a tent roof over her; from outside the tent walls came the sound of strange male voices. She tried to sit up, but her head hurt too much. She waited, breathing slowly, then tried again, ignoring the pain.

As she sat there it slowly came back to her: the attack, the bandits, the horse, the man, her capture. It must have really happened because here she was in this unknown place. Had they taken anyone else? Her mother? Her father? Her brothers?

Rahab was ashamed of the hope that shot through her at this thought. Of course she wished her family was safe, but she didn't think she had ever wanted anything in her life as much as she wanted her father right now.

The flap to the tent opened and someone came in. Suddenly Rahab was terrified. Was it the man who had taken her? What did he want? She was only twelve years old—what good could she be to anyone? She stared at the cloaked figure coming toward her in the dimness of the tent, her heart hammering. When she saw the figure was actually a woman, she felt almost giddy with relief.

"Ah, you're awake," the woman said. She spoke Canaanite, but in an accent foreign to Rahab.

"I want my father," Rahab said, her voice trembling.

"Your father is not here, girl, and you'll have to get used to doing without him. Now, how are you feeling? I'm afraid Sahir hit you a little too hard; you've been out for quite a while."

You'll have to get used to doing without him? What did that mean? Was her father dead?

"Where is my father? My mother? My brothers?" she demanded. "Why am I here alone? Have you dared to hurt them?"

She would kill this woman if her family was dead. She would kill all of these people. She didn't care if she died too. She would do it.

Rahab stared as hard as she could at the ugly middle-aged woman who was speaking to her. "Where are they?" she repeated in a louder voice.

The woman shrugged. "I imagine they are on their way back to wherever they came from. The goods they were transporting so carefully to Joppa now belong to us. And you, my girl, apparently are one of those prizes, thanks to that idiot Sahir."

The woman bent over Rahab and put a hard hand on her forearm. "Get up and come outside. I want to look at you."

Rahab stumbled behind the woman out into the late day sunlight. Her headache ratcheted up as the brilliance of the day struck her eyes.

"Look at me," the woman said sharply.

Rahab, who was almost as tall as the woman, stared at her unblinkingly.

"Ah," the woman breathed as she looked Rahab over from her head to her feet. Then she grasped Rahab's sore chin in her fingers and turned her face slowly from one side to the other. "Perhaps Sahir was right after all. Even he has to be right sometimes, I suppose. You could be worth a fortune to us."

Rahab did not understand what the woman was talking about, but the calculating look in her eyes reminded Rahab of the way she had seen merchants look at wares they were thinking of buying. Her anger died, replaced by an intense, overpowering fear.

The woman took Rahab back into the tent and remained with her for the remainder of the night. Two men were posted outside the tent flap, defeating any hopes Rahab had of escape. Finally she slept.

When she woke in the morning, she could hear the noise from the camp outside. Men were talking and when a donkey brayed someone shouted a curse at it. She sat up, pushed her disheveled hair off her face, and looked around for the woman, whose name she had learned was Aya. The flap to the tent opened and the woman came in carrying a water jar.

"Drink," she said, pouring some of the water into a cup and handing it to Rahab. Rahab finished the cup and asked for more. After Rahab had finished the second cup, Aya said, "We will be leaving shortly. I'll bring you some bread and dates to break your fast."

"Wait!" Rahab cried as the woman started to leave. "You must tell me why you have taken me. You have our donkeys and our wine. You don't need me. Please, Aya, let me go!"

"Idiot," the woman said. "You are never going home to your pitiful little farm. You are going to Egypt, my girl. The great lords there have palaces a poor little peasant like you could never even dream of. You will dine off golden plates, eat perfectly prepared delicacies, and drink only the best of wines. You will be dressed in the finest of white linen and wear magnificent jewels to adorn your beauty. You will be cosseted as much as any grand Egyptian lady. One day you will thank us for what we have done for you. You'll see."

Rahab stared at the furrowed, sunburned face of Aya in amazement. What could she be talking about? Why should she be treated like some grand lady?

"Do you think I am an Egyptian?" she asked, wondering if Aya might be a little muddled in the head.

The woman cast her eyes upward in disbelief at such stupidity. "No, you are not an Egyptian, girl. That face never came out of Egypt. But it will be part of the spice, you see, that you are different."

"No, I don't see." Unlike most girls in her culture, Rahab was accustomed to speaking her mind. As the only girl, and the youngest in the family, she had been indulged far beyond the limits of most girl children. "What are you talking about?" she demanded. She knew her voice was surprisingly husky for one her age.

Aya's slanted brown eyes narrowed. She said slowly and clearly, "We are going to sell you, my dear. One of those debauched Egyptian lords will pay a fortune for a chance to get his hands on you. Sahir knew it the minute he saw your face." Her lips curled in a smile. "You are a defiant little thing too. I hear some of the lords relish a challenge."

Rahab did not fully understand what the woman was talking about, but she understood enough to know that, if these bandits had their way, her future would be horrible. They had something evil in mind for her and her skin prickled with fear. She couldn't help the tears that came into her eyes.

"Let me go home," she begged. "Please, please, let me go home."

The tent fold opened again and this time a man came in. He was dressed in the usual costume of Canaan, a tunic that stopped halfway between his knees and his ankles, with leather sandals on his feet. His hair was mixed with gray but his beard was still mostly brown.

He addressed himself to Aya. "I want to see this so-called prize myself before I go to the expense of shipping her off to Egypt."

Aya gestured toward the trembling Rahab. "There she is."

"Bring her outside so I can see better."

Rahab tried to hold her ground, but Aya pushed her so hard she fell to her knees.

"Get up," the woman said with contempt. "You'll only make trouble for yourself by resisting."

In the part of Rahab's brain that had not been paralyzed by fear, she realized the truth of this statement and walked out of the tent without further protest.

The early morning sky was cloudless. It was autumn, and there was always the possibility of clouds, and perhaps even rain, coming in later, but the bright light showed Rahab the line of men on horseback and the huge collection of loaded donkeys that would make up their train.

Rahab summoned all her courage and said to the man contemptuously, "You are filthy thieves who prey on good, hard-working people, and I despise you."

The man laughed. "I see we have a spitfire here." He grabbed Rahab's chin as Aya had done and held her face up to him. Her instinct was to pull away, but the pain in her jaw reminded her of what these people could do. She stared over his shoulder, pretending he was not there.

"Amazing," the man said. He dropped his hand and Rahab backed away. His eyes raked up and down her body. "How old are you?"

"Twelve."

"You look younger. Which is good—not a child but not yet a woman." He reached out and ran a rough hand down the front of Rahab's tunic. She gasped and pulled away.

"Sweet little buds." He looked at Aya. "She is perfect. We will get good money from the slavers for her."

Rahab finally understood. "No!" she screamed. "No! No! No! I won't be a slave! You can't make me!"

"Oh, I rather think we can," the evil man said. "Tie her up, Aya, but be careful. I don't want her marked; it will affect her value."

"Aye, Ugar. I understand."

Rahab fought, but she was helpless against the strength of the two men who came to help Aya bind her hands and feet and load her into a litter.

Two

"It's a little bigger than Ramac, eh?" Nahshon asked his son, who seemed to have become as tall as he was overnight.

"More than a little," Sala replied as he looked around the teeming waterfront. Gaza was one of the greatest ports on the Great Sea, a stronghold that once was part of Canaan but had been annexed by Egypt years before. Sala's father was a successful merchant in the smaller port of Ramac, farther north on the coast of Canaan, and he was in Gaza to purchase a new boat to accommodate his increasing shipping business. Nahshon might be a Jew, but everyone knew the Egyptians made the best ships in the world. And when it came to business, Nahshon was not fussy about who he associated with.

Father and son stood together under the bright afternoon sun, their eyes taking in the sights in front of them. Dark-skinned porters carried heavy loads on their backs to and from the many ships docked along the wharves; merchants haggled over the prices of their wares, and a crowd of noisy urchins clustered around a man with a bright-colored bird in a cage. Then there were the sailors with packs on their backs shoving their way through the crowds, probably headed for an inn and a jug of wine. Ramac had a busy waterfront too, but Sala had never seen anything as loud, colorful, and crowded as this.

"Come," Nahshon said, and Sala followed his father down the cobbled path to the wharves, where more ships were tied up than Sala had ever seen in his life. His eyes darted from one to the next, admiring the furled colored sails and the gleaming wood. His father stopped in front of a sturdy wooden boat whose broad deck was neatly stacked with barrels of wine and bales of wool. The top of the boat's tallest mast bore the carved figure of a winged woman looking proudly forward.

"This is just the kind of boat I need," Nahshon said with satisfaction.

It was a good boat, Sala agreed, a useful boat for a merchant. But his eyes went wistfully to the long, elegant ship that was just now putting out to sea. It had eight oars on either side and they slid through the water as easily as a knife slides through a piece of fruit. It must be some Egyptian noble's private ship, he thought, his eyes caressing its long sleek lines.

"Time to go back to the inn," his father said briskly. "I have an appointment in an hour."

Sala nodded, his eyes still on the elegant craft as it sailed regally toward the horizon.

Nahshon slapped him on the shoulder. "Look all you want, my son, but that kind of life is not for us. Israelites have not fared well in Egypt since the time of Joseph, and I have been careful to keep my religion out of any dealings I might have with the people here. These ship builders are only interested in my money, but there's no sense in borrowing trouble. They think I am a Canaanite from Joppa, and that's how I want to keep it."

"I understand, Father," Sala said, and the man and boy made their way back up the cobbled steps into the streets of Gaza.

Nahshon had not come to Gaza with just his son. He had brought some of his workers with him, and when they returned to the inn, Sala found himself surrounded by men from home, all of them talking about ships. Sala was interested in ships, but he was also sixteen years old and this was his first time in a city bigger than Ramac. He wanted to look around without someone keeping watch on him. So when his father's appointment, a wide man with a sweaty face and a pungent odor, arrived and the men disappeared into the common room to discuss business, Sala slipped out the back door of the inn.

The warren of streets that wound throughout the city might have daunted another boy, but Sala had been blessed with a keen sense of direction. He did not doubt that he could find his way back to the inn, no matter how turned around the streets might become, and he set off with confidence.

The sun was bright overhead, but the streets were so enclosed that it rarely penetrated into the maze of shops and stalls and markets that made walking in a straight line impossible. *You must be able to buy anything you want in Gaza*, Sala thought as he strolled along the winding streets, taking in the jumble of wares set out for sale. Bakers, weavers, potters, sandal-makers, fish-mongers, and fruit sellers manned the shops. There were also basket makers, barbers, wine sellers, and stonecutters. There was jewelry that Sala thought must be made of real gold, it was so beautiful, and many stalls offered the little scarabs so prized by Canaanites as well as Egyptians.

As he wandered, fascinated, through the crowded alleys and streets, Sala lost all sense of time. He was looking at some honey cakes and inhaling their tantalizing smell when it dawned on him that he was starving. Luckily he had some money with him, and he bought one of the cakes and leaned against the side of an old mud-brick building to enjoy it.

He had just finished the cake and was dusting his hands together to get the stickiness off when he saw a young girl hurrying down the street in his direction. Her long hair was flying loose and she was almost running. There were plenty of girls of all ages, shapes, and sizes in the market, but what caught Sala's attention was the look of sheer terror on this little girl's face.

When she was almost abreast of him, he found himself stepping in front of her and saying in Canaanite rather than his native Hebrew, "Are you all right? Can I help you?"

She pulled up short and tilted her head back to stare at him. Her eyes were dilated and she was breathing hard. She cast a hunted look over her shoulder.

"Let me by!" There was a hysterical note in her voice.

Sala tried to make his voice sound quiet and trustworthy. Her fear was so palpable he could almost smell it. "I can see something is wrong. Please, won't you let me help you? I won't hurt you, I promise."

She bit her lip so hard that blood sprang out. "How can you help me?"

She was young, Sala could see. Her eyes reminded him of a terrified animal, cornered and fighting for its life. "You tell me that. I can see you are afraid. Are you running away from someone?"

If she said she was a runaway slave, he wasn't sure what he could do. But something about her made him think she wasn't a slave. And he wanted to help her.

Her face was damp with perspiration, but suddenly she began to shiver as if she was cold. "I was kidnapped by evil men and they are going to sell me as a slave! I managed to get away but I know they are looking for me."

Sala didn't doubt her. It was well known that girls of good families were often kidnapped and sold into slavery. "Come with me," he said, and reached for her hand.

After the briefest of hesitations, she put her hand in his and let him lead her back into the warren of streets he had just come through. She wanted to run but he stopped her. "We don't want to call attention to ourselves."

He shortened his long stride so she didn't have to skip to keep up with him. "Where were you when you escaped?" he asked, trying to focus his attention ahead and not on what might be behind them.

"I think we were on the outer part of the city. They had a big caravan of donkeys and horses that they put into an open field, but they brought me to an inn." For a little girl, she had a remarkably husky voice.

He tried to sound calm and practical. "I think I should take you back to the inn where I am staying. My father is there and he will protect you. He is an important man; no slavers will dare to question him."

Rahab thought this was an excellent idea. She had prayed to Asherah and the goddess had sent this boy to help her. She gripped his long, slender fingers with her smaller hand and hurried as hard as she could to keep up with him.

He knows exactly where he's going. He has to be a native of this city.

For some reason, she trusted him. His grip was so reassuring. He seemed so grown-up and sure of himself. Her initial terror was fading into a sense of security. This boy and his father would take care of her.

Finally the boy said, "Here we are. This is the inn where I am staying."

It was a much nicer looking inn than the place where the

kidnappers had taken Rahab, and she tried to smooth down her disheveled hair and straighten her robe as they walked into a tiny entry room.

"Remain here, and I will get my father," the boy said.

Suddenly her terror returned. "No!" Rahab grabbed his arm as tightly as she could. "Don't leave me. I want to stay with you."

He looked down into her face and she held her breath. Then he gave her a faint, comforting smile. "Very well. Come along with me."

They climbed the narrow staircase to the second floor and she followed him to a room at the end of a short hallway. He opened the door and peered in.

"Father?" Rahab understood the word, but then he began to speak in a language she did not know. A moment later a man walked into view. Rahab peered at him from behind the boy and bit her lip.

He was tall and stern looking. Rahab waited, poised to run again if she had to. Father and son talked in the strange language, of which she could understand only a few words, then the man looked at her and said in fluent Canaanite, "Come in, little girl. I want to speak to you."

Rahab cast an anxious glance up at her savior. He said softly, "It's all right. No one here will hurt you. This is my father, a good man."

Rahab knew she had to trust him, that she had no other choice, and she walked in the door.

It was a decent size room, with two sleeping mats rolled up in one of the corners. The rest of the furniture was simple wood stools and a large wooden chest that had some clothes neatly folded on top of it.

"What is your name, my child?" the man asked.

"Rahab." Her voice came out as a tremor and she said it again, more clearly, "My name is Rahab."

"A pretty name. And where are you from, Rahab?"

"I am from Ugaru, a village just outside of Jericho."

"Tell me what happened to bring you from Jericho to Gaza."

The story poured out of Rahab. She didn't cry until she got to the part about them wanting to sell her to an Egyptian lord as a slave. "They said they would get a fortune for me. What kind of people would pay a fortune for me? I don't sing or dance. I have no special talents. I think they must have been mad, those bandits. But they wouldn't let me go! They were going to sell me to someone here in Gaza who would take me on a ship to Egypt."

Over her head she saw the eyes of father and son meet. The man said, "Did they hurt you, Rahab?"

She sniffled. "Of course they hurt me! They hit me and tied my hands so I couldn't escape. They are horrible, horrible people."

The man looked for a long time into her eyes. Then he nodded, as if he was satisfied. "They wanted to sell a virgin. That would get them more money."

Rahab shuddered.

The boy asked, "How did you get away?"

She told them about the tiny window and how she had managed to squeeze herself onto the roof and jump onto the ground. "I am skinny and I am a good jumper," she finished proudly. "Even my brothers say I am a good jumper. I once jumped from the top of the stable into the muck pile. It was very far and I didn't get hurt."

"You are an intrepid girl, Rahab," the man said and he smiled. He looked different when he smiled. "My name is Lord Nahshon, and this is my son, Sala. We are from Ramac."

Rahab had never heard of Ramac, but she nodded as if she had.

"I am happy to know you," she said politely, the way her mother had taught her.

Sala said, "We need to return Rahab to her parents, Father. They must be worried about her."

Tears sprung into Rahab's eyes. "Oh, please take me home. My mother will have been crying and crying, wondering what has happened to me."

Lord Nahshon sighed. "I will find some way to get you back to your parents, I promise. You are a lucky girl that you got away from those men. Your future with them would have been bleak indeed."

"I know," she replied in a small voice.

"I will go now and ask the landlady to find a room for you. You need to rest. We will talk later."

"Yes, sir. My lord, that is," Rahab amended hastily. They had lords in Jericho, she knew, but she had never met any. She had lived all her life on her parents' farm and had never been beyond their local village. But lords were important people, almost as important as the king himself.

"Stay with her while I go and find the landlady," Lord Nahshon said to his son in Hebrew. "I had better speak to her myself. This is a respectable house and she will need to be reassured that the girl is not a prostitute."

"Yes, Father."

As soon as they were alone together, Rahab looked up at Sala. He was a very good-looking boy. His hair was black as night and worn shorter than the men of Jericho wore theirs. His nose was thin and elegantly curved and his dark brown eyes looked both warm and intelligent. He was quite tall, taller than her brother Shemu, but slender. She wondered how old he was but didn't think it would be polite to ask.

"What language were you speaking?" she asked instead.

"Hebrew. We are Israelites, Rahab. There are many Israelites in Canaan, but most of them live in small towns in the Judean hills. My father and I live in Ramac, the only Israelite city on the Great Sea. We came to Gaza to buy a new ship for my father's fleet. He is a merchant."

"I do not know about Israelites," Rahab said, careful to pronounce the word correctly. "Are you different from us?"

"Yes, we are different. We do not worship your gods, we worship one God only, the God who created the world."

Rahab frowned. This sounded strange to her. "Is this god like our Baal?"

Sala's lips tightened and for a moment he looked forbidding. "He is nothing like Baal, or any other of your gods. He is the one true God; your gods are just make-believe."

Sala was making her nervous. It was not good luck to say bad things about the gods. Besides, she was sure it was the lady Asherah who had saved her from the bandits. But she did not want to argue with Sala—he was her savior after all. So Rahab smiled and asked a different question and they were still talking when Lord Nahshon came back into the room.

Three

DURING THE TIME LORD NAHSHON WAS AWAY, SALA learned the names and likes and dislikes of everyone in Rahab's family as well as the specifics of her kidnapping. When Lord Nahshon returned, an older woman with a brown, wrinkled face was with him. Sala thought she looked like a shriveled old date.

Sala's father said, "Rahab, this is Hura, and she is going to watch over you while we are in Gaza. We are a group of men and you cannot be alone with us. It would not be right. Hura will show you to the room I have taken for you and then she will bring you some fresh clothing. She has a granddaughter who is about your size."

Lord Nahshon spoke with quiet authority, but Rahab shook her head. "Thank you, my lord, but I don't want to stay here, I want to go home. Please, can't you just send me back to my father?"

Lord Nahshon looked a little taken aback and Sala smothered a grin. His father was not accustomed to having his arrangements questioned by anyone, let alone a little girl.

"When I have decided how to accomplish that, I will inform you," Lord Nahshon replied, looking down his hawk-like nose.

Rahab didn't seem satisfied by this answer. She glanced at Sala and he shook his head slightly, telling her she shouldn't ask anything else right now.

Her lips pinched together and an elusive dimple flickered in her cheek. Then she bowed her head and said, "All right, I will go with Hura." She turned to the door, then stopped, looked back, and added with conscientious politeness, "Thank you, Lord Nahshon, for helping me."

"You are welcome," Sala's father replied.

After the door had closed behind her, Lord Nahshon turned to Sala, shaking his head. "Whatever made you pick that child up, Sala? She is a Canaanite; she has nothing to do with us."

"It was the look of terror on her face," Sala said. "You would have done the same thing, Father. It would have been heartless not to help her. She is a little girl. I couldn't just ignore her."

Lord Nahshon sighed. "Well, I suppose I am saddled with her now. As you say, it would be heartless to turn her loose on the streets of Gaza. A girl child who looks like that, some unsavory character would be sure to pick her up. I wouldn't like having her fate on my conscience."

Sala felt a shiver run up and down his back at the thought of what might have befallen the spunky little girl.

Lord Nahshon said, "Did she tell you anything else about herself?"

"Yes. She comes from one of the villages that are part of Jericho's territory. Her father owns vineyards. Apparently the harvests were excellent this year and he and some of his neighbors decided to ship their excess wine into Egypt. They were on their way to Joppa when they were attacked. Rahab was the only person in the party the bandits took, but they captured many of the loaded donkeys. She has brothers as well as a father, and perhaps someone went to Joppa to look for her, but I doubt they would have thought to try Gaza."

"One of those bandits got a look at her face and saw his

fortune," Lord Nahshon said grimly. "We will have to keep her hidden while we remain in Gaza."

"She's smart," Sala said. "She got away. I doubt many girls would have managed that."

Lord Nahshon pinched his nose. "Do you know how old she is?"

"She's twelve."

"Twelve! She looks younger." He blew out of the nose he had just been pinching. "So, thanks to your gallantry, here I sit with a twelve-year-old Canaanite girl on my hands."

"You'll think of something, Father," Sala said confidently.

Nahshon sighed. "Well, I'm not paying to send her all the way to Jericho. We'll have to take her home with us and I'll dispatch a message to her family asking them to send someone to collect her. That's the best I can do."

Sala smiled his approval. "I'm sure she'll be no trouble, Father. She's only a little girl."

"A Canaanite girl, my son, and a stunningly beautiful one at that." Nahshon shook his head. "I don't know what your mother and sisters will say."

"They will feel sorry for her, as you and I do," Sala replied.

Lord Nahshon grunted. "I hope so. Now let us prepare ourselves for dinner."

After dinner Sala found Rahab in the kitchen with Hura. Her chaperone was helping the other maids clean the dishes, and Rahab was sitting at a scarred wooden table looking gloomy.

Her face brightened when she saw him and she gave him a brilliant, welcoming smile. He joined her at the table.

"You look better," he said as he sat down.

"Hura was very nice. She helped me to wash and she brought me clean clothes." She shuddered. "I didn't want to wear anything those filthy thieves had touched."

"I don't blame you. I came to tell you my father's plan. You are to come back to Ramac with us and then he will send a messenger to Jericho to tell your family where you are. Your father can send someone to bring you home."

Rahab clapped her hands. "How happy they will be to find out I am safe and coming home!"

Sala looked at her radiant face and thought she was the most confident girl he had ever known. He had four sisters, two older than he and two younger, and none of them would have been comfortable sitting in an inn kitchen chattering away to a strange young man as if they were the best of friends. And after all she had been through!

Canaanite girls must be different from Israelite girls, who were kept sequestered from men who were not of their family. Of course, from what he had heard about the Canaanite religion, the women would have to be brought up differently. They certainly seemed looser with their virtue.

"What kind of a house do you have?" Rahab was asking. "Are you rich? You must be, if your father is a lord. We aren't rich but we have some good vineyards. Does your father have many ships? Do you think I could ride on one of them?"

Out of this torrent of questions, Sala picked the one he could answer most easily. "Women are not allowed on ships. It's considered bad luck."

The smile was replaced by a look of astonishment. "Bad luck? Why?"

Sala had no idea why; it was just something he had always heard. He shrugged. "Everyone says it."

"*I* never heard such a thing."

Sala looked down his nose at this girl who barely came up to his chin. "You know nothing about ships. You told me you had never even seen the sea before you came to Gaza. How should you know anything about a seaman's rules?"

She raised her chin. "I know rules like that are stupid. Why should women bring bad luck? Can you tell me one reason?"

Sala stared at her in amazement. *Who does this little creature think she is?*

He said, "They must bring girls up differently among your people. Israelites expect their women to be mild-mannered and courteous."

Rahab mimicked his shrug. "Canaanite women are supposed to be like that too, but my father lets me do whatever I want."

What a stupid man he must be.

"How old are your sisters? Will I like them?"

Sala noticed she didn't ask if they would like her. He shook his head. This Rahab was different from any girl he had ever met. "I have two older sisters who are married and live with their husbands. Then I have two sisters who are younger than I am. There is Rachel, who is fourteen, and Leah, who is twelve."

"I have never heard names like that. They're pretty."

"They are Israelite names. They were named after two of the women who were married to Nahshon, our great forebear."

"And Nahshon is your father's name!"

"Yes."

"Who are you named for, Sala?"

"I am named for my father's father. I was born two days after he died, so I was named for him."

"Sala!" One of his father's men was at the door. "Come. We have heard some news and your father wishes you to hear it." The man sounded excited.

Sala got up. "I will bid you good night, Rahab. I hope you sleep well."

"Thanks to you, Sala, I will."

When Sala walked into the common room, all of the men turned to look at him. Even before he had taken a seat, Nahshon spoke. "I have been telling everyone of something amazing I just heard. A man came to see me, an Israelite who lives in Gaza who knows who I am. He told me the Israelites who escaped from Egypt so long ago have been located! We all thought they must have died in the desert, but it seems that is not the case. They have been living at Kadesh, in the Wilderness of Zin, for many years. And we never knew! None of us here in Canaan ever knew!"

Amos, Lord Nahshon's head mariner, was the first to speak. "But there were thousands of them, my lord, or so we have always heard. How can so many have lived for so long in the desert?"

"There is water in Kadesh, and perhaps there are not so many of them as we have always thought," Nahshon replied.

Sala had been told of the Egyptian Israelites and of the escape that had happened before he was born. But he had always been told they had perished in the desert. It was astonishing to hear they were actually alive.

After the men had departed, Sala went up to his father, questions bubbling up inside him. Lord Nahshon gave him a rueful grin and put a hand on his shoulder. "I am still not used to standing eye-to-eye with you, my son." His face sobered. "This is wonderful news, Sala. I feel as if the heart of our people has just been resurrected from the dead."

"'The heart of our people,' Father? What do you mean by that?"

"Let us sit down, Sala, and talk."

Sala followed his father to a bench at the side of the room. Once they were seated, Nahshon said, "Do you remember the story of Joseph, the son of Jacob, who became a great lord in Egypt? You must remember it; I taught you myself."

"Of course I remember, Father. Joseph went to Egypt because his brothers tried to kill him. And when there was a famine in Canaan, many of the people went down into Egypt, including Joseph's brothers, because they knew there was food there. Joseph, who was now a lord, forgave his brothers and fed all of the Israelites who had come into Egypt. And many of them liked it there and decided to remain in the country as honored subjects of the Pharaoh."

Nahshon looked pleased. "That is correct. Not all of our people went into Egypt during the famine, but well over half of us did and they stayed. However, after Joseph died, the situation of Israelites in Egypt deteriorated, until, finally, they were little more than slaves."

Lord Nahshon looked off across the room as if he was remembering something. "I can clearly recall my father talking about the situation of our Egyptian brothers. His ships frequently sailed into the Egyptian Delta to deliver merchandise, and so he knew all about what was happening to our people."

Nahshon stopped talking, his gaze still focused on that faraway something. After a moment Sala prompted him, "They were slaves?"

"They were being used for forced labor in the building of the city of Ramses. But there was little we Israelites in Canaan could do to help them. All of the cities in this country owe allegiance to Egypt, and we Israelites are only a small number of the Canaanite population."

"I know," Sala said in a subdued voice. This was something

he had often heard, the lament that the land that should belong to his people and his God had been given over to the false gods of the Canaanites.

Nahshon suddenly turned his head and his black eyes glittered as he stared unflinchingly at his son. "Never forget that Canaan is *our* land, Sala, given to us by Elohim Himself. *We* are the people of God, not the Canaanite worshippers of Baal. This is why the discovery of the Israelites from the desert is so important to us. If they are planning to enter Canaan to reclaim the land of our fathers, of Abraham, Isaac, and Jacob, then we must be ready to join with them!"

Sala felt his blood thrill at his father's words. He had been taught the history of his people, but it had always seemed so far in the past to him. Life was different today, or so he had always thought. Now it seemed as if their great days might not be over yet.

Nahshon was going on, "Think of it, Sala! Our Promised Land. A Canaan that is Israelite from border to border. The God of Abraham, the God of Israel, will be restored to His rightful place, and Baal and all his filthy rituals will be swept from our sacred soil."

Sala had never heard his father speak this way. Nahshon had always been a pragmatic businessman, willing to work with anyone if it meant making a profit. And now he was talking about war! About conquest! Sala felt the thrill in his blood turn to fire.

"Do you think the Egyptian Israelites will do that, Father? Do you think they will try to conquer the land of Canaan?"

Nahshon let out a long breath. "I was a young boy when we learned about the escape from Egypt, but I can still remember how excited my father was. It was all anyone could talk about. We kept looking for them and looking for them. It is not that long a journey from Egypt into Canaan, and we expected to see them anytime.

"We knew they could not come by the Way of the Sea—they would have been too visible—they would have to come through the Sinai. But they vanished into the desert and, after a while, we gave up waiting. Everyone believed they had died of disease or starvation. And now—after all these years—to hear of their survival! It is miraculous."

Sala's breath caught with awe. "It *is* a miracle. It must be."

"We must try to contact them, see how many are left, what their plans are." The room had grown darker as they talked and Lord Nahshon's teeth gleamed white as he smiled. "The day of the Lord is coming, Sala. Let us rejoice and be glad."

Four

THE MEN FROM RAMAC REMAINED IN GAZA FOR SEV-
eral more days while Lord Nahshon made arrangements to
purchase a ship. He had been lucky enough to find one already
built by one of the most highly regarded ship builders in Canaan.
The previous owner had died and his widow was anxious to be rid
of it. Lord Nahshon, to his profound satisfaction, got a bargain.

A few of Lord Nahshon's seamen sailed the ship back to
Ramac, leaving Nahshon, Sala, and the rest to return by land
with Rahab. Before they left Gaza, Lord Nahshon sent a message with a caravan going toward Jericho. The message was
to Rahab's family and told them where they could find her to
fetch her home.

"They had better come for her," Lord Nahshon said to Sala
grimly as he watched the messenger set off. "I don't want to be
burdened with a Canaanite girl for the rest of my life."

"Someone will come for her," Sala replied. "I think she's her
father's favorite. He spoils her dreadfully, lets her do whatever
she wants—or so she tells me."

Lord Nahshon frowned in disapproval. "Well, she'll find
things are different when your mother takes her in hand."

Sala laughed.

Rahab had been hoping she would get to travel on the ship, but she refrained from complaining when she discovered Sala would be traveling with her by land. It was not far from Gaza to Ramac, only a two-day journey along the Way of the Sea, the main road from Egypt into Canaan and Mesopotamia. Sala had assured Rahab that the route was so well traveled that it was perfectly safe from bandits, so she could relax and enjoy herself.

Rahab was beginning to regard everything that had happened to her as an adventure. She hadn't forgotten how frightened she had been, but she was proud she had escaped the evil bandits, and she did not fully understand how dreadful her fate would have been if Sala had not rescued her. For now, it was exciting to be so far from home, seeing all these new places and meeting new people. And she adored spending time with Sala.

He was her main companion on the journey. Lord Nahshon had paid Hura to travel with them, but the older woman rode a donkey, leaving Rahab and Sala to walk together. She was curious about his background and religion and he readily answered her unceasing stream of questions as they walked along the busy road.

The Gaza caravan they had joined was going all the way to Damascus and it was huge. There were over two hundred donkeys, and Sala and Rahab stayed close to the front to avoid the dust the animals kicked up as they walked.

"What kind of a temple do you have in Ramac?" Rahab asked. "Our village has only a small one, but my father and brothers have told me there is a magnificent temple to Baal in Jericho, and a shrine to Asherah too. Do you have a big temple to your god in Ramac?"

Sala's nostrils quivered as if he had smelled something rancid. "Israelites do not have temples. Our God is hidden; we do not make images of Him. He is too great for that. It would be impossible to make an image that could capture His immensity."

Rahab's brows knit together. "But how do you know what He looks like then?"

He shot her a quick look. "We do not know what He looks like. He may appear to us in the things of this world, in fire or clouds, but He does not have a form like ours. He is *Elohim*, the Creator. There is no one else like Him."

One of the donkeys in front of them jumped and skittered to the side of the road. The man walking beside him shouted and smacked him with his hand. The donkey brayed loudly and pawed the ground.

"He probably saw a snake," Sala called ahead.

"No," the man shouted back. "He is just stupid."

The donkey finally swung in behind its fellow and the line continued its methodical pace forward.

"But your god must have a mother," Rahab said, her puzzlement increasing. "And a wife and children."

Sala was carrying a walking stick and now he slammed it into the ground and swung around to look at her. He was scowling. "You have no idea how ridiculous you sound. You Canaanites have made up foolish gods who are like people, but Elohim is not like us. He created us, but He is not like us." He stared down his narrow, curved nose at her. "God *created* men and women, Rahab. All of the people in the world are descended from His first creations, but only we, the Israelites, have remained faithful to Him, the real Lord. That is why we are His special people."

"So you only worship this one god, this Elohim, and you don't have any other gods or goddesses—is that what you are saying?" It sounded so strange that she wanted to be certain she had understood him properly.

"Yes."

"But you live in the land of Canaan, the land of Baal—"

Sala cut in before she could finish her thought. "Canaan is

our land, the land of the Israelites! Elohim promised it to our people ages ago. It does not belong to you!"

The conversation was not going the way Rahab had thought it would when she innocently mentioned temples. Sala seemed a different person when he was talking about this god of his.

Rahab stared down at her feet as she thought. Her sandals were covered with dust, as were her narrow toes and instep, but she scarcely noticed. Her mind was busy trying to grasp what Sala was saying.

They walked in silence for a while before she looked up and said in the most reasonable voice she could muster, "But Canaan is the home of the Canaanite people, Sala. You and your father and the people of Ramac are the only Israelites I have ever met, ever heard of. You are small and we are big. This can never be your land."

She watched as Sala lifted his face and squinted up into the intensely blue sky, as if the answer he sought were written there. "You don't understand, Rahab. Once Canaan was ours, the home of the Israelites. Elohim told our forefather Abraham that He was giving this land to Abraham and all his descendants. He made a covenant with us, that He would be our God and we would be His people. And as a sign of that, He would give us the land of Caanan."

Sala turned his head to look at her. There was a line like a sword between his eyebrows. His voice was no longer passionate; he sounded calm and positve. "Canaan should be *our* land, Rahab, the land of the Israelites. You will not hold it forever. Our time will come."

He was making Rahab nervous. She put a tentative hand on his arm and said anxiously, "Surely it can be both our lands? Why can we not live in peace together?"

His brow smoothed out and he patted the hand on his arm.

"I'm sorry. I didn't mean to frighten you. You're just a girl; it's impossible for you to understand these things."

His condescension infuriated Rahab more than all his talk. "I understand perfectly well," she snapped. "You think your god is better than our gods and that Israelites are better than Canaanites. Do you think I am as stupid as that donkey? You couldn't have made yourself clearer. I just think you are wrong."

Sala let out a long slow breath. "I'm sorry. I didn't mean to insult you. Let us talk of something else."

"Perhaps it would be better not to talk at all for a while," Rahab replied. "I think I will go and see how Hura is doing."

She turned her back on him and made her way down the line of donkeys.

Ramac was much smaller than Gaza. The walls of the city were made of mud brick, not stone, but they were very high, and the cobbled road from the gates to the waterfront was straight, with a clear view down to the sea. The houses along the main street were square and substantial looking, and Sala's house was among the grandest of them all. Clearly Lord Nahshon was a rich man.

What Rahab liked best about Ramac, though, was that you could see the water from almost any point in the city. It shimmered in the sunlight, vast and beautiful, the Great Sea. She thought it was the most wonderful thing she had seen in her life.

Rahab stayed with Sala's family for ten days, and much of that time she spent with Sala. His mother and sisters did not speak Canaanite and, since Rahab spoke no Hebrew, the women of the house were unable to communicate with her. Rahab sat and sewed with them for a few hours each morning, but the rest of the time she was in Sala's charge.

She told him she wanted to see the town and the waterfront, and he borrowed one of his sister's cloaks and veils and took her around the various houses and gardens. He even sneaked her down to the waterfront, where women were not allowed. She stood for a few short minutes on a wharf, where she could see the great merchant ships riding at anchor. But she could not get him to take her for a ride on a boat. Women did not go on boats, he told her, and that was that.

Rahab thought this was a stupid rule, but she held her tongue. She did not want to say anything to alienate Sala. He was the most interesting person she had ever met and she loved being with him. He had traveled to Egypt and Ugarit and Damascus, places Rahab had scarcely heard of. She hung on his every word as he described these exotic locales. He also told her about some of the things that had happened to him when he was there. Some of his stories were funny and she would laugh delightedly, loving the way his smiling brown eyes met hers.

Sala was the only son, and his father was grooming him to take over the shipping business when he was older. Rahab was impressed to learn that Sala had learned how to add up numbers and keep books. He had even learned to read. Lord Nahshon was a learned man and he had taught Sala all the great stories of their religion.

Rahab had heard some of the stories of Baal and Asherah and the other gods and goddesses of Canaan, but Sala said Lord Nahshon had his stories written down on papyrus scrolls and he read them out loud once a week to all the men of the town. From what Rahab could gather, this was what the Israelites did for worship. They did not have temples; they got together and listened to the stories of their faith and discussed them. Sala had learned to read so he could take his father's place in this duty as well. It was a position that had long been in their family.

Rahab loved to watch Sala's face as he talked about his Israelite ancestors and how they had learned about their god. He looked so concentrated and intense, as if his very insides were glowing with the power of his words. She could tell that his god, Elohim, meant a great deal to him, that he believed in Elohim with all his heart.

"I'm glad you're here," he said to her one day as they sat together in the garden enjoying the early afternoon sun. "You have given me an excuse to take a holiday from work."

"I like being here too." Rahab had just finished two seemingly endless hours of sewing with his sisters and his mother. "I don't think your mother likes me, though. She took away the shirt I was supposed to be hemming today and ripped all the stitches out. Truly, my work was not that bad. But she gave me an unpleasant look and handed me a dish towel to work on."

His mouth twitched but he didn't respond.

Rahab went on, "I don't think your sisters like me either. They look at me as if I were some kind of strange creature from another world."

"That's not true. My sister Leah thinks you're wonderful. She was so impressed when I told her about your escape from the slavers. She's sure she could never be as brave as that. She said you must come from a family of great warriors."

Great warriors. Rahab snorted. "I hope you told her my family are farmers—not warriors—and certainly not rich merchants like your family. We don't have servants like your mother does. My father and my brothers work in the vineyards and the fields, and my mother and my sisters-in-law work to feed and clothe all of us. We're busy all the time."

Amusement gleamed in Sala's eyes. "What do *you* do, Rahab? Clearly you do not spend your time sewing."

"Oh, I do a little of this and a little of that," Rahab replied, waving her hand. "I help whoever needs help at the moment. I am the youngest, you see, and my father doesn't want me to work too hard. My brothers say I am spoiled." She grinned. "They're probably right, but my papa says one day I will secure all their futures and I shouldn't be worn out in my youth."

The amusement faded from Sala's face. "I see."

"I don't see how that can possibly happen, but I'm certainly not going to gainsay him. I think he just loves me so much he doesn't want me to work too hard. But, of course, if my mother asks me to help her, I always do. I love my mother very much."

Sala was quiet.

She put a hand on his sleeve and said coaxingly, "Tell me the story of Rachel again, and how Jacob served seven years because he wanted to marry her so much."

The sober look left his face. "Why do you always want to hear that story?"

She didn't have to think for even a second before she answered, "Because it shows Rachel was an important person."

"That's a curious answer."

"Why?"

He shrugged. "I suppose I expected you to say something about Jacob's love for her."

"Sala, he only loved her because she was pretty. But he made her important in the eyes of everyone else because of what he did to marry her." She smiled up into his face. "Not too many women are important, so it's nice to hear a story about a woman who was."

He looked at her hand on his sleeve. "Perhaps he loved her for more than her looks. Perhaps he loved her because she was different from other girls."

"Different? How?"

He flicked her cheek with his finger. "Perhaps she wasn't afraid to look straight into people's eyes when they spoke to her.

Perhaps she had all sorts of opinions and wasn't afraid to tell him about them. Perhaps she thought she was just as good as he was and—"

Rahab's eyes widened. "Are you talking about *me*?"

"I never said that." His eyes were dancing with laughter.

She began to laugh back.

"*Sala!*"

Rahab turned and saw Sala's mother, Miriam, standing in the garden door. She sighed as Miriam's angry eyes rested upon her. No, Sala's mother definitely didn't like her.

Miriam said something to Sala in a sharp voice and Sala answered. Then he said to Rahab, "My mother wants you to go with her. She is going to teach you how to hem a shirt properly."

Rahab rolled her eyes at him and began to get to her feet. She saw his lips twitch again before she crossed the garden to join his mother.

Rahab's brother Shemu awaited his sister in the large imposing room of the Israelite merchant who had contacted his father about Rahab's whereabouts. No one in his family knew anything about Israelites, and Shemu had been deeply surprised by the evident wealth in the town of Ramac. So far he had only met the women of the family, who stood in the room with him waiting for Rahab to arrive.

The two girls were pretty enough and had given Shemu shy smiles of welcome. The woman of the house had a face like a stone statue. They spoke no Canaanite, but when Shemu told the servant at the door he had come for Rahab, they had appeared and, from what he could gather from their words, they had sent for his sister.

The three of them stood in silence. Shemu was struggling with mixed feelings. He was glad his sister had been found and was coming home, but he was afraid of what might have happened to her, and not just at the hands of the slavers. Who knew what a wealthy family like this might have felt free to do to a beautiful child like Rahab?

There was a rush of wind in the doorway and then Rahab was throwing herself into his arms. "Shemu! Shemu! I am so glad to see you!"

He closed his arms tightly around his little sister. "I've come to bring you home, little one. We are all so glad you're all right."

Her arms were tight about his waist. A shiver of fear ran through him. "Look at me, Rahab. Let me see that pretty face of yours."

She released her hold and stepped back, looking up at him with the steady clear eyes of the innocent child he remembered.

Relief surged through Shemu and he turned to the three women who were in the room with them and smiled. "Thank you for taking such good care of my sister."

Thank you sounded much the same in both languages, and the girls smiled back, bobbing their heads. The woman's face never changed.

"What is going on here?"

A young man came striding into the room from the same direction Rahab had come. He said in Canaanite, "Who is this man, Rahab?"

"This is my brother, Shemu. He has come to take me home."

The young man approached. Shemu could see that he was sixteen or seventeen years of age and he was handsome. When he stopped in front of them, Shemu also saw that he was tall. Shemu had to look up at him.

Rahab took the boy's hand and said, *"This* is Sala, my

brother. He saved me from the slavers. I was running through the streets of Gaza, not knowing where to go or what to do, when he stopped me and brought me to his father. They have been so good to me! So kind."

Sala's eyes were fixed upon Shemu. "You are not traveling alone?" The words sound like an accusation.

Shemu bristled. "Of course not. My wife and another of my brothers are waiting for me outside the city gates. We have made arrangements to travel with a contingent of Syrians as far as Jericho."

"Good," Sala said. He lifted an eyebrow. "We don't want to have Rahab kidnapped again."

There was something about this boy's tone Shemu did not like. He was making it sound as if it was his family's fault Rahab had been captured.

Shemu said evenly, "That will not happen."

"Good."

Rahab looked from one male face to the other, clearly sensing something was wrong but not understanding what it might be. "Sala saved my life," she told her brother. She looked at the boy. "I can never thank you enough."

He shrugged. "It was your own cleverness and bravery that saved you."

Rahab was still holding the boy's hand. It looked so natural that she didn't even seem to realize she should not be doing such a thing. She looked up at him and said softly, "Will I ever see you again?"

Shemu thought, *A stupid question. Of course she won't ever see him again.*

The Israelite said, "It is in the hand of Elohim. Good-bye, Rahab, and may Elohim keep you safe on your journey home."

Tears sprung to Rahab's eyes. Shemu put his arm around her

shoulders and steered her away from the boy, saying as they went toward the door, "My father has sent you a barrel of our best wine. It is at the inn and I will have it brought over. Thank you for all you have done for my sister. Good-bye."

Rahab stumbled as he led her out into the sunshine and now he could see the tears rolling down her face.

"Atene cannot wait to see you," he said brightly, referring to his wife. "She has brought you some clothes and some of Mother's nut cakes. You know how you love her nut cakes."

Rahab nodded, sniffled, and composed herself.

"I can't wait to see Atene either. I have missed her."

"Those Israelites may have been good to you, but they're not our kind, Rahab. Best to put them all right out of your mind."

"Yes," she said. "I suppose you're right, Shemu." Then she added wistfully, "I'll try to do that."

PART TWO

Second Meeting

Five

RAHAB'S PARTING FROM SALA HAD BEEN SO ABRUPT that she had scarcely any time to reflect upon how she felt about leaving him. And once she was home, she quickly slipped back into the easy ways of her old life. However, as the seasons passed, and Yarih, god of the moon, waxed and waned, the carefree days of her childhood began to run out. Most of the girls her age from the village were betrothed or married, and she knew her turn was near. Her pleasant life as a much-indulged only daughter was coming to an end; soon she would be a married woman with a house to tend and children to rear.

Rahab accepted the reality of her future, but she was not eager to rush it. She did not envy her girlfriends a single one of their husbands. An idea lay hidden in the back of her mind about the kind of man she would like to marry, and she hoped such a man would come along before her father made his choice.

The thing that saved her was that she was late coming into womanhood. Her thirteenth and fourteenth birthdays passed and still she had not shown her first blood.

Girls could not marry until after they were ready to bear children and Rahab knew she could keep her freedom for as long as she remained officially a child. Meanwhile, her mother and father watched her like craftsmen guarding a precious pot. She was into the second month of her fourteenth year when her body, which had been changing slowly, made a dramatic leap forward. Her breasts took form and she had her first blood.

The women of the village held a ceremony in Asherah's grove to celebrate Rahab's changed status. It was the traditional ceremony held for every girl at this time of life, a ritual intended to bless the young woman and help prepare her for the difficult tasks of being a wife and a mother.

The first night of the ceremony, when Rahab had to stay by herself in a small tent, keeping awake and tending the small fire until morning, she was forced to face for the first time the reality of her future. It had been easy to push it aside when she was still slim as a boy, larking around the farm and helping her mother and sisters-in-law with their tasks. But now, almost overnight, she had left the freedom of her childhood behind. Her hips were curved, no longer slender like her brothers'. She was all grown up.

She would have to get married. She would have to get married and she could not think of a single boy or man in her village who attracted her. They were all so boring. She loved her father and her brothers dearly, but she wanted to marry someone different, someone who knew things about the world outside of Canaan, someone who was brave and daring and liked adventures.

Someone like Sala.

He was the ideal who had been floating in her mind for the last two years. She acknowledged this to herself and, at the same time, she acknowledged that she would never see him again. She watched the smoke from her fire going up and out the smoke hole in the tent roof, and for the first time she allowed herself to think about the time she had spent with him in Ramac. Other girls had confided in her how frightened they were of having to stay by themselves in Asherah's grove but Rahab wasn't frightened at all. She was glad of the chance to be alone so she could think.

She rose from her place by the fire and ducked under the

tent opening to go outside. It was the time of year when some days it felt like winter and some days like spring. Today had been a spring-like day and tonight the air was chilly but not cold. Rahab wrapped her cloak around her and looked up at the sky.

All her life she had loved to look at the stars. There was no moon tonight, and the stars shone so brightly and looked so close she thought she should be able to reach up and touch one.

Her father had once told her they were many miles up in the sky, in a place no person could ever go. She had asked him if the gods lived up there, but he had not known for certain.

Rahab shivered. What did the gods care about her? She had been put on the earth to do woman's work: to bear children, to bake bread, to minister to the sick and dying, and finally to die herself. That is what women did in this world. Why should she be different? Why should she long for the impossible? She was only making herself unhappy.

She was a fool to cherish Sala's memory in her heart. He was probably married by now and never gave her a single thought. She must stop thinking about him and be practical about her own future.

She would marry whomever her father picked and make the best of it. That is what all women did, didn't they?

She went back into the tent, sat in front of the fire, and angrily brushed her tears away with her fingers. She was not a baby. She was a woman now and she must act like one. She reached out and put another stick on the fire.

Mepu had already picked a husband for Rahab. His father was a local man who owned cattle and the son desperately wanted to marry Rahab. The negotiations over the bride price started the day after her initiation ceremony was finished, and Rahab's sister-in-law, Atene, kept her informed about how they were progressing.

"They're talking about five hundred silver shekels, Rahab!" she reported one morning as the two young women were spinning dried and stripped flax fibers into yarn. "No one has ever paid that much for a wife."

Rahab's hands slowed. They were working outside in the courtyard, and as she gazed out across the fertile landscape of her father's farm, she sighed.

Atene shook her head. "I don't understand you. Any other woman would be thrilled she was valued so highly. Just think of how well you will be treated. No man will abuse something he has paid so much for."

This comment did not cheer Rahab as it had been meant to. She carefully smoothed one of the longer fibers back into its ribbon and said, "I suppose that is a good thing."

Atene stopped spinning. "I know you love your home, but try to think about how fortunate you are," she urged. "You were born beautiful, and because of that your life will be an easy and pleasant one. As Shulgi's wife you will have a servant to do all the work for you. You should be happy, Rahab, and instead you go round looking as if you've been cursed."

Rahab felt as if she had been cursed, but she couldn't say that to Atene. She couldn't say that she dreamed at night of a different kind of man than Shulgi, with his eager, protuberant eyes.

"Shulgi doesn't know me at all. All he knows is he likes the way I look. We might even hate each other once we are married."

"I'm certain such a thing won't happen."

Rahab looked at her sister-in-law. "Were you happy when you learned you were to marry Shemu?"

Faint color stained Atene's cheeks. "I was happy."

"Did you know him before you were betrothed?"

The color in Atene's cheeks deepened. "Yes, we knew each other from the village ceremonies."

"You liked him," Rahab said, almost accusingly.

"I liked him very much."

"I'm not going to like Shulgi. I know I'm not going to like him."

Atene patted her hand. "You must try to like him, Rahab. Your happiness depends upon it. You must try."

After she and Atene finished with the flax, Rahab went back into the house to see if her mother had any other chores for her. She had entered by the back door, and as she walked down the short hall she heard the sound of voices in the front room. Her father was there with her mother and they sounded as if they were having a disagreement. Rahab stood just outside the door so she could hear what they were saying.

"Do not argue, Kata," her father said. "My mind is made up. If Shulgi is willing to give so much money for Rahab, just think of what the rich men in Jericho would pay."

"You don't know that, Mepu." Rahab could hear distress in her mother's voice.

"Have you *looked* at her lately, Kata?"

"Yes."

"Does she look like a farmer's daughter or a farmer's wife to you?"

"No."

"You were a pretty girl, my dear, but Rahab . . . Rahab is more than pretty. More than beautiful. There is an air about her . . ."

Her mother's voice was sharp as she replied, "I know, my husband. I see how men can't keep their eyes off of her. And I am afraid some rich man will want her for something other than a wife. She is an innocent girl, my husband. We were fortunate to get her back with her virtue unimpaired. I don't want to see her sold—"

Her father interrupted, his voice full of anger. "Do you think I would sell my daughter into prostitution? I would *never* do that. Never. Shame on you for thinking such a thing."

"I am sorry." Her mother's voice trembled.

"We are going to Jericho to find Rahab a *husband*, Kata. Do you understand me?"

"Yes. Yes, I do understand. I am sorry, Mepu. I did not mean—"

"I know, I know." Her father's voice softened. "I love her too, Kata. She is a special girl. Even apart from her looks, she is special, and I want her to have the best."

Rahab turned and went quietly back toward the door she had come in by, a big smile on her face. She was not going to have to marry Shulgi! She was going to go to Jericho! *Anything might happen in Jericho. I might even meet a man I would like to marry. And I am rid of that awful Shulgi. I must go out to Asherah's Shrine and thank her. Thank her for giving me another chance.*

Mepu had a brother who owned a pottery shop in Jericho, and he and Shemu went into the city to ask if his brother might know where they could find temporary housing. It turned out that, besides the shop that he lived over, Mepu's brother owned the house next door. He had rented it for years to the same couple, but the old renters had decided to move in with their daughter and the house would be free.

Mepu looked at the square mud-brick house, which was in the oldest and poorest part of the city. He also looked around to see if other lodgings might be available in a more prestigious area, but what he found was hugely expensive. He ended by renting his brother's house at what he thought was too high a rate, and comforted himself with the thought that Kata would know how to make it cheerful and presentable.

"There was nothing else available," Mepu told his family when he returned home and they were all at dinner. "I had to promise Ilim a good rent, though. He wasn't about to give it to me for free just because we are blood."

"I'm sure he counts on the income for his living," Kata said gently.

Shemu smiled at his mother. "You always think the best of people," he said.

Mepu snorted. "You'd think he could give a break to his own flesh and blood. But Ilim was always a tightfisted scoundrel." He tore a piece of bread in half and scowled at it.

"How big is the house, Father?" Jabin asked.

Mepu gave Jabin a long look. "Only big enough for just Shemu and Atene to accompany us. She will be a help to your mother, and you and your brothers can manage here without us."

Jabin's face fell. He had clearly been looking forward to going to the city. On the other hand, Atene's face brightened. She cast a glance at Rahab, who gave her a quick smile.

"If we leave soon we will be there for the festival of the New Year," Shemu said. His narrow, dark face was alive with anticipation.

Jabin said, "Can't I come too, Father? Just for the festival of the New Year? I have never seen it!"

"We'll see." It was their father's usual answer—not saying either yes or no, just leaving you wondering. It annoyed all of his children to no end, but no one dared to protest.

The family had been to many ritual celebrations at the shrine in their village, but the festival of the New Year, the great Canaanite fertility rite, could only be held if the king was present. It was the king who represented Baal, and his ritual marriage with the hierodule, the woman who had been chosen to represent the goddess Asherah, was the central act of the festival. It was their coupling that would ensure the fertility of the soil, the flocks, and the human family. It was the strength of the king and the life-empowering fertility of the hierodule that would guarantee the prosperity of the kingdom.

"Have *you* ever been to the festival of the New Year, Father?" Rahab asked.

"A few times." Mepu ate a fig so juicy a little of it dribbled down his chin. He wiped it away, then licked the juice from his fingers. "King Makamaron was much younger when I went. He's getting on in years now." Mepu flashed his wife a smile. "As am I."

She returned stoutly, "Makamaron has not lost his powers. The rains have fallen and our harvests have been bountiful ever since he became king. He is still a strong man, and so are you, my husband."

Mepu looked gratified.

"We should sacrifice a young lamb to Baal before you leave for Jericho, Father," Rahab's brother Ahat said. "That will please him and perhaps he will look kindly upon Rahab and your mission."

The rest of the men at the table agreed heartily. They all looked at Rahab, who bowed her head to indicate her gratitude for their good wishes and her obedience to her father's will.

Six

IT WAS A PERFECT SPRING MORNING WHEN SALA AND his father arrived at the gates of Jericho. The sun reflected off the walls of the city and Sala looked up at the massive fortifications, stricken to silence by their magnitude. Lord Nahshon was silent as well. Finally he said, "This is beyond what I had expected."

Still speechless, Sala nodded. The city was built upon a hill, which of itself provided a significant military advantage, but it was the immense wall that made it seem impregnable. As the two Israelites would discover upon further investigation, the wall consisted of several layers. Its base was a fifteen-foot-high revetment of large boulders. On top of the boulders was an eight-foot-high wall made of mud bricks. This double wall was then backed by a massive packed-earth embankment, upon which were built a warren of streets and mud-brick houses. At the top of the embankment there was yet another high mud-brick wall, behind which more houses reached all the way to the top of the hill.

"It's not a city, it's a fortress," Sala said. He sounded stunned.

"It is indeed," replied Lord Nahshon, a similar note in his own voice.

Lord Nahshon and Sala had come to Jericho in the guise of Canaanite merchants from Gaza. The supposed purpose of their visit was to buy local agricultural products in order to make money shipping them to other countries around the Great Sea. Presently Jericho's village farmers sold most of their produce into the city for the use of the city inhabitants, but Lord Nahshon's plan was to approach some of the city nobles to ask if they would buy up large quantities of local products to sell to Lord Nahshon for a reasonable profit. Nahshon would make his profit when he shipped the products overseas.

This was the excuse Lord Nahshon was using to explain his visit to Jericho. The real reason was quite different. For the past few years Lord Nahshon and the men of Ramac had been in communication with the Egyptian Israelites led by Joshua, who had taken over the leadership after the death of Moses. Before he attacked Jericho, Joshua wanted to place a man inside the city to gather information, but he needed someone who could pass as a Canaanite. Lord Nahshon had volunteered.

Joshua needed Jericho if he wanted to enter Canaan, and his plan was for Nahshon to find out all he could about the defenses of the city and the disposition of the inhabitants. Joshua himself would camp on the eastern side of the Jordan, and shortly after the spring New Year, when the hours of darkness matched the hours of light, he would send spies into Jericho to meet with Nahshon and return with whatever vital information Nahshon had been able to acquire.

Nahshon had come up with an excuse for visiting the city, and he had taken Sala with him to bolster his role as representing a family merchant company from Gaza. One of the older men in Ramac had visited Jericho once and he told Nahshon about the location of a popular wine bar in the lower city. The Israelite plan was for Nahshon and Sala to visit this bar every day and Joshua would have his spies seek them out there.

Nahshon and Sala had started their journey to Jericho in beautiful spring weather and, as Sala had ridden through the farms and villages that formed the mainstay of Jericho's economy, he had found his thoughts dwelling on the Canaanite girl he had met two years before. He had never forgotten Rahab. Because of her, most of the girls in Ramac seemed dull and uninteresting. A picture of the fiery, brave little girl whom he had saved from a terrible fate would spring into his mind every time his father or mother sang the praises of someone they considered a good match for him. He knew he was being foolish. The chances of his meeting an Israelite girl who was like Rahab were nonexistent.

He had given in to his parents at last, however, and agreed to become betrothed to the daughter of another wealthy merchant when he and his father returned to Ramac. He knew it was his duty to marry and carry on the family business. But for some reason, the thought of pretty, docile Dinah did not make him look forward to the time when she would be his wife.

Sala and Lord Nahshon were forced to wait at Jericho's huge gate while a chariot clattered through ahead of them, then they were allowed to lead their donkeys through the massive wall and into the streets of the city. They had expected to find an inn easily, but the choices turned out to be limited. Because Jericho was not located on any of the major caravan routes, it was largely self-sufficient. Most outlying farmers had family to stay with when they came into the city, and the few inns that did exist were already filled due to a religious celebration to be celebrated shortly.

The two men finally found an available room on the north side of the city, in what was clearly a poor neighborhood. Many of the small mud-brick houses were built right up against the city wall, which actually functioned as the house's fourth wall. Those houses not pushed up against the wall were crammed together on narrow dirt streets in which groups of children played noisily.

It was not the kind of neighborhood or accommodation to which Sala or his father were accustomed, but they had little choice. They followed the innkeeper up to a tiny room with a ceiling so low Sala felt he should duck his head.

"No sense in complaining, Father," he said, when he saw the expression on Lord Nahshon's face. "At least it looks clean."

Lord Nahshon's expression did not change as he regarded the old rush sleeping mats with disapproval. "I'd rather sleep out under the stars than in here."

Sala felt the same way. He walked the few strides it took him to reach the back wall and looked out the small window, which was really just an opening cut through the mud bricks.

The view of the Judean hills before him was lovely, but what immediately caught his attention was the wall itself. He leaned out to get a better look.

"Be careful," Lord Nahshon called. "You might fall."

Sala drew himself back into the room. "Come and look at this wall, Father. It's only a single brick thick."

Lord Nahshon came to the window, looked, and turned to his son. "You're right! This would be easy to knock down." He leaned out a little himself and looked toward the hills. "We are on the north side of the city, am I right?"

"Yes."

Lord Nahshon smiled. "It looks as if the whole north side of the wall is only a single brick thick. That is something we must let Joshua know about."

Sala smiled back. "Definitely. There is still the stone revetment to deal with, but this section seems vulnerable."

Lord Nahshon glanced around the tiny room once more and sighed. "Let's get out of here, Sala. We should look first for that wine shop where we're supposed to meet Joshua's men. Perhaps we can even get some food there."

"An excellent plan, Father. I'm starving."

"Come along then," Lord Nahshon said, and the two men exited the tiny room.

For several days Sala and his father explored the city, walking down every street and checking the wall from every vantage point. They discovered Jericho was really two cities, the Lower City, where their lodgings were, and the Upper City, where the richer homes were located, as well as the king's palace, the Temple of Baal, and the smaller shrine of Asherah.

Sala had felt an almost visceral repugnance when he first gazed upon the temples dedicated to the false Canaanite gods. However, after his initial revulsion, Sala could not help but be curious to see what the inside of these infamous temples might look like.

He had to admit that the Temple of Baal was an impressive building, with an open court set apart from the street by a stone wall. Inside the court, visitors could see an altar that was clearly used for animal sacrifice and also a tall, narrow standing stone upon whose flat surface was engraved the picture of a more than life-size warrior armed with a lightning spear and a thunderbolt.

Sala stared in both fascination and horror at the picture. He had never before seen a man-made image of a human. Elohim forbade graven images. His people could sing of His mighty deeds—the creation of the world, of man and animals and plants and all living things—but full knowledge of Elohim lay far beyond the capacity of man to comprehend. It would be impossible to show any kind of representation of the God who had created man and the world man lived in.

But this work was so finely done, so harmonious, so pleasing to the eye—

Abruptly Sala realized what blasphemy he was thinking and quickly turned his back on the stone.

"It's probably supposed to be a portrait of Baal," Lord Nahshon said with deep disgust. "I hate to think of what kind of orgies go on during the celebrations they have in this place."

It was well known to all Israelites that the Canaanite religion allowed—even encouraged—sexual excesses. This was the unfortunate reason so many Israelite men fell under the spell of Baal and the Canaanite women who worshipped him. It had been a centuries-long struggle for the Israelites to keep the people of Abraham constant in this land of seduction and temptation.

Asherah's Shrine was much smaller than Baal's, and in its front courtyard Sala saw several young women with long, loose hair who were dressed in flowing white linen tunics. They were playing on stringed instruments and watching the crowds pass by.

"Are they priestesses, do you think?" Sala asked his father. He had heard some astonishing things about the priestesses of Asherah.

A well-dressed Canaanite man who was passing them heard Sala's question and stopped. He cast his eyes over their expensive linen tunics and said, "Pardon me, but are you new to Jericho? I do not remember ever seeing you before."

Lord Nahshon said, "Yes. We are merchants from Gaza and this is our first visit to your beautiful city."

Sala thought the man was about his father's age, with gray in his beard and his thinning hair. There was an arrogance about him Sala did not like.

The man said, "Gaza? I see. That must account for your accent. Gaza is such a mix of races and tribes. One hardly knows what its real culture is."

The man's arrogance spilled over into contempt when he said *Gaza*. Sala was liking him less with every word he spoke.

Lord Nahshon, however, remained affable. "I can assure you we are good Canaanite people. That is why my son and I have come to Jericho, a good Canaanite city. I own a shipping business and I'm always looking for new customers. I have heard the farms around Jericho produce bountiful harvests, so we decided to come here to see if any of your people might be interested in enlarging their markets. We ship into Egypt primarily, but we go to all the other kingdoms around the Great Sea as well."

Suddenly the Jericho man looked interested. "A shipping merchant? *Hmmm*." His sharp eyes went from Lord Nahshon to Sala, then back to Lord Nahshon. "The farms of Jericho usually sell most of their produce directly into the city, but you are right when you say our harvests are usually plentiful." He tapped his finger against his chin. "What are your names?"

Sala's father gave the names they had agreed to assume for their stay in Jericho. "I am Debir and this is my son Arut. We are recently arrived and have been looking around the city a little, trying to orient ourselves."

The man continued to tap his chin. Sala struggled to maintain a courteous expression. Finally the Jericho man said, "Perhaps it is the will of the gods that I have run into you. I only stopped because we in Jericho have been careful about strangers ever since that pack of Israelites started to invade our territory."

"I can understand that," Lord Nahshon said. "We have heard about some terrible battles."

"They will never take Jericho," the man said, waving a hand toward the walls. "But let me introduce myself. I am Lord Arazu, counselor to the king, and I would be interested in speaking to you more specifically about your business."

Nahshon bowed. "I would be most happy to discuss our

business with you, my lord. I can assure you, we are a highly reputable company in Gaza."

"Good, good. If you come to my house later, I will have a few other people there who may be interested in working with you. Where are you staying?"

Sala admired his father's rueful look. "In the only place we could find, my lord, an inn on the north side of the Lower City."

"Ah. Yes. Well, you have come at a busy time. The festival of the New Year is but a week away and people have been coming in from the outlying areas in large numbers."

Nahshon said, "Unfortunately I did not take account of that when I made my plans. I just thought, with most of the grain already high in the fields, it would be a good time to find customers."

"I am not criticizing you, you are right. But we are not a large city and the few good inns get taken fast. I am sorry men of your class have been forced to take rooms in the Lower City."

Lord Nahshon shrugged. "We will be fine."

Lord Arazu gestured to the building behind them. "I noticed you were looking at Asherah's Shrine. Her priestesses are hoping to collect a goodly sum of money for it during the time of the festival. They will be happy to take your donation."

Sala was silent as Lord Nahshon promised to make a contribution.

"You can get directions to my house from anyone," Lord Arazu said. "I shall see you there at five."

Lord Nahshon assured him they would be there and he and Sala watched as the man walked off down the cobbled street.

Sala said, "I hope you don't really plan to contribute to that shrine, Father!"

"Of course not. Those women—priestesses, as they call them—are nothing but prostitutes. They collect money for the shrine by selling their bodies to men."

Sala looked at the young and pretty girls with horror. "They sell themselves out in the open like this?"

As he watched, a man approached one of the priestesses, bowed, and handed her what looked to be a sum of money. The girl received the money, turned, and began to walk back toward the shrine building. The man followed.

"That is disgusting!" Sala said.

"And that is why Elohim wishes us to destroy them and take this land for ourselves." Lord Nahshon's voice was sober. "Such people do not deserve to live."

Sala wholeheartedly agreed.

Lord Nahshon said, "We cannot allow our feelings to show on our faces, Sala. We must remember we need these people to believe we are one of them. We have been tremendously lucky to meet this Arazu fellow. If he is truly a counselor to the king, we may be able to discover a great deal about the temper of the city, how united they are, how willing to take a stand against an attack."

Sala straightened his shoulders. "You are right, Father," then he smoothed his expression to blandness.

"Very well. I suggest we go back to the Sign of the Olive wine shop. It would be good for us to establish ourselves as regular customers there. That way there'll be little notice paid when we finally do meet with the men Joshua will send."

Sala agreed and the two men began to make their way back toward the Lower City.

Seven

RAHAB HAD BEEN IN JERICHO FOR SEVERAL DAYS. THE only cities she had ever been in before were the seaports of Gaza and Ramac, and she was brimming with excitement at the prospect of being able to see all of the sights of Jericho.

This did not happen immediately. The first day of their residence was spent unpacking what they had brought and cleaning the house that belonged to Mepu's brother. The following day Rahab, Kata, and Atene went shopping for food supplies, so it wasn't until the third day of their residence that Rahab was able to tour the city.

On this day the three women, with Shemu as escort, got an early start, beginning their exploration with the Lower City where they were residing. Jericho had two main streets, both of them rising in a series of wide, cobbled steps from the gate in the outer wall to the second wall that encircled the Upper City. The streets in this area of the town were lined with closely packed houses, many of which served both as shops and residences, the shops on the ground floor and the rooms upstairs for family.

The three women barely glanced at the various foodstuffs that had been brought in from the surrounding farms; they had shopped at those stalls yesterday. What interested Kata, Atene, and Rahab were the crafts: the pretty woven baskets; the elegant pottery; the imaginative wooden bowls; the linen and woolen cloth that other women had woven and dyed. Most fascinating of all was the jewelry. They all owned a few bronze pins, but here there were belts and necklaces and broaches and earrings— some even made of gold.

Atene ventured to ask one of the shop owners if the gold was real and received an outraged stare in return. "Of course it is real, madam. Do you think I would sell fakes?"

Atene flushed with embarrassment and began to apologize, but Rahab took her hand and drew her back onto the street. "Don't pay any attention to him," she advised her sister-in-law. "I'll bet there are a lot of fake items being sold in this market. People like us are probably easy marks; when have we ever seen real gold to be able to make a comparison?"

Kata had been outside the shop waiting for the girls, and the three women stood talking while they waited for Shemu to come out of the farm implement shop that had caught his attention.

Kata said, "I heard a few women talking as they passed by and they said there is a meat market on the west side of the city. I was glad to hear that. We certainly don't have room at that house to have our own sheep and chickens."

Kata had not said much about Mepu's brother's house, but she had managed to make it abundantly clear to the rest of the family that she was not pleased with it.

Rahab said, "It seems to me the whole well-being of this city depends upon the work of us farmers. Without us, the people here would starve."

"They most certainly would," Kata said.

Shemu, who had just come up to them, responded to Rahab's remark. "They might need us but we need them too, Rahab. They get our food, but we get our money from selling them our produce. Father always says that is why Jericho is such a prosperous kingdom: the city and the countryside help each other."

Rahab thought about that, then smiled at her brother. "That is a true thing you have said."

Shemu said, "Ready to move on, Mother?"

"Yes, my son. I think the girls would like to look at the shop that is selling statues."

They bought bread and fruit in one of the shops on the way home. Kata had been noticeably unenthusiastic about cooking in the small indoor kitchen area of the house, so, under instructions from his father, Shemu bought them their main meal at one of the food shops along the way. The spring day was delightfully warm and dry and Mepu, who had spent the day conducting some business with his brother, suggested they sit on the front steps to eat and watch the world go by.

Mepu's brother's house was actually bigger than many of the other houses on the street because it had a third floor. The main problem with the house was that the first two floors smelled, and the space on the third floor was filled with a collection of junk left by the previous renters. After their meal was finished, Kata announced that tomorrow the women were going to once more clean the first two floors, which still smelled, and that the men were going to empty out the third floor so they could use it as another bedroom.

No one opposed her scheme. With only two bedrooms available, the women had been sleeping in one and the men in another. If they had a third bedroom for Rahab, the married couples could be together. Shemu was particularly pleased by his mother's scheme and even volunteered to clean the third floor room once it was emptied. He didn't even complain when Mepu said he had an engagement the following day and could not help. Instead Shemu assured his mother he would be happy to do the work by himself.

The family worked hard, and on the following day they were

rewarded when Mepu said at breakfast that he would take them all to the Upper City, home of Jericho's royalty and nobility. Normally it took a special pass to be allowed through the gate into the Upper City, the wealthy of the town having no desire to clutter their streets with riffraff. This rule was relaxed at the time of the festival of the New Year, which was a feast for all the people of the kingdom. For two weeks the subjects of the king were allowed to enter into the Upper City to view the sights.

The sky was blue and the sun bright on the morning Rahab set off for the Upper City with her family. As soon as she passed through the gate that separated the two parts of Jericho, it was clear to Rahab that she had moved from one world into another. The houses that lined the streets here were large and built of stone, not mud bricks. These were the homes of the rich nobility and the priests who, together with the king, governed the small kingdom of Jericho.

The royal palace was the largest of all the houses in the Upper City. Rahab had never seen anything like it. Fronted by a courtyard paved with flagstones, the entrance to the building itself was approached by shallow steps flanked by two wooden columns set in circular stone bases. There were two floors to the huge building and it spread over so wide a space that Rahab could not begin to guess at how many rooms must lie within.

"The king surely lives well," she murmured into Atene's ear.

Her father heard her. "Remember, Rahab, the king is his people's connection to Baal. We only flourish if he flourishes. It is right for him to live as befits his sacred role."

"Yes, Papa," Rahab said, her eyes still moving around the extensive stone edifice.

Eventually they moved away from the other visitors, who were gaping at the palace, and continued along the street. Mepu pointed out a particularly large house and told them it belonged to the high priest. Atene whispered to Rahab, "He does not live too badly either."

Mepu said importantly, "If you will look ahead, you will see the great Temple of Baal itself."

Rahab kept her eyes on the building as they approached it. It was not nearly as big as the palace, but it was still an imposing sight. The street before it was crowded, and when they reached the gate that led into the courtyard, Rahab realized they would have to wait until those inside the courtyard cleared out before they could fit in.

No one would be allowed into the temple itself. That was only for the king and the priests to enter.

They waited patiently in the hot sun, with Mepu and Shemu exchanging polite comments with the men around them. Rahab, like the rest of the women, was silent, but her eyes flicked with interest around the many faces in the crowd.

When finally it was their turn to go in, Rahab found the courtyard was even larger than it had looked. A massive sacrificial altar stood before the shallow stone steps that led up to the great closed door. The other remarkable thing in the courtyard was a tall standing stone, off to the left of the stairs. When Rahab finally got close enough to see it clearly, she saw that the engraving etched into the stone was a picture of Baal himself.

Rahab had never seen anything so perfect. She looked with wonder at the long legs with their long, slender feet, the raised arms holding the spear of lightning and the club that was a thunderbolt, the kilted skirt and bare upper body, the long-nosed profile.

I wonder how the stonemason knew what Baal looks like? Rahab thought. And she remembered Sala's words about his god who could not be contained in a picture because the god who created the world was too great to be known by the mind of man.

"Aren't you ever going to move?" a woman next to her complained. "There are other people who want to see the picture too."

Rahab turned away, murmuring apologies, and went to join Atene, whom she spied standing in front of the temple building. Atene acknowledged her with a glance and said in an awed voice, "Just think, in a short time the king will be making the sacred marriage in the sanctuary inside."

Rahab nodded. There *was* one time when someone else was allowed within the temple besides the priests and the king, she remembered. It was when the hierodule, the woman picked to represent the goddess Asherah, made the sacred marriage with the king at the festival of the New Year.

A woman standing beside them said in a friendly voice, "Your first time here?"

"Yes," Atene said.

"Well, take a good look. You have no chance of getting into this courtyard on the day of the festival."

"I didn't think we would. Do you know who is to be the hierodule this year?"

The woman shook her head and her gaze slid past Atene to Rahab. "You're a beautiful girl. The Lady Asherah would be proud to have you take her role, I think."

Rahab flushed with embarrassment. "I am not high born enough for such an honor."

Truthfully, she could think of few things she would like less than taking part in the sacred marriage. That role was for the priestesses, who had devoted themselves to the service of the Lady. She was just a simple farm girl, a status that felt comfortable to her.

Eventually Rahab and Atene met up with the rest of the family and they began to move along the cobbled street that descended toward the Upper City wall. Suddenly the crowds began to push and Rahab was shoved against her father. Then she heard someone yelling for everyone to get off the street, to make way for the king.

Her father grabbed her arm and the family pressed back against the house wall along with everyone else on the street. Standing on tiptoe, Rahab could see a contingent of guards carrying bronze spears lining up along the street to make certain no one moved. Then, after a few minutes she heard the *clip-clop* of horses' hooves and the *click click* of wheeled bronze chariots coming down the street.

The first chariot to pass was driven by a handsome young man. He wore a white tunic with the purple belt allowed only to royalty around his waist. His hair was combed away from his face, kept in place by a purple headband. Gold bracelets ringed his strong bare arms. He held his horses to a slow trot as they pranced along, almost dancing in their impatience to move faster.

The beauty of the horses awed Rahab. The sheen on their reddish coats glinted in the afternoon sun and their nostrils flared as they held to the slow pace the driver was enforcing. How wonderful it must be to have an animal like that!

The people around her began to shout a name: *"Tamur! Tamur! Tamur!"*

The handsome driver turned toward the crowd and lifted a gracious hand. His eyes flicked over the assembled people, then stilled when he saw Rahab. Deeply surprised, she found herself looking back.

The charioteer turned to the man who was riding behind him and said something. The man nodded, jumped out of the moving chariot, and waited by the side of the road next to one of the soldiers.

"Who was *that*?" Atene asked her father-in-law.

"That is Prince Tamur, the king's eldest son. I have heard

talk that he wants his father to turn the kingship over to him, that he thinks Makamaron is too old and feeble to answer for the welfare of the city." Mepu snorted. "These young men who cannot wait to take their turn at power!"

"How old *is* Makamaron, Father?" Shemu asked, a teasing note in his voice. "Your age, I should think."

At this point the second chariot came into sight. The purple cloak of the occupant and the gold filet that circled his bald head clearly announced that here was the king.

There was no loud cheering, as there had been for his son. Instead people bowed their heads in silent respect as his chariot passed by. The two horses pulling it were not prancing and fighting to move faster; their pace was slow and, to Rahab, they almost looked bored as they passed with listless dignity.

The king himself was a disappointment. *He looks older than Papa. And his belly is as big as a woman's when she is nine months gone with child.* Rahab looked closer. *He's sweating like a pig.* She remembered the elegant picture on the stone in the palace courtyard. *How could anyone think this king is at all like Baal?* After the king passed by, the soldiers fell in behind him and people began to surge back into the street. Kata said in her gentle way, "I am thirsty, my husband. Is there any place where we might get some water?"

The man who had been standing next to them during the procession turned toward them and spoke to Mepu. "There is a shop on the next street where you can get wine, fruit juice, and honey cakes. It's called the Sign of the Olive."

"Thank you, sir," Mepu said.

Rahab saw the man's eyes move to her.

"Your daughter?"

"Yes," her father replied, his pleasant tone surprising Rahab. Usually her father scowled at men who noticed her. Perhaps this man's fine tunic and expensive sandals made the difference.

Then her father added, "We have come into the city from the countryside for a visit."

The man's eyes raked Rahab from her head to her toes. She felt herself flushing and she moved a little so that she was partially concealed by Shemu.

"You must have just arrived," the rude stranger said to Mepu. "Your daughter would not have gone unnoticed if you had been here for any length of time."

Rahab stared in astonishment as her father actually smiled. "I wanted to show my daughter the wonders of our city."

The man's mouth quirked knowingly. "And no doubt you wished to show the city the wonders of your daughter."

Her father shrugged. "As you say, my lord. She has lived all her life on our farm, and now that she is of marriageable age, I thought it was time we made a trip into Jericho."

"A wise decision," the man said. "And you are?"

At this point a young man came up to their small group and said to the rude man with whom her father was being so surprisingly forthcoming, "That is a good question, Lord Hasis. I, too, would like to know who this lovely young woman is."

Rahab felt Shemu put a reassuring hand on her arm, and she flashed him a quick look of gratitude.

The rude man didn't look at all pleased to see the newcomer. He said, "Farut. I saw you jump out of the prince's chariot."

The young man turned his back on Lord Hasis and addressed himself to Mepu. "I am Farut, friend of Prince Tamur. The prince saw your beautiful daughter from his chariot and would like to meet her."

Rahab felt as if someone had just punched her in the stomach. *The prince! What could someone like the prince want with me?*

For the first time her father looked uneasy. "We are farming folk, my lord, from the village of Ugaru. My daughter is but a simple maid, here to see the sights of Jericho. We are not fit company for the likes of the prince."

Farut waved a dismissive hand. "You must let the prince be the judge of that. What is your name and where do you reside?"

Her father answered the questions. Rahab understood he had no choice, but for some reason she didn't want these men to know where she lived.

"Good. Perhaps I will visit you there." Farut turned to Lord Hasis. "I do not see what your interest is here, my lord."

"Perhaps it is the same as yours."

The two men stood staring at each other in unnerving silence. Rahab felt her heart begin to pound. She wasn't sure what was happening, but she knew it concerned her and she was frightened.

Finally Farut lifted an amused eyebrow, turned, and made his way back through the crowd that had lingered to hear the exchange between the two nobles.

Lord Hasis's face was white and tense. He shot one more look at Rahab and then he, too, moved away.

"I think we should go back to the Lower City, my husband."

Kata's soft voice was a welcome relief after the hostility that had crackled between the two men.

"I'm hungry," Shemu said. "Why don't we go to that wine shop we noticed on our way. The food certainly smelled good as we passed by."

"A good idea." Rahab saw her father glance at her mother for confirmation. Kata nodded.

Rahab heaved a sigh of relief. She wanted to be gone from this place.

Eight

THAT SAME AFTERNOON SALA AND LORD NAHSHON PREsented themselves at the house of Lord Arazu. They had dressed in fresh linen tunics, with carefully combed hair and perfectly clean sandals. Arazu had been correct when he had said everyone would know where he lived; the first person they asked was able to direct them.

The noble's house was one of the largest in a neighborhood of large houses. When the servant escorted Sala and his father inside, Sala saw that it was large enough to accommodate an indoor courtyard. Sala had never seen such a thing before. The courtyard had its own roof, which was supported by four posts at each of its corners. A staircase led from the courtyard up to the second floor of the house, which Sala assumed was the family residence.

Two men besides Lord Arazu were sitting in the cool of the courtyard, looking comfortable in their cushioned wicker chairs. Arazu stood to welcome the newcomers and then presented Sala and his father to Lord Edri, the king's treasurer, and Lord Ratu, the high priest. The two Israelites were invited to join them and Sala did so after first giving his father an amazed look. How did they rate this kind of attention from a brief meeting on the street?

All of the men were served wine by one servant while another servant placed a tray of nuts and fruits on a low table next to them. Once the underlings were out of hearing, Lord Arazu turned to Sala's father with a smile.

"You will have guessed from the attendance here, we in Jericho are very much interested in your proposal of shipping our excess produce to other countries. We are fortunate that our farmers are so industrious and we do indeed often have an abundance of grain and olive oil and wine."

Lord Nahshon nodded and remained silent.

Lord Edri, the treasurer, said, "In a city such as this, which is based upon the agricultural bounty of the countryside, we are always looking for opportunities for investment. Jericho is not on any of the main overland trade routes, so our options are limited. However, if you are looking to buy up our produce to sell abroad . . . well, we would be interested."

Something about the way the treasurer expressed himself set off an alarm in Sala's mind. He glanced at his father to see if he was getting the same impression, but Lord Nahshon's expression was unreadable.

His father replied to the treasurer, "Our preference is to buy early in the harvest, and we like to have a guarantee of how much product you will supply. I can provide the caravans to move the food from Jericho to Gaza so you need not concern yourself with that expense."

Sala remained silent as the bargaining went on, but inside he was growing more and more angry. These rich scoundrels were planning to sell the harvest right out from under the people of the city! They would pay their usual amount to the farmers and then turn around and sell the fruit of Jericho's farms for more than twice the price to his father.

Sala held his tongue, but when the discussion appeared to be winding down, he could not resist. Leaning forward, he said,

"Excuse me, my lords, but what will you do if you sell the early harvest and end up with not enough food to feed your own city?"

Three pairs of dark eyes stared at him with veiled hostility.

"We will take care of our own people, you can be sure of that," the high priest said stiffly.

Hah, Sala thought. *You will take care of yourselves, you mean.*

His father reached over and touched Sala's arm lightly. He said to the others, "I think we will be able to do business."

The three Jericho nobles relaxed.

"I just have one more concern," Nahshon said.

"And what might that be?" Edri asked genially, certain he had gotten what he wanted.

"I am a little worried about the stability of your government. I have been hearing rumors that there is a movement to dethrone the king and put his son into his place. Is there any truth to this gossip?"

Lord Arazu flushed red all the way up to his bald head. "It is true there is a group of troublemakers trying to stir up dissent, but Makamaron has ruled successfully for thirty years now. He has the admiration and respect of the citizens of Jericho. This upstart son of his will be king when his father dies, and not one day before."

"I am glad to hear that," Sala's father said. "With the advance of those Israelites who escaped from Egypt, a divided government in Jericho could lay you open to an attack. They are close enough to be a concern—just across the Jordan, or so I have heard."

The treasurer, a skinny man with a long thin nose, gave a short laugh. "Have you seen our walls, sir? And the spring that lies within them? We can hold out against a siege for years. I would not worry about Jericho falling to any enemy."

"A siege would destroy your commerce, though," Sala pointed out.

Arazu glared. "There will be no siege. That ragtag crowd cannot come against well-armed troops, such as we have in Jericho. Put that thought out of your mind, sir. It will not happen."

Sala looked at his father, who said mildly, "I am glad to hear that."

After a little more discussion, and a plan for them to meet again to discuss amounts, Sala and Nahshon made their way out of the impressive house that was at least three times as large as theirs and walked in silence to the gate that would admit them back into the Lower City.

The three Jericho nobles who were left alone immediately broke into discussion.

"So visitors who have been in the city only a few days have already heard of the discord between Makamaron and Tamur," Arazu said.

"Do we know who is spreading this nonsense?" Edri wanted to know.

The high priest gave the treasurer an impatient look. "The prince himself, of course. And that group of malcontents who hang around him."

Edri steepled his hands and looked grave. "I was there when the king and the prince drove down the main street today. The crowd cheered Tamur as if he were some great military hero."

Arazu let out a long frustrated breath and the three of them sat for a while in silence. The servant came in with the wine jug but Arazu waved him away. Finally he said, "If Tamur succeeds in deposing Makamaron, then we are done. The prince will appoint the members of his own circle to take our places."

Edri, the treasurer, slammed his hand down on the wicker

arm of his chair. "There must be something we can do to stop this royal upstart."

The high priest sighed. "It is going to happen eventually. Makamaron is an aging man. With the festival of the New Year coming up, my great fear is that he will fail to complete the sacred marriage. I have asked him if he is adequate to the task, and he insists he is, but I have my doubts. If he should fail to consummate the union, and the hierodule tells the prince he has failed, then Tamur will have solid grounds for deposing his father."

No one disagreed. Belief was strong among the Canaanite people that the fertility and strength of the nation were bound up with the sexual and physical prowess of the king. If the king was impotent, then the land and the flocks and the people would wither. If the king could not make the sacred marriage, then it was time for him to step down and turn his sacral role over to his son.

"Who is the hierodule this year?" the treasurer asked.

"Arsay," the high priest responded.

Silence fell as they considered this comment. Arsay was one of the priestesses of the Temple of Asherah. It was her turn to be the hierodule, the stand-in for the goddess Asherah, who would be the king's partner in the making of the sacred marriage. But Arsay's brother also happened to be one of the prince's closest friends. The chances that she would hold her tongue about any failure on the king's part were next to none.

"We need at least another year out of Makamaron," Arazu said. "If we can make money from this deal with the Gaza merchants, we will be in a much better position when he must finally relinquish the kingship."

The high priest leaned forward as if he had just thought of something. "What if we get a new hierodule? Someone whose loyalty is to us? Someone who will keep quiet if the king proves incompetent."

The others looked at him with respect.

"That is an excellent idea," Arazu said. "But who can we get? I don't believe we can trust any of the priestesses."

"I must think about it," the high priest replied.

Edri said, "We don't have much time. We are within a week of the festival."

"I know, I know," the high priest returned. "It is the only way we can assure Makamaron will keep his throne, however."

The three men agreed and they all decided to give some serious thought to finding a woman to take Arsay's place as hierodule in the coming New Year festival.

"What a collection of villains they are," Sala said disgustedly as he and his father walked away from Lord Arazu's house.

"They are that. But their villainy may work in our favor. A divided city will fall more easily than one that is united."

"But, Father . . ." Sala fixed his eyes on the high wall that protected the Upper City, then moved beyond to the huge embankment and wall that surrounded the entire town. "What that ugly-looking treasurer said about Jericho withstanding a siege has some truth. Look at those walls. This city could hold out forever within walls like this—especially if they have water and food."

"That may be how it looks, Sala, but did it not look just as impossible for the Israelites to escape from Egypt? Yet they did it because it was Elohim's will. We have heard of the terrible plagues Elohim sent upon the Egyptians to force Pharaoh to release our people. Why should He not also lift His hand at Jericho?"

Sala walked beside his father and thought about what Lord Nahshon had said. His father had been on fire ever since he had first met with Joshua, the Israelite leader, and Lord Nahshon had passed his passion along to his son. Sala had no doubts that Canaan was the Promised Land that Elohim had given to Abraham for the Israelite people. When Joshua had asked Sala and his father to go to Jericho in order to discover the military weaknesses of the city, Sala had been both thrilled and honored to accept such an assignment.

Thus far the army of the Israelites had been brilliantly successful, mowing down the armies of Heshbon and Og and destroying all those who lived in their lands. The entrance into Canaan itself lay through Jericho, and Sala understood that Joshua's army would be just as merciless here if it were able to get into the city.

It is only right that this should happen. Elohim is with us and this is what He wishes—His land to be in the possession of His people. I must put my trust in Elohim. If we follow His will, He will always be with us.

Sala and his father had passed through the wall that separated the two parts of the city and the Sign of the Olive was right in front of them.

"Shall we stop for some supper?" Lord Nahshon asked.

Sala agreed and they found a table and ordered food. Sala was eating and watching the people walk by on the street. He took particular notice of one family group, mainly because other people on the street were turning their heads to watch as the three women and two men passed by. As they drew closer, Sala's eyes were drawn to one of the girls. Her head carriage and walk were so proud and lovely that she reminded him of a ship in full sail.

He looked closer and felt his eyes widen. She was an amazingly beautiful girl. Her black hair fell in a shining loose braid over her shoulder, her skin glowed, her full mouth . . . Sala shook his head as if to clear it.

She stopped outside the wine shop door and looked in.

For the first time Sala saw her huge dark eyes. His own mouth dropped open. He remembered those eyes. He would never forget them, filled with terror as she raced down the street in Gaza toward him.

Rahab. He said the word soundlessly. The two men with her were looking around the shop as well, clearly searching for a free table. There were none to be had and the family was turning away when, without any conscious thought, Sala leaped to his feet and ran out into the street to stand in front of them and stop them from leaving. He looked at the girl's startled face and said, "Rahab!"

She looked back and for a terrible minute he thought she didn't know who he was. Then her face broke into a radiant smile.

"Sala! Is it really you?" Her voice was even huskier than he remembered.

"Yes." He tried to laugh. "It is really me."

"What are you doing here?"

They said it at the same time, and then they laughed together. Her teeth were so white, her mouth so delicious.

What had happened to the skinny, brave little girl he remembered?

"I am here with my family for a visit," she said. "What about you? Are you here with your father?"

Suddenly he realized what he had done. *Rahab's family knows we are Israelites. They could reveal our true identities.*

His father's voice spoke from behind him. "Who are these people, Aru?"

"Lord Nahshon!" Rahab said eagerly. "Don't you remember me? I'm Rahab—the girl Sala rescued from the kidnappers. This is my family. You met my brother, Shemu, when he came to bring me home. This is his wife, Atene, and my father, Mepu, and my mother, Kata."

She was glowing with delight at this unexpected reunion. Sala glanced at his father's grim face, then looked back at Rahab. He knew very well that he should not have stopped her, but somehow he could not bring himself to be sorry.

Nine

RAHAB COULD HARDLY BELIEVE HER EYES. IT WAS SALA. Here in Jericho. Right now—right in front of her! She wanted to hug him but settled for a smile.

He looked so good. He was taller than his father now, and so handsome. She liked everything about his face: his thin curved nose, his warm brown eyes, his clean-cut cheekbones. He looked older too, more like a man than a boy.

She heard her father saying, "Who is this man, Rahab?"

"It's Sala, Papa. Remember the time I was a kid—"

"Stop!" Sala's voice was deeper than she remembered it, and he was staring desperately into her eyes. "Don't say any more, Rahab, not until we can go somewhere private."

Lord Nahshon stepped forward and spoke to Rahab's father. "I am sorry to be so discourteous, but my son is right. We must not give out our names until we are sure we cannot be overheard."

"What is going on here?" Rahab's father sounded suspicious, and Rahab suddenly understood what Sala meant. They were Israelites, he and his father. What were they doing in Jericho?

"Father, I know these people too," Shemu said quietly. He looked at Sala's father and asked, "Where can we go?"

"The common room of the inn where we are staying should be empty right now."

And so the two parties formed into one and together they

79

left the cobbled main street of the Lower City and moved into the narrow dirt roads where the poorer people lived. Mepu made Rahab walk between him and Kata, Shemu and Atene followed behind them, and Sala and his father walked last. Rahab wanted so much to turn and look at him, but she restrained herself, knowing how unwise it would be to call attention to their party.

The old inn's common room was indeed empty, and the seven of them sat on benches around two scarred wooden tables they pulled together.

Rahab's father looked grimly at Sala's father. "Now, will you kindly tell me who you are and what this is all about?"

"My son is the boy who saved your daughter when she was running away from the slavers in Gaza," Lord Nahshon replied quietly, his mouth set in a grim hard line. "He should never have accosted your daughter the way he did. I am sorry for his bad manners."

"*Bad manners?*" Kata rarely spoke up in company, and Rahab looked with astonishment at her mother. "If it was not for him my daughter would be a slave in Egypt!" She gave Sala a warm smile. "I am happy to have this opportunity to thank you myself, Sala."

Sala flushed, said, "Thank you," and shot a quick glance at Rahab.

She gave him a brief smile.

Lord Nahshon was going on. "It was not only bad manners, madam, it was dangerous. Dangerous for my son and me, that is. We are Israelites—you know this—and the mood in Jericho right now is not favorable toward my people."

Rahab jumped as her father slapped his hand against the table. "Just exactly what *are* you Israelites doing in Jericho, if I may ask."

Sala leaned forward. "It was because of me, sir. I have always thought your idea of shipping your excess products into Egypt was a good one; it would benefit you and it would benefit us. I talked my father into following up on this venture and that is why we are in Jericho. We did not realize when we set out that the Israelite army was so close."

Mepu looked unconvinced. "If you wanted to follow up on my scheme, why did you not come to my farm to speak to me? Why did you come to the city?"

"We did not know where you lived," Sala replied. "All we knew was that Rahab's family lived on a farm within the territory of Jericho. So we came here to the city itself to see if we might find someone we could talk to who might be interested in the idea." He looked at Rahab. "When I saw you, I was so surprised, I didn't think."

"I am glad you didn't."

Her father shot her an angry look and she lowered her eyes.

Shemu said, "What I don't understand is how you expected anyone in Jericho to want to do business with Israelites. They have been systematically destroying every kingdom they pass through, and now they apparently have the deluded idea that they can take over Canaan. The last person anyone in Jericho would want to deal with is an Israelite."

Sala gave her brother such a charming smile that Rahab blinked. "You see, Shemu, we haven't told anyone we're Israelites. We've said we're Canaanites from Gaza. I assure you that our company can ship out of Gaza too, if we choose, so that part is not a lie."

Silence fell around the table. Rahab sneaked a peek at Sala and found him looking at her. She gave him a quick grin, then looked down at the table and began tracing a deep scratch with her finger.

Finally Mepu said slowly, "So your presence in Jericho has nothing to do with the Israelite army that is almost at our door?"

"Nothing," Lord Nahshon replied firmly. "I do not approve of war. It is bad for business."

Mepu's skeptical look made Rahab nervous. If her father should decide to report Sala, he would be arrested. She shivered at the thought.

She listened as Sala said, "The Israelites would be mad to try to attack this city, sir. The walls . . ." He lifted his hands and shrugged to demonstrate the uselessness of any attack on such a monstrous barrier.

"We know that," Rahab's father answered. "But do *they*?"

"They will once they get a good look," Sala replied. "Believe me, sir, we are here to trade with Jericho, not to collude in her destruction. Jericho's fall will hurt our business, not help us. Self-interest alone demands that we wish you well."

This sounded like an excellent argument to Rahab and she nodded vigorously in agreement.

Atene touched her hand and frowned slightly. Rahab understood her sister-in-law was warning her not to appear to be taking sides, and she nodded.

Shemu was saying, "About your scheme to ship our products, have you had any success in finding a party interested in selling to you?"

Lord Nahshon said, "We have just had a meeting with several of the city's lords and they have indicated they are indeed interested."

Mepu's glare was full of outrage. "The *lords*? What do they have to say about our harvests? It's the farmers you should be speaking to!"

"I should be more than happy to speak to the farmers," Lord Nahshon replied, his voice calm and decisive.

Rahab looked pleadingly at her mother. Kata turned to her husband and said softly, "There is no reason to give them away, my husband. They can help you to sell your extra wine and we owe them so much. They saved your daughter's life, remember."

Mepu stared first at Sala and then at Lord Nahshon, then he said irritably, "I suppose I cannot, in honor, repay them by turning them into the authorities." He focused his hard stare on Lord Nahshon. "But I won't have you buying farm products from the nobles. They'll pocket all the money and we will get nothing."

Rahab had to restrain herself from clapping her hands in glee. It was going to be all right!

Lord Nahshon said, "That most certainly appeared to be their plan."

"We have some talking to do, you and I."

"Yes, indeed we do. Where are you staying?"

"We're renting a house from my brother—it's only two streets away from here."

"Good." Lord Nahshon glanced around the deserted common room. "This is often a busy place. I wouldn't feel comfortable discussing business here."

"It is probably best to meet in a place where no one recognizes us, one of the wine shops perhaps. I will speak to you tomorrow."

Mepu rose, and Rahab and the rest of the family stood up as well. "I will be in touch with you."

Lord Nahshon lifted a hand. "One other thing. We have dropped our Israelite names. In Jericho I am called Debir and my son is Arut."

Mepu's look was sour but he said, "All right."

As her family turned away from the table, Rahab sneaked a look at Sala. He was watching her.

"Rahab!" her father called, and she turned away.

Rahab was so excited that night she could not fall asleep. Now that the third floor had been cleaned up, she had the room all to herself so her wakefulness did not disturb anyone else. She crossed her arms behind her head, stared up into the darkness, and thought about Sala.

She couldn't believe they had actually met. She had thought about him so often in the last few years, she had hoped she could find a husband who would be like him, and now here he was—in person—himself!

She wiggled with excitement. He had recognized her. Perhaps he had thought of her as often as she had thought of him. Perhaps . . .

Her father had brought her to Jericho to find her a wealthy husband. Sala's family was wealthy, she thought. They had a big house in Ramac, and Lord Nahshon owned a whole fleet of ships.

The thought flitted across her mind that perhaps she might marry Sala. Then she thought of the things her father and brothers had been saying about the Israelites.

Everyone she knew hated the Israelites now that they had come back from Egypt and begun to terrorize the local nations. Her father had been outraged when he learned they had killed all the men, women, and children in Og. "They will never take Canaan," Mepu had said. "Jericho will save us."

All of the euphoria Rahab had felt at meeting Sala again came crashing down. Even if by some miracle her father would permit her to marry an Israelite, Sala was probably married already. Married to some Israelite girl of whom his mother approved. She had never approved of Rahab.

Rahab felt tears prick behind her eyes. She would be forced to marry some dull man who thought only about money. Some man whose eyes were cold, not full of warmth and understanding. Some man whose mouth was pinched and tight, not always ready to break into a smile. Some hideous, ugly person she would have to put up with for the rest of her miserable life.

She felt the vitality draining out of her as she thought about her future. But there was nothing she could do. Her father would choose her husband and she would obey. Sala would go home to his wife and have a wonderful life in his pretty town on the Great Sea. His wife would probably even get to ride in a boat!

But he had saved her life. Surely that created a special bond between them. When they had parted, she remembered asking him if they would meet again, and he had answered it was in the hands of Elohim. Perhaps this Elohim had brought him here to Jericho, at just the time when she was here too.

Suddenly Rahab felt how hot and airless the bedroom was. She sat up, lifting her hair off her neck to feel cooler. She wanted a drink of water but she didn't want to go all the way downstairs to get it.

Was there any hope for them at all? If there wasn't, then Rahab thought she might as well be dead.

Ten

PRINCE TAMUR WAS HAVING BREAKFAST AT THE PALace with his closest companion, Farut. The king's residence had some thirty rooms, with three large courtyards and half a dozen staircases leading to the upper floor. The prince had his own apartment and courtyard, completely separated from the rooms used by his father, the king.

Tamur was a tall, handsome young man, with black hair and flashing black eyes. In the last year, as the king had noticeably failed in health, those eyes had grown hungrier and hungrier.

He was tired of waiting for his father to die; he felt he should be the king right now, when they were in danger of being attacked by the Israelites. Jericho needed a young and energetic king, not an old and tired one. The city needed a king who could truly represent the strength, the power, the potency of Baal. Once his father had done that, but he was an old man now. His time was over.

Farut, who was Tamur's age and had been brought up with him, had just come from a meeting with his own father, the commander of the king's army.

"Makamaron will not abdicate to you. My father is certain about that. The king is determined to make the sacred marriage with the hierodule and prove the validity of his claim to retain the kingship."

"What does your father think about this?"

Farut shrugged. "All of these old men are hanging together, my lord. My father says he is convinced that Makamaron is fully capable of completing the marriage act."

"That's not what I have heard from his concubines." Tamur, who had been toying with the fruit on his plate, set his jaw in a determined line. "He was barely capable last year. If he fails this year, then the rains will not come and the land will dry up and the crops will not grow. He is risking the well-being of the whole kingdom with his stubbornness!"

Farut said, "My father says that the power of Baal will overshadow him, that the god will give him strength."

The two young men were meeting in the privacy of the prince's bedroom. The coverings on the carved wooden bedstead were still rumpled from the night, and the table between the cushioned chairs by the narrow window where the prince and his friend sat was set with fruit and breads. Neither man had touched the various honey and nut rolls that lay so temptingly before them.

"What about the hierodule—Arsay?" the prince asked. "You were going to have her brother speak to her. Has Bari done so?"

"Yes. There is good news there. If the king fails in his duty, she will speak up."

Tamur let his breath out as if he had been holding it for a long time. "So. We should be safe then. Once she announces that he has failed, I will demand he step down from his throne so I may sit upon it."

"Bari says we can count on the truthfulness of his sister. *She* does not want to be blamed if the rains do not fall this winter."

"Good." Tamur reached his arms over his head and stretched. "Very, very good. If my father is faced with his failure, he will be forced to concede the rule to me. The city will demand it."

"Many of them are in favor of you taking the throne right

now. The reception you received in the street yesterday was proof enough of that."

The prince looked pleased. Then he tilted his head and gave his friend a considering look. "Do you remember that stunning girl we saw yesterday?"

Farut laughed. "It would be hard to forget her. That mouth! A man could die just looking at her mouth."

The prince drummed his fingers on the tabletop. He was well known in Jericho as a lover of beautiful women.

Farut said, "Her family looked like respectable country people, my prince. Perhaps it would not be wise just now to do anything that might upset the lower classes. You will need them on your side when you become king, especially with the Israelites on our doorstep."

Tamur flung himself back in his chair. "I suppose you're right. Oh well. The girl will keep. Right now, we must concentrate on how we are going to manage the exchange of power."

Sala had not slept well that night and was up the moment the first fingers of light crept into the sky. Lord Nahshon was still sleeping soundly, so Sala went down the stairs and out into the narrow street, hoping the morning air would clear his brain.

The empty street was quiet as only the gentle sliding of night into day can be quiet. He found himself thinking, *Rahab is only two streets away.*

He had thought he remembered Rahab quite clearly, but when he had seen her yesterday her beauty had struck him almost physically. It was hard to reconcile the woman before him with the child he had saved.

But he remembered the joyous smile she had given him when

they met, the quick glance over her shoulder as they left, the lift of her eyebrows when he had looked at her. It was possible, he thought with a lifting of his heart. It was possible that it was truly Rahab behind that new woman's face.

There had always been a special connection between them. Perhaps it was just that he had saved her from the horror of slavery, that he felt responsible for her and in turn she had felt grateful and obliged to him.

He grinned. He doubted Rahab had ever felt obliged to anyone. She had a freedom of spirit he had never found in any other girl. Boys would sometimes have it, but never girls.

She wasn't married. From what he and his father had surmised last night after her family had left, her father had brought her to Jericho to find her a wealthy husband. *He will be successful. That smile would knock any man off his balance.*

Sala scowled at the thought. He did not like the idea of Rahab marrying some arrogant Jericho noble. She should marry someone who would appreciate her special spirit, someone who . . .

His mind shied away from the thought. He and Rahab could never marry. She was a Canaanite. Her religion was anathema to Elohim and His people.

Sala had heard how Moses had treated his own men when he discovered they had participated in the rites of Baal and had relations with the women of Moab. Moses had commanded that every one of the guilty Israelite males, his own people, should be executed. The sentence had been carried out immediately.

Nahshon himself had approved of this punishment when the men of Ramac were discussing it at their weekly gathering. Sala's father was the acknowledged leader of the gathering, and all the others had agreed with his condemnation of any Israelite man who would do such a filthy thing.

What would his father say if Sala told him he would like to marry Rahab?

Sala shuddered. He was mad to even entertain the thought of marriage to a Canaanite. She stood for everything he was against. Her beauty was a temptation he had to resist.

But . . . it was not just her looks that attracted him. It was her spirit. There were beautiful girls in Ramac, but none of them had the joy of life that Rahab had. None of them made him feel he wanted to spend his life with them. In contrast to her, they were dull, dull, dull.

While he had been standing in front of the inn meditating, the street had been waking up. Shops were opening their front doors and women were carrying water jars to fill at the spring. The smell of bread baking drifted to his nose. His father would be wondering where he was.

Feeling no better for this extended talk with himself, Sala went slowly back into the inn.

Mepu and Shemu were also early risers. They washed their faces and hands in the kitchen basin and went outdoors to buy some bread from the bake shop at the end of the street. There was no courtyard at the back of this tiny house, only the city wall, and Kata had refused to try to bake in the miniscule kitchen. In consequence they had become regular customers at the bake shop.

There were a few people before them, and they waited patiently, wearing their shawls against the cool morning air. The day of the festival of the New Year, when the hours of light equaled the hours of darkness, was quickly approaching, and the weather was warming. The flax had already been harvested and soon the barley crop would be ready. The winter rains were gone and the heat of summer had not yet set in. It was the best time of the year.

"It is a shame to be cooped up in a city on such a day as this," Shemu murmured to his father.

"I know. But it will be worth it if we can get Rahab settled."

"Another good thing has come out of our visit. We found out about those greedy nobles trying to sell our crops out from under us," Shemu said.

Mepu nodded, looked around at the other customers, then gestured for Shemu to hold his tongue. His son nodded.

They bought bread and nut cakes and took them back to the house. There was a small room just inside the front door that served as the family gathering place, and Mepu put the basket of breads down on the single low table. The seating in the room consisted of cushions on the floor, and the two men each lowered themselves with the ease of long practice to a cross-legged position.

Mepu said, "I have been thinking. I do not like it that those two Israelites are here in Jericho. The boy was glib enough about their business scheme, but the more I think about it the more I do not like them being here."

Shemu, who was waiting for his father to take the first bite of food, replied, "I thought their reason for coming sounded plausible enough. It was our own scheme, remember, and it was a good one."

Mepu took a bite of nut bread and chewed reflectively. "It might be plausible, but it still makes me uneasy. There is an Israelite army less than twenty miles away, and we all know what they have done to the kingdoms south of us. No one has been able to stand against them. And now they are poised at the very entrance to Canaan and we have two Israelites walking around Jericho. Disguised as Canaanites."

"It could be coincidence that they decided to come at this time."

"Perhaps." Mepu did not look convinced.

Shemu bit into his own crusty slice of fresh baked bread. "What do you think we should do?"

"We could turn them in to the authorities, I suppose, but Rahab was right. I cannot forget the debt I owe them. Without that young man's intervention . . ."

Shemu nodded. "They were good to her. The son saved her from the slavers and the father kept her safe. No one molested her. And he sent for us to come and get her. There was no reason except for kindness for them to have been so careful of her welfare."

Mepu looked glum. "I know."

"They are rich too, Father. I saw their house in Ramac, and Rahab said the father owns many ships. Families like that might hesitate to throw in their lot with a group of barbarian invaders. The Israelites have lived in this country for as long as we have. Why should their loyalty be to this foreign group and not to us?"

Mepu took another bite of bread. "Perhaps you are right, Shemu. In truth, I do not know what to think about them."

Shemu said, "Let us look at this situation differently. If they are here as spies, they will be planning to report whatever they find out to the Israelite army. Is this not so?"

Mepu nodded agreement.

"But what is there to report? They will have to inform the Israelites that the walls of Jericho are unassailable, that the city is stocked with grain, and, finally, that one of the finest springs in all of Canaan lies within the safety of our walls. Even if the whole of the surrounding countryside moves into the city, we can withstand an extended siege."

"They would be spies who bring only bad news to their people."

Shemu smiled. "Perhaps it would not be a bad thing for them to carry that news to our enemy."

"Clever thinking. Very clever."

Shemu looked pleased. "And there is always the possibility they are not spies at all. They might be here for the reason they gave us. They might want to do business with us."

Mepu's jaw tightened. "If that is the case, we must be certain they deal with us and not with the greedy nobles. Those bloodsuckers would buy up all of our produce and sell it at an inflated price."

"They said they had already spoken to a few nobles. We must act quickly if we are not to lose out."

"Yes. I said I would be in touch with them. After breakfast you must go to their inn and see if you can set up a meeting."

They both turned their heads as they heard the sound of steps on the stairs. It was Kata. She gave them an approving smile as she came into the room. "I see you have been to the bake shop already."

"We have, Mother."

"Did you sleep well, my husband? Did you sleep well, my son?"

Both men assured her they had.

"Good. I will get the water and the fruit from the storage room. Rahab and Atene will be down soon."

As she left the room, Shemu said softly, "What are you going to do about Rahab, Father?"

"What do you mean?"

"The prince noticed her yesterday."

Mepu didn't reply at first. Finally he said, "I don't want Rahab to have anything to do with the prince. He will not be looking to marry her, and I do not want your sister to be some man's courtesan. She was not brought up for that."

"We need to find her a husband without delay then. Otherwise there will be little we can do if royalty wants her."

They both turned their eyes to the staircase. Rahab's voice could be heard from the second floor. Mepu said, "We must not be here if the prince's messenger comes. If she is unavailable he may forget about her."

Shemu agreed as Kata came back into the room with the jug of water and some cups. As she was putting them on the table beside the basket of bread, Rahab and Atene came into the room.

Mepu looked at his daughter. It always amazed him that he could have produced so beautiful a child. She was his treasure.

She smiled at him. "Good morning, Papa."

"Good morning, daughter," he returned.

"Will you have some fruit, Rahab?" Kata asked and Mepu watched as she took the platter from her mother. She deserved a rich husband, he thought, and it was his duty to make certain she got one.

Eleven

When breakfast was finished Kata set Rahab and Atene to work cleaning. This house would never be the same as her house in the country, but she was determined to get every speck of dirt that had accumulated over the years out of the floors and the walls.

Her mother liked to clean but Rahab did not. As she worked, her thoughts were far away. What was Sala doing today? Would she get to see him? She hoped her mother wouldn't want to stay home and clean all day or she would never have a chance of running into him in the city.

They had only been at work for an hour before Mepu came to tell his wife that the women should get dressed, they were going out. Rahab's heart leaped at this news.

Kata put her pail down with a thump. "We are cleaning the house, my husband."

"You can clean the house anytime, Kata. It's a beautiful day today—not hot, not cold. A day to be outside."

"Where are we going, Father?" Atene asked, looking up from the floor she had been scrubbing.

"We are to meet with the Israelites in the same place where we saw them yesterday."

Rahab's heart jumped.

"The Israelites?" Atene was surprised.

"Yes. We have business to discuss. Don't take forever to get ready. Shemu and I will be waiting for you in the front room."

As Mepu disappeared down the stairs, Atene said to Rahab, "That's odd. Why would the men want to take us with them if they are going to talk business?"

Rahab didn't care if it was odd or not, all she cared about was that she was going to see Sala. She began to gather up the cleaning rags and tried to think which of her tunics would be most flattering.

Her mother said, "It is not for us to question your father. Go and get ready, girls, and don't take too long."

Rahab put on a freshly washed long tunic of white linen and gathered it at her waist with a wide blue sash. She took her favorite blue shawl downstairs so Atene could drape it gracefully over her left shoulder. Then she asked Atene to braid her hair. When Atene was finished, Rahab asked anxiously, "Do I look all right?"

Atene laughed. "You never ask about your appearance, Rahab. What's gotten into you?"

Rahab turned away to hide the flush that colored her cheeks. "Nothing."

The midday weather was cool and pleasant as the family made its way up the cobbled street. The wine shop they were heading for was located in the Lower City but only a few feet away from the walls that divided it from the Upper City. The street was busy but Rahab hardly noticed the people who crowded around her as she followed in the wake of her father. Her heart was beating fast and her stomach was fluttery. She had never felt like this before. She wanted to smile until her cheeks hurt, but she contained herself and trailed along behind her father and Shemu, trying to look unconcerned.

When finally they reached the wine shop designated for

the meeting, Mepu went inside to see if the Israelites were there while Shemu waited outside with the women. When Mepu came back out, Sala was with him. Rahab could not contain her smile.

Mepu said to Kata, "It is too crowded inside for all of us, so Sala—*Arut*, I mean—will escort you to the south garden to wait for us."

"Yes, my husband."

The smile died away from Rahab's face. Sala's eyebrows were drawn together, forming a crease over his nose. Clearly he wanted to stay in the wine shop and not have to go with the women.

Kata said timidly, "I am sorry you have been inconvenienced by us."

At Kata's words the line disappeared from between Sala's brows and he looked embarrassed. "I am sorry if I seemed ungracious. I am delighted to be of service to you ladies. I believe the garden is this way, so if you will come along . . ."

He began to walk toward the wide, shallow steps that led into the Upper City.

Rahab's chin was up. He didn't want to be with her. And she had been so joyful at the thought of seeing him! Angry and hurt, she let Atene step forward to walk beside him while she remained behind with her mother.

The garden was a charming spot of green in the midst of the great stone buildings that comprised the Upper City. It was situated on the south wall, a half-acre pocket of linden trees with stone benches set under their softly rounded canopies. A flagged walkway set the park off from the city streets.

Rahab spread her skirts and took a seat on one of the benches. Atene and Kata sat on a second bench to discuss a recipe. That left the seat next to Rahab for Sala.

Sala sat. Rahab stared straight ahead and ignored his existence. After a long silent moment he said, "Are you angry at me?"

"No."

Silence again.

"Well then, why won't you look at me?"

"You don't want to be here with me so I thought you would appreciate it if I didn't bother you with my chatter."

More silence. A boy with a small wooden sword in his hand ran down the path in front of them. From the park area near the wall they could hear the sound of children's voices.

Sala sighed. "Rahab, it's not that I don't want to be with you."

She turned her head fractionally. "Then what is it?"

He looked back at her and a muscle jumped in his jaw. "It's just . . . well, I am learning the business from my father and I thought I should listen to the discussion."

"Oh." She returned her head to its forward position. He had no interest in her, she thought dismally. What a fool she had been to think he might want to marry her. He didn't even want to talk to her; he'd rather talk about business. She blinked hard and told herself fiercely she would not cry.

Two young men, obviously noble, were strolling toward them. One of them glanced at her casually and stopped.

Rahab looked at him in surprise.

He smiled. "I beg your pardon, I know it is rude of me to speak to you when we haven't been properly introduced—"

Rahab didn't care for the condescending note in his voice and was about to say so when Sala cut in. "You're right, it is rude. I suggest you be on your way and leave the lady alone."

Affronted, the young man turned his eyes to Sala. Rahab looked at him too. Her breath caught. He looked . . . dangerous.

The young man took a quick step back. "I meant no harm. Are you her brother? Your sister is beautiful."

"I am her betrothed," Sala said, "and my advice to you is to be on your way."

The young man's companion said, "Come along, Charzu. Don't make trouble."

The young man let himself be led away by his friend. As soon as they were out of sight, Rahab turned to Sala and said lightly, "I didn't know we were betrothed. When exactly is our wedding day?"

Spots of color stained his high cheekbones. "I'm sorry, it was the best way I could think of to get rid of him."

From the next bench Atene, who had observed the scene, said to Sala, "Everybody stares at Rahab. Even the prince noticed her yesterday from his chariot. He sent his friend to find out where she was staying."

Sala's brows snapped together.

Rahab wanted to tell Atene not to say such things, but fortunately Kata, who was seated on the other side of Atene, said something and Atene turned away. Rahab silently blessed her mother and turned once more to Sala.

He had swung around so his back was to the women and his body blocked Rahab's face from their view. "Is that what you and your father are aspiring to then, the hand of a prince?"

She looked into his eyes, trying to decipher his mood. "That's a ridiculous thing to say. First of all, the prince would never stoop to marry a farmer's daughter. And I wouldn't marry him even if he wanted me to. I would suffocate having to live the rest of my life in this walled-up city."

"I thought your father brought you here so he could find you a rich husband."

"I have to marry somebody, Sala." Rahab was all sweet reason. "That is what girls do with their lives."

He looked down at his hands. "What kind of man do you *want* to marry?"

Rahab kept staring at him, not sure what she should answer. Should she expose her heart? She knew it would hurt her cruelly if he rejected her, but . . . if she did nothing, if she never let him know how she felt, then he might simply go away and she would have lost him forever.

That would be worse.

She held his gaze and said bravely, "I want to marry a man who can take me on a boat."

Sala went pale. He swallowed. "Rahab." His voice was unsteady. "No matter how you may feel, or how I may feel, you and I can never marry. My father would never permit it."

Rahab ignored the last part of his statement and went right for the important part. "Do you want to marry me?"

"I've always thought of you as a child." She could see he was trying to be as honest as she had been. "But then, when I saw you again yesterday . . . well, I realized that you are the reason I was never eager to marry any of my father's choices. None of the girls were at all like you."

Her heart began to sing. *He does want to marry me. He loves me. That is all that matters. He loves me!*

She put all of her happiness into her smile. "I have thought about you, Sala. I have always remembered you."

But instead of looking happy, he looked anguished. "You don't understand. My father—"

"I know there are obstacles, Sala. My father does not like Israelites and your father probably does not like Canaanites. But don't you see, what is important is how *we* feel. Not them."

"You have no idea of the obstacles, Rahab." His face looked thinner, older. "If I were to marry a Canaanite woman, it would be as if I put a dagger through my father's heart. Everything he believes— everything *I* believe—would be outraged by such a union. I am his only son, Rahab." He shook his head. "I am his heir. I am to follow him not only in the business but also as *Chazzan* in our prayer meetings."

Rahab could feel herself growing colder and colder as he spoke. "You are going to be a priest?"

"Not a priest. We have had no priests since our people became so separated. But in Ramac we have always met, to pray and to talk about our scriptures, and the leader is the one who can read those scriptures. I am the one whom everyone expects to replace my father someday. I cannot—"

He stopped talking and looked at her.

"Do you love me?" Rahab asked, feeling small and fragile.

There was a white line around his mouth and his nose looked pinched. "Yes," he said.

"And I love you, Sala. You are the only man I wish to marry."

"I wish we had never met again," he said wretchedly.

I can't believe this is happening. How can he be saying such things to me?

"I thought your father liked me," she whispered.

"Yes, he liked you. But you are not an Israelite. He would think my marrying a Canaanite woman would forever defile me in the eyes of Elohim. I would be dead to him, Rahab. It would be as if I were dead."

Rahab turned her face away. People were coming by them on the path, the children by the wall were calling out to each other in a game, and Kata and Atene were chatting about food. But for Rahab the world had changed.

I would defile him.

To her great relief, she heard Atene say, "Here come the men."

Rahab jumped to her feet and everyone else followed. Suddenly all she wanted was to feel her mother's love, and she went to stand close beside Kata. Her mother put her hand on Rahab's arm and smiled at her. Rahab wished desperately that she was a child again and that her mother's smile could make everything right. But that was no longer true.

Twelve

LATER THAT AFTERNOON, MAKAMARON, KING OF JERICHO, was alone in his private reception room, staring out the open door that looked out into his private courtyard. He had been king since he was twenty years of age and now he was fifty-two. Thirty-two years of leadership and now his own son was trying to pull him down. Makamaron had at least had the grace to wait until his own father died, but not Tamur. His greedy son wanted to grasp what did not belong to him, and he had chosen the worst time possible to make his bid for power.

Makamaron considered the threat the Israelites posed. Jericho could withstand a siege, but he was concerned about the logistics of dealing with a city crammed with hundreds of people from the countryside as well as its own residents. Too many people in tight quarters always made for restiveness. They would have to ration water and food, never an easy matter. Rationing always fostered corruption, which would lead to more unrest—particularly among the farmers, whose homes and fields would surely be burnt by the advancing enemy.

Jericho had armed troops, of course, probably far better armed than the Israelites were. But from the information that had come to him from Edom, Moab, Sihon, Og, and Ammon, his troops would be greatly outnumbered. That had been the case in those kingdoms, all of which had fallen to the invaders. If the military of Jericho took the fight outside the walls and were slaughtered, as had happened elsewhere, it would panic the city. And Makamaron knew how dangerous panic could be.

To add to all of this, the festival of the New Year was upon him and he knew he was going to have to rouse his tired old body to complete the marriage act with the hierodule. It had been difficult enough for him to complete his duty last year, when the hierodule was cooperative, but this year he would be dealing with Arsay, a girl whose family was loyal to Tamur. She was unlikely to do anything to help him along.

He was vulnerable. Had not King Keret, greatest of all Canaanite kings, been similarly challenged by his son when he was lying ill and helpless with age?

The Keret stories were part of the cultic rituals of Makamaron's people, and everyone in Jericho would have heard the high priest speak the well-known words of Keret's son as he challenged his father: *Come down from your kingship that I may be king, from the throne of your dominion that I may sit on it.*

It was a deeply rooted belief of Makamaron's people that the fertility and strength of the nation were bound up with the sexual and physical powers of the king. If Arsay announced he had failed to complete the sacred marriage, Tamur would certainly overthrow him.

Come down from your kingship that I may be king, from the throne of your dominion that I may sit on it.

Makamaron closed his eyes, imagining the sound of those dreaded words on his son's lips; imagining the look of triumph in Tamur's glittering black eyes.

He could not let it happen! He was strong. All he needed was a woman who could stir him, not freeze him as Arsay was certain to do.

He had to get rid of Arsay and find another girl to be the hierodule.

One of his servants came in to announce that the Lords Arazu, Edri, and Ratu had asked for an audience with him. Makamaron smiled. He would discuss his idea with these three men whose loyalty he did not doubt. Perhaps, among them, they could come up with a solution.

The morning after Rahab's conversation with Sala in the garden, Kata asked Atene and Rahab to go to the market to buy some flax. Rahab's mother was beginning to find it irksome to spend her days in what she considered idleness. They had no garden to weed and no animals to care for, but they could buy flax that had come in from the countryside. They would spread it on their flat roof to dry and then they would strip it and comb it and make it into yarn. That would at least be useful. After all, how many times could they just parade around town looking at things?

Mepu grumbled at his wife's idea. He wanted Rahab to be seen by the people in the Upper City, not to waste her time playing with flax. None of them was so in need of new clothing that Kata had to worry about making yarn! However, Mepu knew his wife. She was the mildest and most pliable of women, but she hated not having something to occupy her. So he gave his permission for the girls to go and buy some flax.

Shemu went with them. He let them walk in front so they could talk while he took in the ever-fascinating street scene.

Rahab walked beside her sister-in-law and, unlike her brother, she saw nothing of her surroundings. All she saw was the fog of her own misery.

Finally Atene said, "Rahab, is something wrong? You've been

so subdued that you have me worried. It's not like you. Are you all right?"

"I'm fine," Rahab said.

"No you're not. You haven't been yourself since we came back from our visit to the garden yesterday. Did something happen there to upset you?"

They passed by a shop selling leather belts and the owner leered at Rahab from his doorway. Shemu snapped at the man to keep his eyes to himself.

Atene said, "Was it Sala? Did he say something to hurt you?"

Rahab turned toward her sister-in-law. She and Atene had lived in the same house since Shemu's marriage four years ago. They had always liked each other but they had never shared confidences. The years that separated them, and the fact that Atene was married, had always been a barrier. But Atene was the closest thing to a sister she had, and Rahab needed someone to talk to.

She said, "I can't tell you here. When we get home."

Atene took her hand and squeezed it. "Fine," she said.

The flax market was concentrated in one small square in the midst of the maze of streets that comprised the Lower City, and when they found it they ordered the amount Kata had specified and asked for it to be delivered. Then Shemu escorted them back to the house that was their temporary home.

Before he opened the front door, Shemu said to Rahab, "Father told me he wants to take you to the Upper City this afternoon, but I don't think Mother will budge from here. She's seen enough buildings, she says."

Rahab didn't want to go either. When they first came to Jericho, it had been fun to see the markets and visit the great temples and the palace, but the excitement had quickly faded. She hated the bold way men looked at her. In her home village she had always been regarded with respect. She was Mepu's daughter, and that counted among his friends and neighbors. But the men in Jericho had no respect for her or for her father. If it wasn't for Sala, she would be begging Mepu to take her home.

She said nothing to Shemu, however, and passed into the house to tell her mother they had purchased the flax.

Kata was preparing the midday meal. After a few days of purchasing prepared food, she had decided she would cook their food after all, even if the kitchen was so small she could scarcely turn around in it. It was too expensive to keep buying their meals, she said, and the food wasn't half as good as hers. Since everyone agreed with that assessment, and since Kata wouldn't let anyone else in the kitchen because there was no room, Rahab and Atene had some time to themselves.

They climbed up to the roof, which was shaded by the city wall that formed the house's back wall. Tomorrow they would have to start hanging the flax, but for now it was deserted up here, and private. The girls reclined on two rush mats and raised themselves on their elbows to look at each other. Atene said, "You never mope, Rahab. What is wrong?"

Rahab felt tears sting behind her eyes. She blinked them away. "You were right. It *is* Sala who has upset me. I've never stopped thinking about him, even though I thought I would never see him again. But he saved my life, Atene, and I thought he was wonderful. I still think he's wonderful. He's the only boy I have ever wanted to marry."

This confession had spilled out of her as fast and furious as a waterfall rushing down a mountainside. She felt tears threaten again, and again she blinked them away.

Atene said, "I thought that might be what it was."

"I love him! And he says he loves me too. But he says we can never marry, that his father would not allow it. He said marriage to me would *defile* him, Atene. Can you believe that?"

Atene eyes widened in horror. "Why would he say such a dreadful thing to you?"

"It's because of his religion. The Israelites believe in only one god, Elohim, and they think Baal and Asherah and Mot and all of our other gods are evil. They think *we're* evil because we believe in them. That's why Sala can't marry me. He's his father's only son, and he says he can't go against his father's wishes."

Atene was silent. Rahab looked up at the sky, which was deeply blue with scarcely a cloud in sight. How could the world be so beautiful and she so unhappy?

"These Israelites believe in only one god?" Atene sounded both surprised and curious.

Rahab sat up and rested her chin on her knees. "Yes. When I was staying with them, Sala told me about him. He said this one God, Elohim, was the creator of the whole world—the sea, the sky, all of the plants and the animals and the men and the women. Then, yesterday, he told me Elohim only allows Israelites to marry other Israelites. That for him to marry me—a follower of Baal—would defile him in the eyes of Elohim and his family."

This time she could not stop the tears and they began to drip down her face.

Atene spoke gently. "But, Rahab, we don't like foreigners either. In fact, your father would probably feel the same as Sala's father. Mepu wants you to marry a wealthy man from Jericho. He wouldn't be at all pleased to learn you wanted to marry an Israelite from Ramac. And he would take you so far away from us too."

"But I love Sala!" Rahab cried desperately. No one had ever loved as she did. She was sure of that.

Atene looked away. "Unfortunately, we don't always get what we want in this life."

There was a note in her voice that made Rahab momentarily forget her own misery. "But you wanted to marry Shemu, didn't you?" She had always believed her brother and Atene were happy together. They seemed so close.

"I wanted to marry Shemu very much. And I wanted to give him children."

"Oh, Atene." Rahab suddenly felt terrible that she had been heaping her problems on her sister-in-law. "You are still a young woman. You will have children."

Atene shook her head. "I am beginning to give up hope, Rahab. And I think Shemu is too. We have been married for four years, and I have never once been with child."

Rahab leaned forward, trying to think of something comforting to say. "Shemu loves you, Atene. I know he does. I can see it in his eyes when he looks at you. He would never divorce you."

"I don't think he would," Atene agreed. "But I know he wants to have children, and I have failed him." She bent her head and lowered her voice. "Sometimes I think he should divorce me and marry a woman who can give him a family."

"Do not think that way. You must pray to the Lady Asherah. She will help you."

"I have prayed to her. I have been praying to her for years. I don't think she hears me."

The girls sat in silence for a while as the sun hit the edge of the rooftop. Then Rahab said, "Sala says that his God hears all prayers. He told me that one of their ancestors, a man named Abraham, had no children and when he prayed to his God, his wife, who was well beyond childbearing years, conceived. And they had a son."

Atene looked at Rahab, her eyes wide with interest. "Is it so?"

"That is what Sala said, and he knows everything about his religion."

"Are there special prayers one must say to this God?"

"I'm sure there are, but Sala said you can also pray to him from your heart."

"What is the name of this God again?"

"They call him Elohim, which means Creator, but that is not his name. He is so great that Sala says he doesn't have a name."

Atene sat up and looked solemnly at Rahab. "I wonder what would happen if I prayed to this God? Would he be angry to hear prayers from a Canaanite woman?"

Rahab sat up too and they faced each other, close enough to touch hands. "I am sure it wasn't just Abraham who prayed for a son—his wife must have prayed as well. The Israelites don't believe their God has a wife. He is too great to have anyone share his power. If the Lady Asherah is not answering you, perhaps it would be well to try this Elohim."

"I think I will," Atene said.

"I will too. Perhaps I can convince him it would be good for Sala to marry someone who loves him as much as I do. I will tell him that if he lets me marry Sala, I will give up Baal and only worship him."

They stared at each other, having made this momentous decision.

Atene whispered, "Do you think Baal will be angry with us for praying to another god? Will something awful happen to us or to our families?"

Rahab lifted her chin. "I am willing to take the chance. If Sala is right, and his God is the only God, then there is no Baal. Is this not so?"

Atene let out a long breath. "How can that be?"

Rahab shook her head. "I don't know. What can we know about gods? We are only two women who want to be with the men we love. How could any god be angry at that?"

Atene held out her hand. "Let us pray to this Elohim together."

"Yes," Rahab said and took Atene's hand into hers. Solemnly, the two girls bowed their heads and started to pray.

Thirteen

AFTER THE MIDDAY MEAL WAS FINISHED, MEPU, ALONG with Rahab, Atene, and Shemu, returned to the Upper City, leaving Kata behind to clean up the kitchen. Rahab's father had decided he would take the bold step of calling upon Lord Arazu, who had always been one of Mepu's best wine customers. Of course, Mepu had never transacted his business directly with the noble—he dealt with Arazu's steward—but he hoped a surprise visit might get him an interview.

Mepu had two reasons for wanting to see Arazu personally. He wanted to find out if the noble was involved in Lord Nahshon's scheme to sell Jericho's farm products to the supposed Gaza merchants, and he also wanted Arazu to see Rahab. Since arriving in the city, Mepu had realized that to succeed in finding a husband for his daughter he was going to need a formal introduction into the city's wealthy community, and he was hoping Arazu might provide it.

When Mepu stated his name and his business about the wine to the servant who opened the door of Lord Arazu's grand house, the servant raised his eyebrows and said condescendingly, "You mean you wish to see my lord's steward. You may inquire after him at the servant's entrance. Lord Arazu does not deal directly with farmers."

"Lord Arazu will wish to speak directly to me," Mepu

returned firmly. "Just go and tell him who is here and why I have come."

The servant hesitated, not really believing Mepu but concerned not to make a mistake. "One moment," he murmured, and closed the door in their faces.

The family waited in silence. When the door reopened, the same servant told Mepu woodenly that Lord Arazu could spare him a few minutes. Mepu stepped through the door, followed by Rahab, Shemu, and Atene. Startled, the servant held up his hand. "My lord expects to see only the man Mepu. The rest of you must wait outside."

"This is my daughter and my son and his wife," Mepu replied. "We are together today and I never leave them alone. They will be no trouble."

The servant started to object again, looked at Rahab, then said, "Very well, you may come in. Lord Arazu is in the courtyard."

Rahab followed her father into the same inner courtyard that Sala and Lord Nahshon had visited just days before. Two men were sitting there, and one of them, who must be Lord Arazu, addressed Mepu, asking him to state his business.

Rahab glanced at the other man and blinked. He looked exactly like a rodent. She looked quickly away, feeling badly for having such a thought. The poor man could not help his looks, after all. He was probably quite nice.

She looked back at Lord Arazu to find that his eyes were fixed on her. "Who are these people you have brought with you?" he asked her father, his tone of voice more pleasant than it had been.

"This is my son, Shemu; his wife, Atene; and my daughter, Rahab."

Rahab nodded politely to Lord Arazu and gave an especially nice smile to the man who looked like a rodent, to make up for her unkind thoughts.

The friend's name was Lord Edri and his nose twitched when he looked back at her. Just like a rodent.

Suddenly Lord Arazu became a considerate host. He commanded the servant who had escorted them to bring other chairs so they could all be seated. He asked Mepu if he wished something to drink and, when her father refused, he turned solicitously to Rahab and asked the same question. She refused as well.

Rahab took her seat, folded her hands politely in her lap, and listened as Mepu broached the reason for his visit. The two men spoke for several minutes and it soon became clear to Rahab that Arazu was indeed interested in purchasing far more wine than he usually did. She glanced quickly at Shemu. His mouth was set in a grim line.

So, what Lord Nahshon and Sala had said was true. These nobles were going to buy up the produce of the local farms and sell it out from under the noses of the city population. How horrible, Rahab thought, that rich men could have so little concern for the welfare of people less fortunate than themselves. What they were planning to do was . . . well, evil.

When the discussion had concluded, Mepu made as if to rise. Lord Arazu motioned him back into his chair. "I am wondering how a lovely girl like your daughter is still unmarried. She is unmarried, I take it?" He was speaking to Mepu, but his eyes were on Rahab.

"Yes, my lord, she is unmarried, although not for lack of suitors. But she wants to live in the city, not the country, so I have brought her into Jericho to see if she might find a man more to her liking."

Rahab almost jumped out of her chair in outrage. Not want to live in the country? She would far rather live in the country than cooped up within the walls of this city. The longer she stayed in Jericho, the more Rahab realized she didn't like it here at all.

"That is perfectly understandable," Lord Arazu was replying silkily. "Such beauty should not be worn out by the hard life of a farmer's wife. She is a gem who needs the adornment of a rich man's home to show her off."

Mepu smiled for the first time during the interview. "That was precisely my own feeling, my lord. It is why I brought her with me to Jericho."

Rahab's clasped hands were now clutching each other tightly. She knew if she said anything to alienate this noble, her father would be incensed. She bit her lip to keep her mouth from opening and the furious words from pouring out.

She was so angry she hardly heard the rest of the conversation. There was one thought only in her mind: *I am not going to marry some boring old noble. I am going to marry Sala. I am not going to marry some boring old noble. I am going to marry—*

"Rahab!"

Her head jerked around to meet her father's eyes. "It is time we were going."

Rahab jumped to her feet. She couldn't wait to get away from here. Atene was gracious and Shemu was polite and manly. Rahab didn't say a word, she just followed her family out of the courtyard, out of the front door, and into the street, where she finally felt as if she could breathe again.

After Mepu and his family had left, the two nobles sat in silence, waiting until the front door closed behind the visitors. When the faint echo of wood settling into wood reached them, they both sat up a little straighter. They were ready to talk.

The first part of their conversation dealt with Mepu.

"I wonder what precipitated that visit?" Lord Arazu said.

"Was it just that he wanted to show me his daughter or has he met those Gaza merchants? He might have been trying to discover if we had spoken to them too."

They both thought about this possibility.

Lord Edri said, "If he has, it's not good for us. He might alert the farmers not to sell to us, that they should sell directly to the merchants for more money."

Arazu's eyes narrowed in thought. "I find it hard to believe a simple farmer like that could have come into contact with the merchants. He is so clearly beneath their social level."

His words trailed away and he lifted his hands as if to say such a meeting would be impossible.

Edri frowned. "Merchants are clever about money, though. They must realize they could buy directly from the farmers more cheaply than they can buy from us."

Arazu thought about this. "That may be so, but merchants like the two we met want to do a transaction with as little fuss and bother as possible. They don't want to travel around from farm to farm haggling with peasants."

"True." Edri steepled his fingers. "Also, there may have been a reason for that visit that had nothing to do with wine." His little black eyes glittered in the sunlight.

Arazu nodded. "The girl."

"Yes, the girl."

Arazu moistened his lips with his tongue. "A daughter like that can be worth more to a father than a thousand barrels of wine."

Edri's nose quivered. "Quite so. And he has brought her to Jericho to show her around. Peasants may be stupid in some ways, but they are shrewd in others. What did you think of her?"

Arazu lifted his eyebrows. "I thought exactly as you did, my dear Edri. She is astonishingly beautiful and delicious as a ripe fruit. No man could see her and remain unmoved."

The two men looked at each other, the same idea in both their minds. It was Arazu who spoke the thought out loud.

"She may be just what we need for the king."

Edri stood up and began to pace around the courtyard, his hands behind his back. "If any woman can rouse Makamaron's manhood, that girl is the one."

Arazu leaned back in his chair and watched his colleague pace. "And even if he fails, we can make sure she never tells. What we need to do is buy all of her father's wine. We'll offer him an extravagant price. Even if we don't make a profit selling it on to the merchants, we can still afford it. We'll be making huge profits on the grain and olive oil harvests."

Edri swung around, frowning. "Why overspend for the wine? The man should be thrilled his daughter has been chosen to be the hierodule. It is the greatest honor a woman can attain; to be the goddess herself in the sacred marriage."

"That is so." Arazu looked over his shoulder at his friend and complained, "Will you please sit down and stop pacing? My neck hurts from trying to follow you." After Edri had resumed his place, Arazu went on. "Will we have a problem because she's not a priestess?"

Edri waved his hand, dismissing the notion. "Not if the high priest says she is called to the office, which of course he will. And there have been precedents. Don't you remember the time Makamaron fell in love with one of Salu's daughters and insisted she be the hierodule? The priestesses were not happy, but once the high priest said it was all right, there was nothing they could do."

"The prince will complain," Arazu said. "He is counting on Arsay to expose Makamaron's inability."

"He may complain, but there will be nothing he can do."

Arazu nodded. "Good, then. We discredit Arsay, then bring this girl forward. We can buy the father off if necessary, but he should be delighted. He wants her to make a good marriage, and once she has stood in the place of Asherah, no woman will be more exalted. She will have her pick of the young men of the nobility."

"It's a good plan," the treasurer agreed. "But we must show the girl to Makamaron first. He is the only one who can name her as his hierodule."

Arazu nodded. "What was the girl's name again?"

"I believe the farmer called her Rahab."

Fourteen

WHEN RAHAB AND HER FAMILY ARRIVED HOME, THEY
found Sala and Lord Nahshon waiting in front of their door.
Lord Nahshon told Mepu he wished to speak to him, and Mepu
invited him inside. Shemu followed them but Sala remained
outside with Rahab. Atene, seeing this, remained behind to
chaperone.

Sala said to Rahab, "Your mother said you had gone to see
Lord Arazu. Please don't tell me your father actually allowed you
into that man's company?"

Rahab, who was trying to quench the thrill the sight of him
had produced in her, gave him a haughty stare. "What my father
does is no concern of yours, Sala."

His nostrils flared. Clearly he was in a temper. *Too bad,*
Rahab thought. *He can't insult me and then think he can tell me
what I can and cannot do.*

Sala said, "I am *concerned* because I care about your welfare. A noble like Arazu is not interested in you as a marriage
prospect, Rahab, although he might well want you for something else, now that you have been flaunted before him."

Suddenly Rahab was furious. "My father is not flaunting me
in front of anyone! And don't pretend that you care about what
happens to me. I have no intention of *defiling* you by expecting
you to marry me, and my father has every right to present me to

117

whatever man he deems suitable. All I want from you, Sala, is for you to leave me alone so I can forget you ever existed."

The two of them glared at each other.

Atene said, "Lower your voices. You are attracting attention."

Rahab glanced around, then looked back at Sala, prepared to continue the battle with a muted voice. She stiffened with surprise when he took her hand in his and held it tightly. When he spoke his voice had lost its anger. "Listen to me, Rahab. I'm sorry if I offended you, but you must listen to me. You and all your family must get out of Jericho. And not to your farm—you must go someplace else, someplace where you will be safe."

She stared at him, knocked off balance by the change of subject. She heard Atene ask, "Why are you saying this? Why wouldn't we be safe in Jericho or at our farm?"

Before Sala could answer, the front door was pushed open and Lord Nahshon stood on the threshold. He scowled when he saw Sala holding Rahab's hand.

She jerked it away. "Atene and I must go indoors. My mother will be looking for us."

Without another word, the two girls went into the house, leaving Sala and his father alone in front of the closed door.

Lord Nahshon looked bewildered. "What was going on here? I came to see what had kept you from joining us and I find you holding Rahab's hand?"

Sala had admired his father all of his life. He had done everything his father asked of him, had followed him around like a shadow, because all he wanted was to be as great and good a man as his father was. He had never disagreed with anything his father had said, not even in the secrecy of his own heart. But he knew he had to be careful about what he said now and how he said it.

"Father," he began, "somehow we must convince Mepu to get his family away from the city before Joshua attacks."

Lord Nahshon's eyes opened wider in stunned surprise. "Sala, you know we cannot do anything that might give away Joshua's plans to the Canaanites! I cannot believe you would even consider such a thing."

"We won't be giving away Joshua's plans." Sala made his voice as persuasive and reasonable as he could. "Everyone knows the Israelite army is poised to strike at Jericho. That is no secret in Jericho."

"Then let Mepu make his own decision. If he is worried, he can take his family away on his own."

"That is the problem, Father. No one in Jericho is worried! They think they can withstand a siege. None of them understand that we are the army of Elohim and that we cannot lose."

Lord Nahshon was silent, his eyes searching Sala's face. Finally he said, "Mepu is not a fool. If I tell him to take his family and leave the city, he will suspect I have secret information. He may even give us up as spies."

Sala set his jaw. "He would never do that."

Lord Nahshon put his hands on Sala's shoulders and said with the calm certainty that Sala had always admired and obeyed, "I understand your feelings, Sala. I like these people too, but they are Canaanites. They stand in the way of the will of Elohim and therefore they are disposable. What you ask is impossible. You will see that for yourself if you stop and think about it."

Lord Nahshon's hands on his shoulders felt like heavy weights to Sala. His father had just called Rahab's life disposable. He looked down into Nahshon's eyes and said steadily, "I saved Rahab's life once. You helped me to save her. How can you think she is disposable?"

Sala kept looking into his father's eyes. Rahab was not for him. He knew that. But he would not let her die. He would *not* let her die.

His father said, "Soon Joshua will secretly send men into Jericho to bring back the information we have gleaned. When that is accomplished, he will better understand how to move against the city. We cannot risk drawing attention to ourselves in any way, Sala. Perhaps I can speak to Mepu later, when our plans are certain. But we cannot do anything that might alert him now. If we are discovered, then Joshua's spies will not have access to what we have learned."

Sala didn't think they had learned much and he said this to his father.

Nahshon said, "We have learned that the north wall of the city is the most vulnerable place and should be the target of Joshua's attack. We have also discovered there is a split between those who support the king and those who support the prince. Nothing makes a city riper for destruction than division among the rulers. And we are not yet finished. By the time Joshua's men come, I hope to have even more information to pass along."

His father's logic was impeccable and there was nothing more Sala could say. His heart was bursting inside him, but he could find nothing to refute his father's logic.

He said, "But you will talk to Mepu after the spies are away?"

"Yes," Lord Nahshon said.

It shocked Sala to his core to discover that he did not believe his father's promise. In all his life, Sala had never felt so desperate. "Joshua will kill everyone in the city, Father. That is what he has done elsewhere."

"This is not their land, Sala. This is our land. And if we leave the Canaanites alive, there will only be more fighting and more Israelite deaths. Better to cut off the head of the enemy than to leave it wounded but able to overcome its injuries and strike at us again."

Sala, his father's son, knew this was true. But Sala, who loved Rahab, felt as if he were being ripped apart.

He lay awake for most of the night, wrestling with himself. What he was thinking of doing was traitorous. He knew very well what he owed to his father, to his people. The fall of Jericho would be the greatest moment for the Israelites since Elohim gave this land to Abraham. He should do nothing—nothing!— that might compromise that victory.

It was almost morning when he came to the most momentous decision of his life. After the spies were safely gone back to Joshua, *he* would tell Mepu to take Rahab away from Jericho. He had saved her life once and he would do it again. As the sun began to creep in at his tiny window, Sala finally fell asleep.

The following morning four soldiers came to the door of Mepu's house and told him the king had sent for his daughter, Rahab. Mepu was stunned.

"What are you talking about? What has my daughter to do with the king? You must be mistaken."

"There is no mistake," the soldier who had first spoken said. "The king has sent for your daughter. We have a litter waiting. Tell her to hurry, we must not keep the king waiting."

Mepu looked beyond the bronze helmeted men to see that there was indeed a litter waiting in the narrow street.

"I don't understand," he said.

"You don't have to understand, you just have to get your daughter."

"Wait here," Mepu said and closed the door.

The family was gathered in the small front room and they had heard the whole of the conversation. They stared at Mepu with bewilderment and fright.

Rahab crossed her arms around herself tightly and said, "I'm not going."

Mepu pulled himself together. "You have no choice. If the king has asked for you, you must go. But you must not go alone. Your mother will go with you."

"To see the king?" Kata looked terrified. "I don't under-stand—what is happening, Mepu? Why should the king wish to see Rahab?"

Shemu said, "Father has been taking her all over the city for the last week. Clearly someone who saw her told the king about her."

Rahab looked from her father's face to her brother's and realized there was nothing they could do. Her chest was tight with fear. What could the king want with her?

Atene said, "I will go with you, Rahab. Mother is too upset."

There was no one Rahab would rather have with her than Atene. "Thank you," she breathed.

The girls looked at Shemu, who nodded his approval. "A good idea."

Kata fluttered her hands helplessly. "You must change your clothes, Rahab. You cannot go to see the king in that old tunic."

A hard, impatient knock came on the front door. Rahab shuddered.

Mepu said, "There is no time for changing clothes. She must go as she is." He looked at his daughter and spoke reas-suringly, "Come, Rahab. I'm sure the king has heard about your beauty and only wants to see you. Don't worry. All will be well."

But Rahab saw the fear in her father's eyes, and she did not believe him.

Rahab and Atene sat pressed together in the narrow litter as the porters carried them through the streets. Rahab had seen many such litters in Jericho, but they were for women of the nobility. She had never thought she would be riding in one of them. She wished with all her heart she weren't.

Atene took her hand and squeezed it encouragingly. Rahab tried to give her a courageous smile.

"The king won't do anything to hurt you," Atene said. "I'm sure Father was right; he just wants to see if you are as beautiful as people say."

Rahab stared at the linen curtains that hid the passengers of the litter from the view of people in the street. "I wish I looked like a frog. What's the use of being pretty if it only brings you trouble?"

Atene said sensibly, "You are not of the nobility, but your father is a successful farmer, a man of some substance. No one will be able to do anything to you without his permission."

Her words made Rahab feel better. It was true that girls were under the rule of their fathers and she knew her father cared about her. He would never let anything terrible happen to her.

The litter was lowered to the ground, and one of the soldiers opened the curtains to let the women out. As Rahab stood up she looked around, always curious no matter how frightened she may be.

They were in an inner courtyard, which was covered by a

roof supported by four stone columns. All around the courtyard rose the sheer white walls of the palace.

"It's so big," Atene breathed and Rahab nodded silent agreement.

A man came down the stairs that led to the upper rooms of the palace and approached the one guard who was still standing with them. Rahab recognized the man as Lord Arazu, the noble she had visited yesterday with her father. She began to breathe more easily. Perhaps it was true, perhaps the king only wanted to see her and then she could go home.

Arazu dismissed the soldier, then turned to Rahab with a pleasant smile. "We meet again, Rahab." His eyes moved to Atene. "I see you have brought a friend."

"This is my sister-in-law, Atene, who has come with me." Rahab's voice was firm. "She was with us yesterday when we came to your house."

"Ah, yes." Clearly Arazu had no memory of Atene. "If you will both come with me, I will show you to your room."

Rahab didn't move. "What do you mean, my room? I have no room in this house."

Arazu's eyes flicked up and down Rahab's tunic. "You cannot expect to be presented to the king until you have been dressed properly."

I don't like this man. I don't like anything about him, Rahab thought. But she didn't know what else she could do except obey.

"I want Atene to come with me," she said.

"Of course." Arazu smiled. "She can attend your bath."

Bath?

Rahab and Atene stared at each other.

"Come," Arazu said, and Rahab and Atene followed on unwilling feet as he led them up the stairs and into the residential part of the palace.

124

Fifteen

TWO HANDMAIDS WERE AWAITING RAHAB IN THE ROOM to which Arazu brought them. He waved the frightened girls in, then closed the door behind them. Rahab could hear the sound of his feet as he walked away.

The room itself contained a stone basin set on the floor, a table with a large jug of steaming water, and a pile of linen towels. The two women looked stonefaced at Rahab and bowed slightly.

"Is that the bath?" Atene muttered, her eyes on the stone basin.

One of the women took Rahab by the hand and led her to the basin, motioning for her to step in. When they began to take off her robe, she pulled away and ran back to Atene's side. "What are you going to do?" she demanded.

The older handmaid, a heavy-set woman with a hooked nose, said, "We are going to bathe you, my lady. Then we will dress you in clean robes so you will be fit to meet the king."

Rahab and Atene exchanged alarmed glances. The only bathing they had ever done was in a stream during the summer and out of a small hand basin during the winter.

Atene said, "We bathed before we came to Jericho and I washed her hair myself. She is perfectly clean."

The younger handmaid sniffed contemptuously.

"Her hair looks glossy enough," the elder handmaid

admitted. "We can leave it as it is. There is too much of it to dry properly anyway."

Rahab considered refusing. If the king wanted to see her, then he could take her as she was. She had no desire to make a good impression on him. Suppose she didn't let these women touch her? What could happen to her if she did that?

She looked longingly at the door. But she had to think of her family. If she angered the king, he was likely to take it out on them. Slowly she moved forward and stood once more in the center of the basin.

For what seemed like forever she stood there naked while the maids poured water over her and scrubbed her skin from her forehead to her toes. She had been brought up to be a modest woman, and standing nude before these strange women made her uncomfortable.

As the ablutions went on, Rahab began to wonder what all these preparations could be about? She could understand that she might need to wear nicer clothes to meet the ruler of Jericho, but why this bath? She asked the maids if everyone who went to see the king had to have a bath, and they looked at her as if she were a simpleton.

"Of course not," the older maid said condescendingly, as if Rahab were a dairy girl and not a farmer's daughter. Rahab looked at Atene. She was beginning to feel really frightened. There was something more going on here than a mere visit so the king could admire her beauty. She noticed Atene was looking worried too.

After Rahab was dry, the maids gave her a plain robe to put on and began the process of combing out her hair. Rahab had worn it braided, and the combing out was painful. The maids were not satisfied until it was falling down her back in a waterfall of shining black.

Then they took away the plain robe she had worn to have

her hair done and gave her an exquisite linen tunic to put on. They placed a circlet of what looked like real gold on her head and slipped a pair of beautiful leather sandals on her newly scoured feet.

Both maids regarded her with satisfaction, pleased with their work. "You look like a noble woman," one of them said.

Rahab scowled. She did not want to look like a noble woman. She wanted to look like herself.

"I will go and inform Lord Arazu that she is ready," the younger maid said to the older.

Atene came to stand beside the transformed Rahab and took her hand. "Have courage, my sister."

"But what can this be about?"

"I don't know. It is certainly strange."

"You are going to come with me, aren't you?"

"I will if they will let me."

The maid came back into the room. "I will take you now to Lord Arazu, my lady."

Rahab said, "I want my sister-in-law to come with me."

The maid shrugged. "That will be up to Lord Arazu. Come, now, and we will go to him."

Rahab, with Atene beside her, followed the maid along the outside balcony. They walked for quite a distance before they came to another door. The maid knocked and a male voice answered, "Come." The maid pushed the door open and stepped aside for the girls to enter.

Lord Arazu was alone inside. Rahab looked around quickly and saw that the room was small but richly furnished, with a beautifully woven wool rug, elegantly carved chairs, and a table with a lamp. Beyond it was yet another door.

Lord Arazu frowned at Atene. "The king only wishes to see Rahab. You should not be here."

Atene replied in a steady voice, "Rahab's father sent me as a representative of her family. If the king does not wish to see me, then I will wait here until Rahab comes out."

Rahab felt a flash of admiration for Atene's outward composure. If her sister-in-law wasn't intimidated by these surroundings, then she told herself she wouldn't be either.

Arazu turned his back on Atene and spoke to Rahab. "The king will receive you informally, but you must be certain to fold your hands at your waist and bow your head when you come before him. Do not look up until he speaks to you. Do you understand?"

"Yes."

"Then come with me." Lord Arazu gestured Rahab toward the closed inner door, sparing only two words for Atene. "Wait here."

Rahab's mouth was so dry she didn't think she would be able to speak at all, but she walked as straight and steady as she could through the open door that led into the king's private reception room.

Makamaron was seated in a high-backed bronze chair with images of unusual animals on the feet and arms, in a chamber where he often met with his friends and advisors. When Arazu came into the room with the girl at his side, Makamaron was prepared to be disappointed. No woman could be as beautiful as his friend had promised. However, she might be pretty enough to give him an excuse to put aside Arsay, who was definitely a danger to him.

"My lord king," Arazu said when the door had closed behind them, "may I present Rahab, daughter of Mepu, one of your faithful subjects."

The girl folded her hands, bent her head, and was silent. The thin linen tunic showed Makamaron that she was slender but beautifully curved. The skin of her bare arms revealed by the tunic glowed with youth and health.

"You may approach me, Rahab," the king said graciously.

As the girl came toward him, he noticed with approval the fluid grace of her walk. When finally she reached his chair and lifted her face, he was stunned. Vaguely he heard her say, in a charmingly husky voice, "I am honored to have this opportunity to meet you, my lord king."

Makamaron was having trouble with his breathing. For the first time in many moons he felt his sexuality stir. This girl . . . this girl was amazing.

He cleared his throat in an attempt to get his speaking voice back to normal. He said, "Rahab. That is an unusual name."

"It was my mother's mother's name," she replied.

"I see." Makamaron was still short of breath. He struggled for normality. "And your father, what does he do?"

"He is a grape farmer, my lord king. We live south of Jericho, near the village of Ugaru, where my father's family has owned vineyards for many generations."

The girl's huge dark eyes were fixed on him. He watched her mouth as she spoke in that wonderful voice. His mind was already made up. This was his hierodule. If anyone could help him complete the sacred marriage it was this Rahab. She must have had some experience. He knew sometimes Canaanite girls slipped off into the dark with young men after the important nature ceremonies. They could not do such a thing after they married, of course, but when they were young it happened. A girl like this would have been much in demand.

He looked at his advisor and said simply, "She will do. Arrange it."

"Yes, my lord king," Arazu replied.

The king smiled at Rahab, showing his bad teeth. "We will meet again, Rahab. You may go now and Lord Arazu will make arrangements for you."

The girl's face went still. There was a watchful look in her eyes. "Arrangements, my lord king? What arrangements?"

Makamaron lifted his brows at being questioned. "I am bestowing on you the greatest honor a Canaanite woman can have, Rahab. You will be the goddess Asherah in the sacred marriage to take place at the New Year festival. We will notify your father and your family. Now, go with Lord Arazu, please. I have other engagements I must attend to."

The girl was as pale as her tunic. "I do not deserve such an honor," she said, not adding "my lord king" to her comment.

Makamaron frowned; he did not like having his pronouncements questioned. "You must let me be the judge of that." He looked at Arazu. "Take her out."

"Come, Rahab," Arazu said commandingly, and he began to lead the girl toward the door. Before they left, Makamaron called his advisor's name. "See to it that Lord Edri and the high priest come to see me." He paused a moment, then added, "And you had better bring the head priestess as well. I will meet with you all in one hour's time."

"Yes, my lord king," Arazu replied and almost pushed the girl out of the door.

The small group that gathered in the king's private reception room an hour after he had met with Rahab was both serious and determined. There was only one day left until the sacred marriage, the most significant ritual of the New Year festival, and much had to be done. Makamaron sat in his bronze chair and the others sat on carved wood stools around him as they began to discuss the situation.

The head priestess, Umara, who had held her position for the last twelve years, understood what was being planned. Arazu had told her about their scheme to replace Arsay as hierodule and she was skeptical. Umara had been a priestess for twenty-five of her forty years and was well acquainted with the power struggles in Jericho. Her own main interest lay only in promoting the importance of Asherah and the goddess's shrine in the life of the city.

She looked now at the king and said, "Arsay will not step down voluntarily. She will go to her brother, who will go to the prince, who will make a scandal if he can. We must do nothing that will taint the sacred marriage."

Ratu, the high priest, answered in his sonorous voice, "We are all aware of the importance of the ritual, High Priestess. We wish to safeguard it, not to damage it. However, our king must complete the marriage act in order for the benefits of the ritual to bless the country, and we are convinced Arsay will do everything in her power to keep that from happening. She might even lie and say that the act had not been accomplished, that the king was incapable. Can you imagine the chaos the city would be thrown into should such a thing occur?"

"We cannot allow that to happen," Umara returned immediately.

"We agree. That is why we have met here today. We must find a way to remove Arsay." Ratu's face was as hard and ruthless as his words.

"We cannot harm her," Edri, the treasurer, warned. "There would be too much talk and the king cannot afford to be compromised in any way."

Silence fell as the group contemplated their problem.

Arazu turned to the head priestess. "Can you announce that you have found some fault in Arsay that makes her ineligible to be the hierodule?"

Umara was dubious and said so.

Makamaron said decisively, "I have decided what I will do. I will announce that Arsay has displeased me and that I have found someone else whom I wish to be the hierodule. I have done it before, so it is not unheard of. And, since the time is so short, I do not think the prince will be able to organize any kind of effective protest. I am still the king, no matter what my son might think. And when the people lay eyes upon Rahab, no one will wonder why I chose her."

The king's advisors let out a silent breath of relief, but Umara frowned. "I will go along with this because I agree with you about Arsay. But why can't you choose one of the other priestesses, my lord king? Why this outsider?"

Arazu said, "When you see her, Head Priestess, you will understand."

"She is so beautiful?"

"Yes."

"If she is truly to be the hierodule, I must see her immediately. She has to be prepared for her role and there is not much time. I must get to work right away."

Makamaron said, "You may see her after I speak to her father, Head Priestess. I have sent some men to bring him to me. He is only a farmer, but he is her father and has some rights in her disposal. I doubt there will be any trouble. What man would not rejoice at having his daughter raised to such a height? But still, it is a courtesy that must be followed."

Shocked, the head priestess stared at the king. "You have chosen a farmer's daughter to be hierodule, my lord king? Surely not!"

"Wait until you see her," Arazu said.

Umara knew when she was beaten. She tightened her lips and said, "I see you are determined. Very well, I will do my best."

Makamaron stood and his advisors rose with him. "That will be all for now," the king said. "I will send for you, Umara, after I have spoken to the father, and you may take Rahab into your charge."

The head priestess bowed her covered head, and the advisors exited, leaving Makamaron alone with his thoughts.

Sixteen

WHEN THEY HAD LEFT THE KING'S RECEPTION ROOM, Lord Arazu did not take Rahab back to Atene. Instead he turned her over to two women who were dressed in the flowing white garb of priestesses.

"Where is my sister-in-law?" Rahab demanded of Arazu as the two priestesses moved in on either side of her. "I am not going anywhere without her."

"You will see her soon," Arazu replied. "Go now with these women. Your father will be meeting with the king shortly and then you may see him and your sister-in-law as well."

Relief flooded Rahab when she heard her father was coming. Papa would not let them do this to her. She—the hierodule! It was madness. That was for a priestess, not for a farmer's daughter. Even if the king did want her, her father wouldn't allow it. She had not been brought up to do such a thing. She had no experience of the fertility rites of the goddess. How could anyone expect her to be the goddess and make the sacred marriage to the king? She thought of Makamaron's wrinkled face and brown teeth and spotted hands and shuddered. It couldn't happen. Her father would save her.

The priestesses took her to the women's part of the palace, which was largely empty. Makamaron had not had a queen since his third wife had died some years before. There were two young princesses who still lived in the palace, but they were rarely seen.

A royal daughter's life was important only because of the marriage that might be made for her. It had long been tradition for political alliances to be cemented by royal marriages, and that was what daughters were good for. Nothing else.

Rahab walked between the priestesses, looking carefully at her surroundings. If she managed to get away, she would have to know which way to run. They finally stopped at a room that had two palace guards in front of it. One of them opened the door and held it for the three women to go inside.

The priestesses led Rahab through an antechamber and into a large luxurious room clearly furnished for a woman. There was no stately bronze chair here, just slim, elegant cushioned furniture and a thick soft rug. Near the roof there was a line of small openings to let the air circulate.

Rahab stared at the openings with dismay. She had been thinking of how she escaped from the slavers, but she would never be able to reach those air vents. Even if she could, she didn't think she would be able to fit through them.

"Sit and make yourself comfortable," the older priestess said. The woman's icy voice echoed the cold expression on her face. The priestess was not happy. *Well, neither am I*, Rahab thought.

"Why am I being called to be the hierodule?" she demanded as soon as she was seated. "That position is for a priestess, not for someone like me."

The priestess exhaled a long hissing sound. "So, it is true. The king is putting away Arsay and making someone else the hierodule."

Both women glared at Rahab.

Rahab glared back. "Believe me, this was not my decision. I have no desire to take your friend's place. I don't want to be the hierodule. I can't understand why the king should want me to do this."

"Stupid girl," the older priestess muttered. "Do you think we will believe you? Of course you want to be the hierodule. Every woman in Jericho would leap at such a chance."

Rahab spaced her words for greater emphasis. "I. Do not. Want. To be. The hierodule. Besides, my father will never allow it. He will tell the king I belong at home with my family, and that will be the end of this ridiculous plan. Your priestess will be the goddess. I certainly don't want to be!"

The younger priestess looked at her with pity. "You are a stupid girl. Your father will never defy the king."

But Rahab trusted her father. He loved her too much to make her do something as big as this if she did not want to. She could always count on her father to keep her safe.

When the soldiers arrived back at Mepu's house and told him the king wished to speak to him, he felt sick with fear. First they had taken Rahab away and now they wanted him. What could have happened to bring his family to the attention of the king? Had he said something on his visit to Lord Arazu that had insulted the lord? Did they perhaps suspect Mepu was aware of their plans to buy up the whole wine crop? If that was the case, what were they going to do to him? To his family?

Mepu was not given the privacy of a litter. Instead he was forced to walk in the midst of a foursome of guards through the streets of the city so everyone could see him. By the time he reached the palace, Mepu was sweating profusely and trying not to show his terror.

Like Rahab, he was brought through the king's anteroom into his reception room, where he found Makamaron sitting in his imposing bronze chair. Mepu fell to his knees as soon as he passed into the room, bowed his head, clasped his hands so tightly his knuckles went white, and breathed in a trembling voice, "My lord king."

"You may rise and approach me, Mepu," the king said. His voice sounded genial. Mepu peeked at him uncertainly, then rose to his feet and came forward a few steps.

He had never been this close to Makamaron and he was surprised the king looked so old. The flesh sagged on his heavy face and his stomach swelled under the perfect folds of his tunic. His color looked pale and unhealthy.

The king said, "I have just had an interview with your daughter, Rahab. She is very beautiful."

"Thank you, my lord king," Mepu replied cautiously. Perhaps this was not about the wine after all.

"She is so beautiful, in fact, that I am going to make her the hierodule for the sacred marriage in the coming New Year festival."

Mepu's eyes stretched wide and his mouth fell open. "The hierodule?" he repeated, wanting to make certain he had heard right.

"Yes. It is right that the goddess be represented by the most beautiful woman in the city, and your Rahab is undoubtedly that."

Mepu's head was reeling. Did the king know he was only a farmer? His mouth was so dry that his voice came out like a croak. "It is true she is beautiful, my lord king, but I do not want you to choose her under false pretenses. My family, my daughter's family, is not noble. I have large vineyards in the countryside that are profitable, but we are not noble."

The king smiled graciously. "This I know, and I have thought for some time that such an honor should be extended beyond the temple priestesses and the nobility. It will be good for all my people to see that I view them as valuable and important."

Mepu was stunned by this astonishing reply. So stunned that he couldn't think of an answer.

Fortunately, the king was continuing, "Let me make it clear that you needn't worry about your daughter's future after the festival is concluded, Mepu. I shall see to it that she marries a man of stature in the city, a man with the financial means to keep such a beautiful creature as she deserves to be kept. Once she is seen, there will be a crowd clamoring for her hand."

Mepu moistened his lips with his tongue. It was true; this was really happening. The king wanted Rahab to be the hierodule in the sacred marriage. Mepu went down on his knees again. "Thank you, my lord king. This is beyond anything I had ever dreamed of. To think that my daughter should represent the goddess herself, that she should participate in the sacred rite that will bring life and prosperity to the kingdom. I am overcome."

Makamaron smiled, showing his stubby brown teeth. "You may see your daughter briefly to assure her of your blessing. One of my guards will take you to her. And I will send men to escort you and your family to the palace tomorrow so you may have a good viewing place for the festivities. Now you may go."

The king picked up the gold-plated staff, which had reposed beside his chair, and thumped it once upon the floor.

Mepu rose to his feet and bowed deeply. "Thank you, my lord king." He backed out the door that had opened behind him at the thump of the king's staff.

Rahab and the two priestesses had been sitting in icy silence for over an hour when the quiet was broken by a knock on the door. It came so suddenly that Rahab jumped.

The younger priestess went to the door and opened it a

crack. When she saw who was there, she opened it all the way and Mepu came into the room, accompanied by Atene.

"Papa!" Rahab ran to throw herself into her father's arms. She started to sob with relief that he had come to take her home.

He patted her back. "Now, now, Rahab. There is nothing to upset you, unless you are crying for happiness."

Happiness. Of course she was happy that he had gotten her out of this terrible situation. She controlled her sobs and pulled away so she could look up into his face. "You saw the king? You told him I could not possibly do this thing?"

A puzzled frown creased her father's forehead. "Why would I say such a thing to the king, my daughter?"

Rahab's eyes went from him, to Atene, to the two priestesses who still hovered by the open door.

"Please leave us," she said to the two women. "I wish to speak to my family in private."

The priestesses' return look was openly hostile, but they went out and closed the door behind them.

Rahab turned back to her father. "Didn't the king tell you he wants me to be the hierodule, Papa?"

"Yes, he did, my daughter. And it is a great honor, not only to you but to our entire family. I am still stunned. I never thought such a great thing would come of my bringing you to Jericho."

Rahab stared at her father in disbelief. "You cannot mean that you agreed to it!"

The puzzled look returned to Mepu's face. "Of course I agreed to it, Rahab. How could I possibly reject such an honor?"

Rahab looked to her sister-in-law, and the pity on Atene's face frightened her even more than her father's words. Atene said, "You are going to have to do this, Rahab. There is no way you can decline such a command from the king. Nor can your family decline for you."

A sick feeling began to rise in Rahab's stomach. She turned back to her father. "But I don't want to do this, Papa! Didn't you at least ask the king if you could speak to me before you agreed?"

Mepu was looking annoyed. "I don't know what you are talking about, Rahab. You have just been offered the highest honor a woman can achieve. You are to represent the goddess Asherah in her marriage with Baal. Because of you, life and fertility will bless the lands of Jericho. How can you not be thrilled by such a great distinction?"

Rahab looked into her father's genuinely bewildered face and did not know what to reply. What he said about the importance of the sacred marriage was true. But . . .

"I don't want to do it, Papa," she repeated. "The king is old and disgusting. I don't want him to touch me . . ."

A wrenching sob tore through her body.

"Now, now." He reached out and drew her back into his arms. "There is nothing to be afraid of. It will not be the king who comes to you, but the god. And think of this, Rahab, your future is assured! After the New Year festival the king has promised me that he himself will choose a husband for you from among the most noble and rich men in the city. Everything I hoped for you will come true—even more than I hoped for, because I never dreamed you would be chosen by the king to be the hierodule."

He is not going to help me. He is going to let me be the hierodule and there is nothing I can do to stop it.

Was there something wrong with her that she was so horrified by this so-called honor? For her father was right—in the eyes of all the Canaanite people, it was a great honor. Yet her whole body and soul flinched away from it. She was not the goddess, she was Rahab, and she did not want to be with that old man. Even if he became Baal, she didn't want him to touch her.

What will Sala think when he hears this? What will he think of me? I will truly be defiled in his eyes. I will be defiled in my own eyes. This is all wrong. They should not be asking me to do this against my will. What have I got to do with gods and goddesses?

Her father's voice interrupted her thoughts. "You are frightened now, my daughter, but the spirit of Asherah will enter into you as the spirit of Baal will enter into the king, and you will make the sacred marriage with triumphant joy. Believe me when I tell you this."

But she didn't believe him. He was a man—how could he know how she felt?

"Go away," she said and turned her back on him.

She felt him hesitate, then Atene said, "Come, Father, let us give Rahab some privacy." She felt Atene's gentle hand on her shoulder. "Have courage, my sister."

Rahab nodded and briefly put her hand over Atene's. Then Mepu and her sister-in-law were gone and Rahab was left alone with her anger and her fear.

Seventeen

SALA HEARD THE NEWS ABOUT RAHAB BEING NAMED hierodule later that day when he and his father were on their way to a meeting with Lord Arazu to discuss Nahshon's phantom shipping deal. They were early for the meeting, so they stopped first at the Sign of the Olive, where they had established a presence as steady customers.

Sala was standing with his father in front of a high counter, their wine cups perched in front of them, when a uniformed palace guard entered the shop and stood by the door, waiting for the customers to fall silent.

It was not long before the gathered men realized the guard's presence. When the official saw that he had everyone's attention, he waited a dramatic moment before announcing in stentorian tones, "I have come to bring all the men of the city a message from our revered king, Makamaron."

The silence in the room was profound, as if everyone had stopped breathing. A message from the king to the populace, delivered in such a fashion, was unheard of. Sala and his father exchanged glances. Could this be news that the Israelites had been sighted? Was Joshua getting ready to attack so soon? If so, he was going to need their information and there had been no sign of his messengers.

The official continued with his announcement, spacing each

word so it was clear and separate from the one before: "Be it known to all the population of Jericho that Arsay, daughter of Elhu, has offended the king in such a way that he has rejected her as hierodule in the New Year festival."

An audible wave of shock ran around the room, with men murmuring their amazement and looking at one another. Nothing like this had ever happened before—not on the very eve of the festival! The official paused, waiting until silence fell once more. When quiet had been restored, he continued, "Be it further known to all inhabitants of Jericho that King Makamaron has chosen a new hierodule. Her name is Rahab, daughter of Mepu, and she is the most beautiful woman in all the kingdoms of Canaan. It is right that such perfection should assume the sacred role of Asherah, and the king believes that the goddess herself has sent this Rahab to heal the contention in the city and to bring the blessings of fertility upon all who live and work under Makamaron's rule."

At the mention of Rahab's name, Sala's hand jerked and he knocked over his wine cup. Nahshon grabbed his wrist and hissed, "Pull yourself together, Sala! You have gone as white as your tunic. We can't call attention to ourselves."

Sala didn't hear a word his father was saying.

They are going to make her prostitute herself with the king. These were the words going around and around in his head. The image of Rahab rose before him, as clear as if she had been standing there in the flesh. He saw her beauty, but he also saw her enthusiasm, her laughter, her bravery. He remembered the light that had been in her eyes when she told him she loved him.

He loved her too. He could not marry her, but he loved her. He loved her as he would never love another woman, no matter how long he might live.

He turned to his father and said fiercely, "They can't do this to her. We must stop it."

The guard by now had left and moved on to the next gathering place. Nahshon put an arm around Sala's shoulders and said, "Come with me."

Sala walked out of the wine shop with his father, aware of nothing but the buzz of fury in his brain.

Nahshon shook his arm hard. "Sala! Listen to me! We have an appointment with Arazu. You must compose yourself."

Sala stared at his father, making no attempt to hide his rage. "Didn't you hear what that guard just said? They are going to make Rahab into a whore! I have to stop this, Father. She doesn't want to do this—I know she doesn't!"

Nahshon moved his hand to Sala's shoulder and grasped it so tightly it would leave a bruise. "How do you know how she feels? This Canaanite religion makes a holy thing out of promiscuous sex, and Rahab is a Canaanite woman. She is probably thrilled to be singled out by the king for such an 'honor,' and these people will admire her, worship her even. They live in such a filthy world that a woman like that becomes a goddess to them."

Sala did not attempt to pull away. The pain felt good, it kept him focused. He said, "You're wrong, Father. Rahab does not wish to do this disgusting thing. I know this because she loves *me*. She told me so. And I love her. I cannot let this terrible thing happen to her." He shut his eyes in anguish. "What can I do to stop it?"

Lord Nahshon dropped his hand and took a step away. "Do you dare to look me in the face and tell me you love a Canaanite woman?"

Sala opened his eyes. "I do love her, Father. I think I have always loved her."

Blood rushed into Lord Nahshon's face. "*What?* Has she slept with you, Sala? Has she ensnared you with the charms these Canaanite women know so well? How could any son of mine let himself be so deceived?"

Sala was not surprised by his father's reaction, but he hated it. "We have done nothing," he said. "I know I can never marry her. I know that, Father. But I cannot just stand by and let this happen to her!"

"So," Nahshon said in a cold voice, "it has come to this. For the sake of this Canaanite woman you want me to endanger Joshua's plans to take the city of Jericho. You want me to help you save her from one of the filthy rites that make up her own religion."

Sala shook his head, denying his father's tone more than his words.

Lord Nahshon went on relentlessly, "Don't confuse lust with love, Sala. She is the kind of woman every man wants to lie with, but not you! Not my son. You are an Israelite. Don't you know what Moses did to the Israelite men who lay with the women of Moab in the rites of Baal? He executed all of them for their betrayal of Elohim. They were executed, Sala, for lying with pagan women. And Moses was right to do this. Too many of our men have been seduced by the blatant sexuality of this so-called religion. And my son will not be one of them!"

Suddenly Sala felt so sick that he was afraid he was going to vomit right there on the street in front of the wine shop. He said, "I am your son. I would never lie with Rahab outside of marriage, and I will never marry her. I know my duty to you and to my people. But if I can help her, I will do that. And nothing you say will stop me."

Sala turned away.

"Where are you going?"

"To her house. To find out what has happened."

"What about the meeting with Arazu?"

Sala glanced back at his father. "You don't need me for that. Go yourself." And he walked down the street in the direction of the Lower City.

Atene's heart ached for Rahab. She knew it would be impossible for her to plead her sister-in-law's cause to Mepu. In the eyes of her father-in-law, which were the same as the eyes of all Canaanite men, his daughter had just been given a tremendous honor, an honor that reflected back onto her family. Rahab would not just play the role of the goddess; during the enactment of the sacred marriage she would *become* Asherah, just as the king would become Baal. It was a marriage of the gods that would take place at the New Year festival, and it was called sacred because that is what the people of Canaan believed it to be.

But Atene did not think it was going to be sacred this time. The hierodule had to be willing, and Rahab was not. She loved Sala and she would not be able to forget him, just as Atene would not be able to forget Shemu were she in Rahab's position.

Atene had loved Shemu since the moment he had taken her hand, smiled down into her eyes, and led her into Asherah's grove during the autumn festival in their village. They had married the following spring and he was the only man she had ever lain with. And she knew Shemu loved her too. All of these years and no child, yet he had never once hinted that he might wish to divorce her, as was his right under the law.

Atene had seen the way Sala looked at Rahab when he thought no one was watching and she knew he loved her back. So once they reached home, Atene remained in the front room, keeping her eye on the street so she would see Sala when he came, as she was certain he would. When she spied him in front of the house, she opened the door before he could knock.

"Don't go in there," she said. "Come with me and I will tell you all that has happened."

Sala followed her into the tiny dirt strip that separated Rahab's house from the one next to it that belonged to Mepu's brother. The shadow of the two houses sheltered them from the view of anyone on the street.

A muscle jumped in Sala's jaw and he said in a shaking voice, "I was in the wine shop when one of the palace guards came in and announced that Rahab was going to be the new . . . whatever that name is for the woman who has to prostitute herself with the king."

Atene summoned up the calmest voice she could manage. "This is what happened. The king's men came to our house this morning and told Rahab she must go with them to the palace, that the king had sent for her. She wanted me to go with her, and they allowed it. Neither of us had any idea what the king might want with her. I thought perhaps he had heard of her beauty and wanted to see her for himself. But then, when we got there, we were met by Lord Arazu."

"Arazu!" Sala's voice was filled with loathing.

"Yes. We had been to his house the previous day, you see. My father-in-law wanted to speak to him about selling his wine." Atene bit her lip. "At least, that was what Mepu said was the reason. I think the real reason was to show Rahab to Arazu so he might be moved to find a husband for her."

Sala said something in his own language that Atene did not understand, but she was quite sure it was not a compliment of Mepu's judgment.

She did not ask for a translation but continued, "So that is how Arazu met Rahab. He must have gone to the king and told him about her."

"But why would Makamaron make such a change at the last moment? This other woman was probably chosen a long time ago. Why would the king risk alienating her family for Rahab, whose family is of no importance?"

"Rumor says that Arsay's family is of the prince's party, and so Makamaron didn't trust her. Rahab's lack of influential family is probably one of the reasons he picked her. She has no ties to any of the factions in the city."

The muscle in Sala's jaw jumped again. "If she didn't want to do it, then why didn't she just refuse? It's not like Rahab to agree to do something she doesn't want to do."

"You must understand, Sala. After her father had approved, there was nothing she *could* do. I haven't been able to see her since they took her to the shrine, but I know she is heartbroken. She loves *you*, Sala. She does not want to be the hierodule, but she has no choice. If she refused to perform this role, the king would surely take his anger out upon her family. She can't risk that."

Sala stared down into Atene's face. "What kind of religion do you people follow, that you could force a young girl to do such a thing? To prostitute herself! That is all this is, Atene. No matter how you try to pass it off as religion, this is nothing else than prostitution. Her pay for the use of her body will be patronage for her family. Am I right?"

"Perhaps," Atene replied in a low voice. She gathered her courage and spoke aloud the thing that had been preying on her mind all day. "Sala . . . Rahab and I prayed to your God yesterday. She told me some of the things you had explained to her about your beliefs, and, well, we prayed to Elohim. Rahab prayed you would marry her and I prayed that he would send me a child. And then, this morning, Rahab was taken away." She bit her lip. "Sala, I'm afraid Baal was angry with us for turning to another god. I think that might be why this is happening to Rahab."

Sala was stunned. "Rahab prayed to Elohim?"

"Yes. She said you had told her it was all right just to pray from the heart, so that is what we did. But now that this awful thing has happened, I'm afraid we made a terrible mistake. And

I encouraged her. We did it together . . ." Her voice broke and she looked away.

She felt Sala take her hand into his and she looked up. "You did not make a mistake, Atene. It was Mepu who made the mistake, by taking Rahab to see Arazu. If Rahab has put herself under the guidance of Elohim, then there is still hope for her. We must believe this. We must believe that when Elohim heard Rahab's prayers, He listened and He set her feet upon this path for a purpose."

The ring of belief in Sala's words both surprised and comforted Atene. He truly did believe in this Elohim. "Do you really think so?" she asked.

"Yes, I do." His brown eyes were deep and grave. "And we must continue to pray for her, Atene. Both of us. We must ask Elohim to give Rahab the courage to follow His wishes and give us the knowledge of how we may help her."

"I . . . I will try," Atene whispered.

"You did the right thing, Atene. There is only one God, and He is Elohim, the Creator of us all. Believe that. And pray for Rahab."

Atene could almost feel physically the power of his faith. Perhaps he was right. Certainly her prayers to Baal and Asherah had never been answered.

"I will pray to your God, Sala. I will."

"And so will I," Sala replied. "If Elohim has called Rahab to be one of His own, He will save her."

Eighteen

FOR ALL OF HIS FINE WORDS TO ATENE, SALA FELT sick every time he thought of Rahab and what she was being forced to do. He had told Atene that if they prayed to Elohim, Rahab would be saved, but he could not ignore the trickle of doubt that crept into his mind as soon as he began to walk back to the inn. Rahab was not an Israelite and she was engaging in a pagan rite. Would Elohim care about her? Would He see in her some part of His plan? Or would He see in her only the false religion He hated? Elohim despised His people when they fell into the worship of pagan gods. But surely He must see that Rahab was different!

He began to pray:

She is a good woman, Elohim. She seeks to find the truth. She seeks to find You. I beg You to take pity on her and help her. She does not deserve to be defiled by this false religion that she is turning her back upon. Save her, Elohim. I beg You, save her!

That evening after supper he went out to the inn courtyard and looked up into the clear night sky. The brilliant stars seemed so close, but he knew they weren't close; they were far, far away. They belonged to Elohim, not to men. Elohim had made the stars and the sky and the sun and the moon and the great water upon which his father's ships sailed. How could people believe that such beauty and precision could have come into being through

150

the quarreling of childish gods? Did they not understand the great gap that lay between men and the God who created them? When Elohim created the world, He had put into it the nature of plants to grow and the nature of animals and men to procreate. These ignorant Canaanites thought they had to imitate their gods in order to bring about what the One God had ordained to happen from the beginning of time.

Sala looked up at the beautiful, mysterious sky and prayed with everything in him that Rahab would be saved from this unclean act, saved for herself, and saved so she could know the One True God, Elohim, the God of Israel.

Alone in her room at Asherah's Shrine, Rahab's thoughts were on Elohim as well. The priestesses had explained to her what would happen at the festival and how she must conduct herself. As she listened, everything in her mind and heart and body had recoiled from the picture they were painting. She did not feel like an empowered goddess; she felt like a sacrifice. She wanted to fight. She wanted to scream at these white-clad priestesses that they were wrong, that there was no holiness in what they were doing, but the thought of her family and their vulnerability held her back. The priestesses believed in this ritual. That was the difference between them and her. They believed and she did not.

Rahab arose from the carved wooden bedstead she had been given for the night and walked over to the wooden statue of Asherah that was the room's only decoration. As was usual with statues of Asherah, she was nude, with her hands tucked under her breasts. Instead of a torso and legs, her lower body consisted of a straight cylindrical column decorated with snakes, symbolic of the goddess's power of renewal.

All of Rahab's life she had revered and prayed to Asherah. The statue she was looking at now was the same as dozens of other statues of the goddess that Rahab had seen. She shut her eyes and felt with her mind for some connection to the goddess she had grown up with.

There was nothing.

"I am not going to become you tonight," she said out loud. "I am going to be me, and whatever the king does with me is not going to cause the grain to grow or the beasts to bear."

The empty eyes of the statue looked straight ahead, not seeing Rahab at all. The girl took one step back and then another. She had nothing in common with this blind wooden replica. It was not Asherah; it was just something that had been carved by men.

Rahab shivered in her thin white gown and wrapped her arms around herself to stop shaking. Once again she thought of Sala's God, Elohim. There were no statues of Elohim because His greatness could not be captured in wood or stone. He did not even have a name. He was the Creator. Did that mean He had created her? If He had, if He had really created her, then wouldn't that mean He cared about her?

She didn't know. All she knew was that she was in the worst trouble of her life and she didn't know where to go or what to do. Sala had said his God had done miracles for his people. He had sent plagues on the Egyptians so the Israelites would be freed from slavery. He had parted the waters of the sea so that they could escape from the pursuing Egyptian army. He had fed the Israelites in the desert. Surely, if this God could do all of these things, He could save her from the sacred marriage.

Rahab shut her eyes and whispered to Elohim that she would become His faithful follower and do whatever He asked of her, if only He would send a miracle to save her from the king.

Prince Tamur was furious when he learned about his father's ploy to get rid of Arsay. He, his friend Farut, and Arsay's brother Bari met in the prince's apartment in the palace early that evening to discuss what they might do to rescue their plan.

"It's too late. The news is all over Jericho," Farut said grimly. "Makamaron had messengers go to every gathering spot in the city. No one is talking about anything else and everyone is agog to see this Rahab who has taken Arsay's place."

Bari said, "I have tried to speak to Arsay, but she is being kept somewhere here in the palace. I know she is not at Asherah's Shrine; the new hierodule is there, being instructed on how to behave in my sister's place."

The prince cursed loudly and jumped to his feet. The two other men watched him as he prowled restlessly around the luxurious room like a giant cat, his stride long, his feet quiet on the carpet. Finally he swung around to look at them, his dark eyes flashing with barely contained fury.

"We had it planned perfectly. At the banquet the morning after the ritual, all Arsay had to do was stand up and announce that the king had been unable to consummate the marriage. It would have been the ideal moment for me to step in and demand that he come down from his throne so that I may take his place. An impotent king is not fit to rule. Everyone understands that."

Farut said, "Makamaron has outmaneuvered us."

"We can still protest that this sacred marriage is not lawful," Bari argued. "No one has ever heard of this girl. She is not noble—someone told me she was the daughter of a shepherd! The spirit of Asherah will not enter into the body of such a low-born creature. We have every reason in the world to call this supposed sacred marriage a sham."

Farut took a long drink of the wine in his cup before he turned to his friend. "Have you seen the girl, Bari?"

"No. I hear she is beautiful, but so is Arsay." The young man slammed his hand down on a table in his rage. "Jericho is filled with beautiful women who are not the daughters of a shepherd! Why did this happen?"

"Her father is not a shepherd," Farut said. "He owns large vineyards near the village of Ugaru. It's true he is not noble, but he is a man of some substance."

"He's still just a *farmer*," Bari protested. "My sister comes from one of the noblest families in Jericho. And I'm quite sure she is just as beautiful as this shep—farmer's daughter the king has chosen."

The prince said, "You are the one who saw her up close, Farut. How do you answer Bari?"

Farut smiled wryly. "Her beauty is not in question. The king chose her because he knew he could not trust Arsay. Is there any possibility of us getting to her so we can convince her to denounce the king at the banquet?"

The prince shook his head. "No. My father will have her tightly guarded at the shrine. We won't be able to get near her."

Farut put his wine cup down on the table. "Then we must hope Makamaron does indeed fail and that this new hierodule will say something." His lips curled cynically. "Perhaps her farmer father has brought her up to tell the truth."

It was the prince's turn to slam his hand down on the precious inlaid table next to him, causing his wine cup to tip and the remaining wine to drip onto the luxurious rug on the floor.

"We were so close!" Tamur said furiously. "So very close!"

"Do not give up, my prince," Farut said, getting up and

walking toward the door. "Things may still resolve themselves in our favor." He opened the door and called for a servant to come mop up the wine.

The three young men sat in silence while this chore was performed. After the door had closed behind the servant, Farut said to the prince, "Soon the Israelites will be coming against us. Many misfortunes may happen to the king if Jericho becomes a city under siege."

Prince Tamur nodded slowly. "That is so, Farut. For certain, I will be better able to direct the defense against the Israelites than that old man will."

"A true word," Bari said.

Farut said, "Larger numbers of people are starting to come into the city from the surrounding villages. I've been told that many of the people who came in for the festival are planning to remain until after the Israelite threat is gone. We are now facing overcrowding and everything it entails, and Makamaron has done nothing to prepare for it."

"He must be disposed of," Tamur said forcefully. "The welfare of Jericho depends upon it."

His two friends agreed, and they poured more wine into their cups.

Nineteen

THE DAY OF THE NEW YEAR FESTIVAL DAWNED AS bright and hot as if it were already high summer. The king had sent guards to escort Mepu and his family into the temple court-yard, where the great altar of Baal stood before the steps that led up to the sanctuary. The courtyard was packed with most of the aristocracy of Jericho, and it was so hot and airless that Atene felt as if she might faint. Of all the family, she was the only one who was not jubilant about Rahab's honored place in the coming ceremonies.

"Look at all these people," Shemu said to her in a low voice. "To think it is my little sister who is to be the goddess on such a day as this."

Atene glanced up into her husband's face. There was noth-ing she could say. Everything in his upbringing told him this was a great honor for Rahab. Everything in Atene's upbringing told her that too. But since she and Rahab had prayed to Elohim, Atene had begun to wonder. The idea of one god being in charge of all the world . . . Atene liked that idea. Somewhere deep inside herself she thought it made sense.

The city streets outside the walls of the temple were jammed with people by the time the door to the temple sanctuary opened and Makamaron made his appearance. This yearly festival was the most important religious and political occasion for Jericho's king. This was the day when he was reinvested with his authority as the representative of Baal on earth. This was the day that he reasserted his kingship.

Makamaron proceeded with slow dignity to the high-backed, carved wooden chair that was set before the temple doors at the top of the stairs. His tunic had been dyed with the precious purple that came from Tyre and was only worn by kings. A circle of gold sat upon his bald head, and the wide bracelets on his arms and the rings on his fingers glittered gold in the hot sun.

"He doesn't look well," Atene murmured to Shemu. "His face is gray."

Shemu said, "Well, he's not young anymore. He's been king here for twenty years."

Poor Rahab, Atene thought. The glory of the king's clothing could not disguise his age or his unhealthy bulkiness to Atene, and she shuddered at the thought of having to lie with so repulsive a man. She reached out to grasp Shemu's hand. He looked at her in surprise, then smiled and closed his fingers around hers.

Atene watched with the rest of the crowd as a magnificent bull was led into the courtyard. The animal walked quietly and Atene thought it must have been given some kind of herb to make it so docile.

The bull only roared once when the high priest brought the ax down on its neck. Then it slumped down on the altar, twitched once or twice, and was quiet. Atene felt sick as she watched the sacrifice. She had seen animal sacrifices before, as they were a part of the village rites of Baal and Asherah, but the blood from this large animal seemed torrential. She closed her eyes so she didn't see the high priest fill a cup with the blood of the sacrifice and climb the stairs to the king's chair to anoint Makamaron on the forehead with the mark of Baal's thunderbolt.

Once the sacrifice and anointing were finished, the part of the festival the crowds most enjoyed began. For several hours the high priest stood on a platform that was raised higher than the temple walls so the people gathered in the city streets could see and hear him. From this perch he recited the extensive collection of holy stories that told about Baal and the various other gods who made up the Canaanite religion.

Other platforms had been set up in different places outside the walls, and lesser priests recited the stories to those who were not close enough to the temple to hear. As the stories progressed, the adventures being described were enacted by mimes to the delight of the populace. The people threw themselves into the stories, weeping and lamenting when Baal was hurt or defeated, and shouting and rejoicing at his victories.

Sala and his father were in the crowd watching these proceedings along with the believers. Lord Nahshon had not wanted to come, feeling that to do so would make him unclean, but Sala had threatened to go alone, so his father had reluctantly accompanied him. The two of them listened to the priest nearest to them with a mixture of incredulity and horror. How could these people believe that the wonders of this earth had come into being because of these brainless, power-hungry gods they had created out of their own imaginations?

The first story the high priest recited had been about Baal and his conflict with Yam, the god of the seas and rivers. After Baal's victory over Yam, there came the long story of the building of Baal's palace in the mountains. Then the priest went on to tell about Baal's summons to Mot, the god of death. When Mot refused to come to Baal's palace, Baal went searching for him.

All of the other gods took sides and there was extensive fighting among them until Mot apparently devoured Baal and killed him.

This particular part of the story called for shrieks of mourning from the women in the crowds and much beating of the breast from the men. The crowd surrounding Nahshon and Sala quieted a little when they heard of how Asherah, who was both Baal's wife and his sister, went searching for Mot and killed him with a sword.

This provoked many cheers for the redoubtable Asherah and snarls for the hated Mot. Then, to the crowd's delight, Asherah learned from the sun goddess, Shapash, that Baal was not dead. The goddess sought out her brother and her mate and finally found him, still alive.

This evoked huge rejoicing among the crowd. The priest had to wait a long time until the noise died down before he could finish his tale. It ended with the happy news that Asherah and Baal then retired together to his mountain so he could take his rightful seat upon his throne.

When the storytelling was over, the crowd was in a highly emotional state. There was shouting and laughing and dancing, much of it fueled by the wine that had been going around.

Sala had not been prepared for this kind of display. Among his people, worship was serious. The Israelite religion was concerned with the behavior of Elohim's people, about following the laws of the Creator, about being upright and just and open to the word of God. This display . . . this was outrageous. Disgusting. Offensive in every way to Elohim, who had commanded that Joshua crush these polluted worshippers under his feet like the dirt that they were.

And Rahab. His beautiful, brave Rahab was trapped in the net of this filthy ritual. It made Sala sick to his soul to think about it.

Save her, Elohim. I beg this of You. Save Rahab from this deg-radation. She has turned to You for help. Save her, Elohim . . .

A sudden roar came from the crowd, distracting Sala from his prayer. He heard someone cry, "The hierodule is coming!"

Sala's stomach turned over. They were parading her in front of this drunken crowd. How could this be happening? How had things come to this?

But it was happening. They were bringing Rahab from Asherah's Shrine to the Temple of Baal for the culmination of the festival, the sacred marriage. The noise of the crowd had grown so great that it was impossible for Sala to hear what his father was saying to him. He saw the king's guards using their spears to push back the crowd to make a pathway for the raised chair carrying the hierodule.

Sala and Nahshon were shoved back with the crowd, but Sala was tall enough to see over the heads of those before him. He looked at the opened path and wondered if he could bear to watch this. It would tear his heart out. But even if he wanted to, he could not move, he was so hemmed in by the mass of people around him.

Then he saw it, moving at a measured pace along the path cleared by the guards. Sala could not look away. The chair was anchored to two long poles and four priests were carrying the poles on their shoulders. And sitting in the chair was Rahab. The hierodule.

She did not see him as she passed by. She sat straight-backed in the painted cedar chair, her great brown eyes staring straight ahead. Her glorious black hair was loose and flowing over her shoulders and down her back. The pure white tunic she wore brought out the warmth of her skin and the heavy gold necklace, the slender delicacy of her neck. The lineaments of her face were utterly without expression. She actually looked like a goddess, so remote did the shouting people appear to her in her aloof and transcendent beauty.

Such fury filled Sala that he thought he would explode with it. "They can't do this to her!" he shouted to his father. "I won't let them do this!" He shoved the man in front of him hard, trying to get past, and kicked the next one in the legs in a frantic effort to reach Rahab.

"Sala!" Nahshon caught the edge of his son's tunic to haul him back, but Sala pulled away. He was so filled with rage that the air in front of him looked stained with red. He wanted to pummel, to smash, to destroy, to kill; he wanted to murder every person in the world who had done this to Rahab.

Several men came to the aid of Sala's victims and he went after them as well. He fought like a demon, but he was only one man and they managed to hold him long enough for a guard to reach them. When Sala tried to kick the guard, the king's man used his spear to administer a blow to the head and Sala went down.

By now Rahab's chair had passed and the attention of the crowd turned to the maniac who had begun the fight. Sala was sprawled on the ground, unconscious, with blood running from the wound the spear had opened. Nahshon knelt beside him and, when he saw that his son was still breathing, tears of relief and thanksgiving filled his eyes.

"What was the matter with him?" the guard growled. "Too much to drink?"

"Yes." Lord Nahshon leaped at the excuse. He stood up to address the guard. "I apologize that my son put you to so much trouble. If you will allow it, I will take him home and sober him up. He is not usually so aggressive, but . . ."

The guard nodded and looked for a long moment at Sala's recumbent figure. Lying still on the ground, the slender young man looked completely harmless. It was hard to believe he had caused so much damage.

"Don't let him out of the house until tomorrow," the guard warned Nahshon. "If he makes any more trouble, he'll be for the prison."

"I will take care of him, I promise," Lord Nahshon said. "Thank you."

The guard moved away and Lord Nahshon once more knelt beside Sala. He felt his son's heart, which was beating normally. But the wound on his head was still bleeding. Lord Nahshon looked up, almost frantic with worry. How was he to get Sala away from here?

An elderly woman knelt beside him and said practically, "Here, I have some water. Let me clean that wound." A younger woman joined her, kneeling on Sala's other side. "Here, use this scarf, Mother; it's clean."

"Thank you. Thank you very much."

Lord Nahshon was surprised and truly grateful for the help of these good women. He moved to get out of their way, but his eyes remained fixed on his son's unconscious face.

The older woman looked up to smile at Nahshon. "Some boys should not drink more than a cup. One of my sons is like that. As soon as he drinks too much wine he starts fighting." She shook her head. "He's calmed down now that he's married and has a family, but he gave us a hard time when he was younger."

"I was not watching him closely enough." Lord Nahshon was happy to continue with the excuse that Sala had been provoked by too much to drink.

The older woman finished cleaning the wound, and then the younger one pressed the scarf over it tightly, to stop the bleeding.

"Do you think it's serious?" Lord Nahshon asked, his brow creased with worry.

"No." The woman with the water was washing the rest of Sala's face. "The guard only broke the flesh. The bone underneath is untouched. He will be all right, although he will probably have a scar on that handsome face."

The people who had been watching the little scene began to drift away and Lord Nahshon looked around. The streets were still noisy and crowded; there was little or no chance of finding a litter to take Sala home.

A man came up beside Nahshon. "Ah, there you are, Mama," he said to the kneeling woman. He looked down into Sala's unconscious face, then put a hand on the woman's shoulder. "Always the one to help." His voice was full of affection.

Lord Nahshon said to the man, "I am grateful for your mother's kindness. I'm afraid my son got carried away by the excitement of the festival."

"You have to watch how much they drink," the man said practically. "They just keep going and don't keep count."

"I fear that is what happened," Lord Nahshon said.

The younger woman who had supplied the scarf said, "Our boys are around here somewhere, my husband. See if you can find them. This poor man will need help getting his son away from here."

The man nodded and said to Nahshon, "Don't worry, I'll find my sons and we'll help you get him home."

"Thank you." For the first time in his life, Lord Nahshon looked at a Canaanite with real gratitude. "I would appreciate that greatly."

The man laughed as he moved off. "He'll have a headache that will split his skull in the morning."

Lord Nahshon said, "Yes. I'm sure he will."

By tomorrow morning it would be done, he thought with grim satisfaction. The girl would be defiled and that would be that. He shut his eyes briefly. If only he had just sent the girl back to her family while they were still in Gaza. Why, oh why, had he brought her to Ramac with them and given Sala a chance to get to know her? It had been the worst mistake of his life, and he would give his entire fortune if he could reverse that thoughtless decision and so save his son from all this unnecessary temptation and pain.

Twenty

When Rahab's chair arrived at the Temple of Baal, the courtyard was still packed with people, although the king had left. The priests carried her through the opening in the crowd that had been created by the guards and rested it on top of the sanctuary steps, where the king's chair had stood just a short time before. The priestesses who had followed the hierodule in the procession helped her from the chair, then turned her so that all the people in the courtyard could see her.

A murmur went up from the gathered nobles, but all Rahab cared about was locating her family. This time it was not her mother she wanted, however, it was Atene. Her sister-in-law was the only person in the world who might understand what she was feeling, and she wanted the comfort of Atene's compassionate gaze. But she couldn't find her in the sea of people who were staring at her so eagerly.

After a few moments the priestesses turned her so she could pass through the great sanctuary door. This was the only day in the year that women were allowed into Baal's temple, and the priestesses looked eagerly around the room, taking in the statues and splendid carved wall decorations, trying to absorb everything while they had the chance.

Rahab looked at nothing. She was aware only of the quick beating of her heart and the buzzing in her ears. She dug her nails into her palms, hoping the pain would keep her from fainting.

The priestesses led her into one of the side rooms that opened off the outer chamber. Inside the room was a raised pool of water, larger and deeper than the one she had used yesterday in the king's palace. It was the bath for the ritual cleansing of the hierodule.

As Rahab looked around the graceful bathing room, a sense of crushing defeat settled over her. She had never felt so beaten, not even when she had been kidnapped as a child. At that time she had truly believed the goddess would save her, and that belief had kept her fighting spirit alive. But she didn't believe in the goddess anymore. She was now, as she always had been, just Rahab.

She wondered how other hierodules who had gone before her had felt. Had they believed they turned into the goddess while making the sacred marriage? Or had they just pretended? They must have pretended; they were just girls who wanted to be important and so they told everyone they had felt the goddess enter into them. But Rahab didn't think that had happened. The girls had lied.

She was lost. There was no Sala to help her and no way she could help herself. To resist would be to bring certain destruction on her family. No king would allow himself to be so humiliated without seeking retribution.

As the priestesses helped her into the pool and washed her body carefully with scented soap, she thought of Sala. She had been trying so hard not to think of him, not to imagine what he would think of her for doing this. Even worse, what would his father think?

It would defile me to marry you.

Those words had hurt her. They had hurt her worse than anything else in her life. And he had said that before . . . this.

Sala believed in Elohim. Rahab had prayed to Sala's god last

166

night, but He had not listened to her. He had let this terrible thing happen to her. She was a Canaanite woman, and He must not care about Canaanites.

Perhaps Sala would pray for her. If he did, perhaps Elohim would listen to Sala if He would not listen to her. Rahab shut her eyes tight and hoped with all her heart that Sala was praying for her.

When the bath was over, the priestesses dried her, dressed her in a fine linen robe, and combed out her hair.

The head priestess, who had been supervising the bath, looked at Rahab and lost a little of her sour expression. "Asherah will be pleased. Now do you remember the prayers I taught you to say while you wait for the king?"

"Yes." Rahab, who had no intention of saying those prayers, nodded.

"Then come with me."

Rahab followed the head priestess back into the outer chamber. The door to the inner chamber was guarded, but when the sentry saw who it was, he opened the door to allow the women to enter.

The first thing Rahab noticed was the scent of cedar. The second thing was the wide bed in the middle of the room. It was covered in pure white linens with pillows scattered along the top.

Rahab stopped.

The head priestess turned to her with a frown. "Come along. I must arrange you in the bed before the king comes. Do not delay."

A rush of nausea roiled through Rahab's stomach. *Perhaps if I get sick all over the bed the king will reject me,* she thought a little hysterically. *Surely goddesses don't vomit.*

The head priestess must have seen her sudden pallor, for she guided Rahab to sit on the side of the bed. "Put your head in your lap and take deep breaths," she commanded.

Rahab obeyed, trying hard to get control of her stomach. Much as she would like to throw up all over the bed, and the king as well, she knew that would be fatal for her family. So she took some sips of the water the priestess brought her and her stomach began to settle down.

As the priestess took the cup back she looked deeply into Rahab's eyes. "It is not surprising that you are overcome by this moment. When the king enters this room, it will be Baal coming to you, and that is certainly enough to overwhelm a simple girl like you. But remember, you are no longer Rahab, the daughter of a farmer; you are Asherah, the goddess who is Baal's wife and his sister. You will feel joy to see him, and the consummation of your union will assure the life of our country."

Rahab returned the head priestess's look and saw that she believed absolutely in what she was saying. Rahab breathed deeply once, twice, then again. She nodded. "I am all right now."

She let herself be as easily manipulated as a doll while the head priestess arranged her in the bed. Once she was lying properly, Umara spread her hair over the pillow and then folded back her robe so that her body was partially uncovered.

Finally the priestess left. Rahab lay as still as the dead, stared up at the ceiling, and told herself that all she had to do was endure. After all, it couldn't take long.

Don't think about it, don't think about it. Just do whatever has to be done so that it will be over. Don't think of Sala. Don't think of anyone. Pretend you are on a boat flying across the water. Feel the sun on your head and the spray in your face. You're not here in this suffocating room, you're—

At that moment the door to the inner sanctuary opened

again, and this time the king came in. Rahab's head and shoulders were propped up against the pillows so she could see him clearly in the flicker of the rush lights.

He wore a white robe and his face and neck and chest were wrinkled and dotted with ugly brown spots. His stomach was so big he looked as if he were carrying a child.

Rahab shut her eyes tightly. Everything inside her seemed frozen with horror.

She opened her eyes and saw that the king was standing next to her. She heard his breath catch. "You are so beautiful, Asherah, my goddess, my wife. Just looking at you has given me the might and the potency of Baal."

She felt his fingers touch her skin and she shut her eyes again. With all her being she wanted to shove him away from her and run.

I have to do this, she kept repeating to herself. *I have to do this, I have to . . .*

She felt the heavy weight of the king crush her into the softness of the bedstead. She shuddered. He was lying on top of her and his breath smelled rotten. He pushed her robe away and began to rub himself against her. It was awful, more awful than she had ever imagined. She could feel his bare flesh against her and she wanted to scream.

Suddenly he raised himself and let out a deep, gutteral moan. Then, as she laid still beneath him, he made a strangled sound and collapsed on her with his full weight. He didn't move and was quiet.

Rahab lay there, rigid as a board. She was terrified. What had just happened?

"My lord?" she whispered at last.

There was no answer.

Rahab tried to push him a little, to take some of the weight off of her, but he just lay there, inert, his face against her neck. A horrible suspicion rose in her mind. He couldn't be . . . he couldn't be dead?

"My lord!" She spoke louder and pushed harder. Still no response.

Rahab panicked. She was trapped here under a dead man! She pushed and shoved with all her might. He was heavy but finally she managed to shift him enough so that she could get out from under him. When she was finally standing on the floor, she bent over him to check if he might still be breathing.

His eyes were open, but they did not see her. His chest was motionless.

Rahab raised shaking hands to her mouth. He was dead. The king had tried to make the sacred marriage with her and had died doing it. What was she going to do?

Slowly, slowly she backed away from the bed, her eyes on the unmoving figure sprawled among the rumpled sheets. When she was halfway across the room, she whirled and ran to the door. She pushed it open and burst into the outer chamber. Two temple guards were at the door and they gaped at her as if she were a madwoman.

"The king!" she cried. "I think the king is dead!" The horrified expression on the guards' faces was the last thing she saw because, for the first time in her life, Rahab fainted.

The guard nearest the door ran into the sanctuary while the other guard knelt next to the fallen girl. When the first guard came out, he was pale to his lips. "She's right. The king is dead."

The second guard looked up from Rahab's unconscious body. "Get the prince. I'll stay here."

Rahab's eyes were still closed when Prince Tamur came striding into the temple, followed by more guards. He took a quick look at the recumbent Rahab, then demanded, "Where is the king?"

"In the sanctuary, my lord."

The prince went inside and when he came out his face was grave. "It looks as if he died in the act." He came over to Rahab and knelt down next to her.

At that moment her eyes fluttered, opened, and she looked up at him. He asked quietly, "Are you all right? You've had quite a shock."

"The k-king," Rahab stuttered. "He . . . he . . ."

"Yes, we know. You will need to tell us what happened," Tamur answered.

"My lord!"

Tamur looked up to see Farut coming across the room. "You sent for me? What has happened?"

"My father is dead." The prince jerked his head toward the inner sanctuary. "In there."

Farut went immediately into the room and when he came out he, too, was pale. "We must send for the high priest. He must declare the king dead before we can move his body."

"Yes, and I want a priestess to examine this girl. Her robe is stained with my father's seed. I don't think he was able to finish the act."

Farut squatted next to the prince and looked into Rahab's dazed face. "Rahab. Please, can you tell us what happened?"

She replied in a thin, frightened voice, "He was lying on top of me, moaning and pushing at me, and then he just stopped moving and lay still. I didn't know what had happened. I didn't do anything! Truly, I didn't do anything! I only pushed him away after a while so that I could get up. Then I saw that he was dead."

Farut and the prince looked at each other. "He didn't manage it," Farut said.

"No, the trying killed him." The prince stood up and began to issue orders to the guards that now filled the room. "Go fetch the priestesses to take care of this poor girl. And bring my father's counselors here as well. I want everyone to see what happened so there can be no rumors of assassination."

"Yes, my lord," the head guard replied and began to snap out orders to his underlings.

Rahab tried to get to her feet and Farut bent to help her. When she was standing the two men looked at her. The thin robe could not hide her body and her pale face made her eyes look larger and blacker than ever.

Farut said, "Beauty killed him."

The prince nodded. "What a piece of luck for us. If the priestesses confirm that the sacred marriage was not accomplished, then I can ascend the throne and truly become the king and progenitor of this land."

Farut bowed low, until his forehead almost touched his knees. "All hail to the king!" he said loudly. And all of the guards in the room repeated the words with him. "All hail to the king."

Twenty-One

IT WAS AFTER MIDNIGHT WHEN THE NEW KING MET with his closest friends, along with the high priest and head priestess, both of whom had been supporters of his father. Makamaron's body had been removed from the sanctuary and taken back to the palace. Tamur had called this group together to decide how to handle the problem that had so stunningly arisen. He was clever enough to realize that he needed to divert any possible rumors of assassination, thus it was important to have an answer for any questions that might be raised by skeptics as to the way his father had died.

The council was meeting in one of the small side rooms of the temple and Tamur, who was seated on a carved stool with the others gathered around him, addressed the high priest first. "What say you, High Priest? How should we inform the city of my father's death? And how should we phrase our announcement?"

Tamur's voice had been respectful and Ratu's tight mouth relaxed a little. He said, "We cannot tell them he died attempting to complete the sacred marriage. Such a statement could easily spread fear that Baal is angry with the city, and we cannot risk that, especially now, with the Israelite threat so close."

Tamur looked at the others. "I agree with the high priest. With the Israelites waiting to attack us, we cannot do anything that might take the heart out of our people."

Farut said, "The important question is—can we trust the girl to keep her mouth closed? We do not want to say anything that might taint the sacredness of the ritual, and the king falling dead in the midst of the act . . ." He shrugged. "It would be best if the city did not know that."

All of the men turned to the head priestess, who had earlier removed Rahab from the temple and taken her back to Asherah's Shrine.

Umara's slanted brown eyes narrowed. "She was frightened and I think she will do as we tell her." She pinched her lips in disgust. "It was mad to name an ignorant girl like that to be hierodule."

Murmurs of agreement came from the prince's men.

Umara continued, "Leave her to me. I will tell her if she says anything about the king dying in her bed, people may think she killed the king herself. Given that caution, I think we can count on her remaining quiet."

"We can always send the whole family back to their farm," Farut said.

The high priest disagreed. "I don't think that is a good idea. I heard from one of my informants that most of the village people who came into Jericho for the festival are planning to remain until the threat from the Israelites is over. If we send this girl and her family back to be butchered, it might give rise to just the kind of rumors we want to avoid."

Farut reluctantly agreed.

"There is one vital fact that I must know," said Tamur, turning to the head priestess. "Did my father manage to complete the sacred marriage before he died?"

"No, he did not. I examined the girl myself and she is still a virgin."

Tamur's eyebrows flew upward in surprise. "A girl who looks like that—she was a virgin?"

"Yes, my lord. She was and she still is."

"So the sacred marriage was never accomplished?"

"No, my lord. It was not accomplished."

"That is good news," Tamur said.

The high priest said, "If that is the case then we must have another sacred marriage, a real one. Every part of the festival must follow its proper order. We cannot risk the anger of Baal, not now when we lie under the threat of a siege." He turned to the young man who was now king of Jericho, Baal's representative on earth. "You must complete the ritual, my lord. It is not too late. We can bring the hierodule back and start over again."

"I agree," Tamur said. "It is imperative that we assure the people that every part of the ritual has been accomplished."

Farut said, "I think this is how we should proceed. We tell the people that Makamaron's heart ceased to beat before he even went into the sanctuary. Before he even saw the hierodule. Thus we can assure them that the kingship passed untainted from father to son, and Tamur, their new king, accomplished the sacred marriage in the place of his father. We can assure them that Baal and Asherah have come together and that our land will be blessed for the coming year."

Everyone agreed with this plan.

Tamur said to the head priestess, "There is still time to do this, Head Priestess. Can you get the girl ready quickly?"

The head priestess looked thoughtful.

Tamur said sharply, "Did you hear me, Head Priestess?"

"I did, my lord, and I do not think you can use this girl as your hierodule. She has been shocked and frightened—she is a virgin, remember. She is in no state right now to allow the goddess to enter into her spirit. The sacred marriage will not fulfill its purpose if she is part of it."

"She will feel differently with me, Head Priestess. I am not an ugly old man and I know how to woo a woman."

The priestess shook her head. "Believe me, it would be a great mistake. The hierodule must appear at the banquet in the temple courtyard tomorrow morning, and you do not want a pale and shaken woman sitting beside you, my lord king."

Bari, who had been quiet thus far, now spoke. "Get Arsay to do it. My sister was supposed to be the hierodule in the first place, until Makamaron replaced her with this farmer's daughter."

The high priest looked at Bari in approval. "An excellent idea. Arsay will know how to conduct herself. That would be best."

"How shall we explain the change in hierodules to the people?" The king's voice was crisp. His biggest concern was to have answers to any questions that might arise as to the naturalness of his father's death.

Umara said, "We will say she was your father's choice, but your choice is Arsay, a priestess of Asherah's Shrine. No one will question the legitimacy of such a decision."

Farut, ever practical, said, "What shall we do with the other one then? Lock her up to ensure her silence?"

The high priestess regarded the young man as if he were about two years old. "It would be unwise to make her a prisoner when we may need her to back up our story that Makamaron died before he came to her. She will say what we tell her to say as long as we return her to her family, I'm certain of that. Odd as we may find it, she never wanted to be the hierodule in the first place."

A thoughtful silence fell, then the king said, "I will listen to your advice, Head Priestess. Send the girl home and make certain she knows what she is expected to say."

Umara bowed her head.

Tamur once more looked around the hastily summoned

council. "So this is what I will do. I will say that my father's heart stopped while he was preparing to go to the hierodule. I will say that after his body was seen by the high priest, it was respectfully returned to the palace. I will say that I, the new king, made the sacred marriage with a priestess from our own temple."

Murmurs of approval as the men nodded their heads.

"I will deliver this announcement at the banquet tomorrow morning, and I will also announce that the banquet will be shortened so that my father's funeral rites can take place immediately." Tamur paused. "Are we agreed?"

"Yes, my lord," came the unified response.

"Very well," the king said. "Then we had better start to prepare for the second sacred marriage."

"I will get Arsay," the high priestess said, and the council broke up.

It was after midnight and Rahab lay curled into a tight ball in the middle of her bed. The rush light in the room had burned out earlier leaving her in darkness, but she could not go to sleep. She had scrubbed all traces of the king off her skin, but he was not so easily banished from her thoughts. The nightmare events of the day kept running ceaselessly through her mind.

They had taken her from the temple and brought her here to the shrine, where she had endured a humiliating encounter with the head priestess. The woman had wanted to verify whether or not the king had had intercourse with her. Rahab didn't think he had, but in her innocence she wasn't quite sure.

Her relief upon hearing that the king had not defiled her was enormous. It was only after Umara had left her alone that the idea crept into Rahab's mind that because she was still pure perhaps they would make her be the hierodule again with the new king.

At this thought, Rahab flung herself onto her back and stared up into the darkness, her fists clenched at her sides. "I won't do it." She said it out loud, to emphasize her resolve. "I don't care what they do to me, I will not be the hierodule again."

They will not want an unwilling goddess, she told herself, struggling to hold back panic. *I will tell them that I am sick, that my experience with the king dying while he was lying on top of me has shattered my nerves, that I am not fit to welcome Asherah into my heart. They will see the reasonableness of that. They must! These people truly believe Asherah comes into the person of the hierodule. They will not think I am fit.*

Her experience tonight had stripped Rahab of her belief in any rituals of Baal, and her thoughts turned next to Elohim, Sala's god. When she was chosen to be hierodule, she had believed Elohim hadn't heard her prayers, that a god of the Israelites would have no concern for her, a Canaanite woman.

Then the king had died before he could defile her.

Elohim *had* heard her. He had heard her and He had saved her from the king.

Rahab closed her eyes and prayed with all her heart: *Help me now, Elohim, as You did before. I believe You are the one God, Creator of us all, and I promise I will be Your follower. Please help me to get away from these false worshippers. Help me to get home.*

At this moment, the door of Rahab's cell swung open and the head priestess came in. She was carrying a rush light, which she put on the wooden chest. The small light flickered, leaving pools of darkness in all the corners of the room.

"We must talk," Umara said.

Rahab, who had sat up as soon as the door began to open, nodded speechlessly.

The priestess remained standing by the chest so Rahab could see her face in the flickering light. Umara said, "It has been decided that you may return to your family, but you must first agree to certain conditions."

Joy ignited inside Rahab and she clapped her hands in delight.

The priestess said, "Don't look so happy yet, you have not heard the conditions. Are you listening?"

Rahab tried to stop smiling. "Yes, Head Priestess. I am listening. I will do whatever it is you ask of me."

"This is the condition: you must never tell anyone that the king died in your bed. We are telling the people that he died while in his room, before he came to you. It is important that the people be assured the sacred marriage was not desecrated in any way. There is enough fear in the city because of the Israelites and we do not want to add to it. Do you understand?"

"Yes, Head Priestess, I understand."

"If anyone asks you, you are to say you never saw the king at all, that you were informed of his death while you waited for him to come to you."

"Yes, Head Priestess," Rahab repeated.

"Before the night is out, King Tamur will make the real sacred marriage. We must be certain the New Year rites have been completed so the city will be protected."

Rahab stiffened. *I will not be the hierodule again. I will not!*

"Arsay will take your place as hierodule," Umara said. "It would not please Asherah to have a distressed woman represent her, and it would only be natural that you should be distressed by the events of this evening."

"I am extremely distressed, Head Priestess," Rahab said quickly.

For the only time since they had met, a flicker of approval showed in Umara's eyes. "Will you swear to me now, by the sword of Baal, that you will never say aught of what happened at the temple tonight?"

"I swear by the sword of Baal that I will never tell anyone about what happened at the temple tonight," Rahab repeated fervently.

"Very well." Umara picked up the rush light. "When Shapash makes her first appearance in the sky, I will send for your father to come to bring you home."

Rahab's heart was bursting. "Thank you, Head Priestess."

She sat on the bed until the sound of footsteps died away, then she got up and went over to the window. Looking up toward the sky, she prayed with all her heart and soul, *Thank You, Elohim, for listening to my prayers. From this moment forth, You will be my God and I shall be Your faithful servant. Whatever You may call upon me to do, I will do it as I bless Your name.*

Twenty-Two

WHEN MEPU HEARD SOMEONE BANGING ON HIS DOOR just after dawn, he leaped up from his sleeping mat, his heart hammering.

Rahab. Had something happened to her?

Kata was sitting up too, her hands clutching her throat. "What is it?" she asked.

"I'll go and find out," he said.

"Wait! I'm coming with you," Kata cried and, pulling a robe around her, she hurried after her husband.

When Mepu opened the door and saw a palace guard standing there, his knees weakened. Was the guard here to arrest him? Had Rahab done something she shouldn't have?

"Y . . . yes?" he croaked.

"You are Mepu, father of Rahab?" the guard asked in a gruff voice.

"Yes, I am Mepu." He managed a more normal tone this time.

"You are to come with me immediately to Asherah's Shrine."

Kata clutched her husband's elbow. She was so afraid for Rahab that she spoke to the guard directly.

"Is this about my daughter? Is she all right?"

The guard ignored her and said to Mepu, "You are to bring her home. Get your cloak and come with me."

"But what about the morning banquet . . . ?"

The guard gave him an impatient look. "I was told to bring this message to you and that is all I know. You had better hurry."

"Yes, yes, I will be but a moment." Mepu closed the door on the guard.

Kata was still grasping his arm. "What can have happened? Rahab was supposed to attend the banquet this morning. We were to go too. Why are they sending her home?"

Mepu put his hand over his wife's to calm her. He was alarmed by this summons, but he did not want to frighten Kata any further. He said, "You know Rahab. She probably begged them to let her come to see us before the banquet starts. I'm sure it's nothing more than that."

Kata's face relaxed a little. "That sounds like Rahab. Perhaps you are right. But to awaken us at this hour! Something does not seem right to me."

Shemu had also heard the noise at the door and he came down the stairs as his father was speaking. "They want you to bring Rahab home?" he asked, his brows knit together in a worried frown.

"Yes. I am to go right away."

"I'll come with you," Shemu said, and Mepu felt a deep relief that he would have his son's company. Clearly Shemu also believed something was wrong.

The guard had a chariot waiting outside the door, which worried Mepu even more profoundly. Something was indeed wrong if they were being taken by chariot.

No one spoke as the chariot rattled along the empty streets. The guard drove them to Asherah's Shrine and stopped outside the courtyard.

"Go in. Someone will be waiting for you."

Mepu and Shemu stepped out of the chariot and entered into the courtyard. Umara, the head priestess, greeted them.

"You are Rahab's father?" she said to Mepu.

"Yes, I am."

"And who is this?" She looked at Shemu.

"I am Rahab's brother, Head Priestess," Shemu replied. "May I ask why we have been summoned here like this?"

The head priestess looked as if she had eaten something sour as she proceeded to relate the events of the night.

Shemu interrupted the tale. "The king's heart gave way? Do you mean he died?"

"Yes."

Mepu exchanged an astonished look with his son. Neither of them had dreamed of this!

The head priestess continued, "Since it was vital that the sacred marriage take place, our new king went ahead with the ceremony. Your daughter"—she tossed Mepu a disdainful look—"was too upset to be the hierodule, and so one of our own priestesses took her place. So the New Year festival has been successfully completed and we do not need your daughter any longer. Since she shows no interest in remaining here as a priestess, I thought it best to simply send her home."

Mepu's emotions were mixed as he listened to the head priestess. He was grievously disappointed that his daughter had been cheated of the honor that had been promised her, but he was also immensely relieved that Rahab had not done anything that might bring evil consequences upon her family.

The two men remained silent as they waited in the courtyard. At last Rahab came out, escorted by a priestess. Her face was as white as desert sand and there were dark shadows under her eyes.

No wonder she looks so unhappy, Mepu thought. From being the highest woman in the land, she was being thrust back into the obscurity of her ordinary home and family. The new king might not even keep his father's promise to find her a noble husband.

Mepu frowned as another thought crossed his mind. Perhaps no one would want to marry her now. Even if it had been no fault of hers, Rahab would always be associated with the death of Makamaron. Mepu thought bitterly that perhaps it would have been wiser to accept a husband for her from among their neighbors back in Ugaru. Who knew what could happen to her now?

He was thinking these things when Shemu stepped forward and held out his arms to Rahab. She ran into them, threw her arms around her brother's neck, and buried her face in his shoulder.

"It's all right, little one," Shemu said, patting her on the back. "You're coming home and that's all that matters. You will be safe with us."

Mepu stood awkwardly by as Rahab burst into tears in her brother's arms. After a bit Mepu also patted her on the shoulder. "Come along now, my daughter. There is supposed to be a litter waiting for you in the street."

Rahab rode in the litter and the two men walked alongside of it. Kata and Atene were waiting inside the door of the house when Rahab walked in, and both her mother and her sister-in-law hugged her tightly. Everyone cried.

Finally Kata served breakfast and Mepu related what the priestess had told him. When Mepu finished, Kata said, "I think we should take Rahab back to the farm. This city has not been good for her. It has not been good for any of us, I think."

Over Kata's head, Mepu looked at his son. It was Shemu who said gently to his mother, "We cannot go home, Mother. There is news that some Israelites have been seen at the Jordan crossing. Once the river subsides to its normal flow, their whole army will cross onto the plains of Jericho. All of our villages and farms will lie helpless before their advance. They are known for destroying everything that lies in their path, and we cannot risk returning home. I am afraid we are going to have to remain in the city for the time being."

Kata's face crumpled and she turned to Mepu. "But I hate it here."

Mepu said gruffly, "You don't want to be killed by the Israelites, do you?"

Kata sniffled and shook her head.

"Well then, we must stay."

Once breakfast was finished, Rahab and Atene went up to the roof, ostensibly to check on the drying flax. As soon as they were alone, Rahab said urgently, "Have you seen Sala?"

"I saw him briefly, right after the news about you being chosen was announced. I told him how it had happened."

Rahab's chest felt so tight she could hardly breathe. "What must he think of me, Atene, being paraded through the streets like that? Even worse, what will his father think? He will tell Sala I am contaminated, that he must never come near me again."

"You are not contaminated, Rahab! Being chosen hierodule was hardly your fault. And as it turned out, the king never even touched you. Lord Nahshon will hear that. The story is going to be all over the city within the hour."

"He hated me even before I became the hierodule. Why should he change now?"

"I told Sala that you had prayed to Elohim and that I had prayed to Elohim as well. He was so happy, Rahab! He told me he thought Elohim would save you, that he and I must continue to pray for you. He said we must put our trust in Elohim."

"He said that?" Rahab breathed.

"Yes, he did. And once his father knows you have turned

your back on Baal and now worship the god of the Israelites, his feelings toward you will change. How could they not?"

Last night Rahab had thought she would never be happy again. Now she could scarcely contain the joy that flooded throughout her being. "Do you really think so, Atene?"

Atene nodded. Then, in a slow and gentle motion, her hands cupped her flat stomach. "I hope Elohim answers me too."

Rahab hugged her sister-in-law. "He will, Atene. I think Elohim wants us to belong to Him. I feel it in my heart."

"I want a baby so much, Rahab." Atene's voice broke. "So very much."

Rahab held her closer. "Let us pray again—together."

Atene nodded, and Rahab slowly released her embrace. Quietly and solemnly, the two girls clasped their hands and began to pray.

When Sala awoke the morning after the festival, his whole body ached from his bruises and he had a raging headache. His father showed little sympathy.

"You asked for it," he said. "Do you remember how you started a fight with the men around you? Finally one of the guards subdued you by hitting you on the head with the handle of his spear. You're lucky he didn't kill you."

Sala was sitting on his sleeping mat, holding his head in his hands. "I remember," he mumbled. And he did. He remembered the look on Rahab's face as she passed by, and the same fury he had felt then swept through him again. He shut his eyes. It would all be over by now. Rahab . . .

He had moaned her name aloud and the word seemed to enrage Nahshon. "How can you be so stupid, Sala? That girl has turned you into someone I don't even recognize! A trouble-maker. Even worse—a disobedient son."

Sala winced. His head felt as if a knife were stabbing into it.

His father said, "Can you come downstairs with me?"

Sala began to shake his head, then moaned. "No. My head hurts too much." After a moment he added pitifully, "I'm thirsty."

"I'll bring you some water," Lord Nahshon said in a grim voice and left the room.

Sala slept for the rest of the day, and when he awoke the following morning he felt slightly better. At least he could stand up without feeling as if his head was going to explode.

He went downstairs with his father to have breakfast. The courtyard was packed with people. They found a place at a table with two other men and sat on the bench to wait for their bread and fruit.

Nahshon said to their neighbors, "I don't believe I've seen you before. Did you come to Jericho for the festival?"

The men looked like farm workers with their shaggy hair and work-worn hands; not the sort of people who visited Jericho, even at festival time.

One of the men picked up the slice of dark bread in front of him and took a bite. "No, we came in yesterday, along with a lot of others from our village. Haven't you heard?"

"Heard what?"

"The Israelites have been seen at the Jordan crossing. It looks as if they are preparing to cross the river. The whole countryside will soon be on the move, coming to shelter inside the walls. The word is that the Israelites are vicious; they kill everything in their path: men, women, children, animals . . ."

Sala's attention suddenly focused on the conversation.

"They won't be able to get into the city, though," the other farm worker was saying. "Not with these walls to protect us."

A man from the next table, who had been listening to the conversation, leaned across. "Now that we have a young warrior for a king, our defense will be even stronger."

Sala's head snapped around. He didn't even wince at the pain. "What do you mean? What new king?"

"Where have you been that you have not heard? Makamaron is dead and his son, Tamur, has taken his place."

Makamaron dead? Sala's heart began to slam in tune with the pounding in his head. "No, I have not heard. What happened?"

The speaker smiled with satisfaction at this chance to impart news. "It happened on the night of the festival. Makamaron died before he could make the sacred marriage with the hierodule. Tamur had to step in and do it." He chuckled lasciviously. "That's what Makamaron gets for choosing such a gorgeous girl to be hierodule. Just thinking about her probably stopped his heart."

Sala stared at the men, trying to make sense of what they were saying. "Do you mean *Tamur* made the sacred marriage with Rahab?"

Lord Nahshon put his arm around Sala's shoulders. "You're as white as your tunic. Come upstairs."

Sala pulled away. "No!" He turned again to the men. "What happened?"

The first man burped, then coughed. "He didn't make the sacred marriage with the first one. That would have been unlucky. He made it with the priestess who should have been the hierodule in the first place. They sent the other one home. Everyone is talking about it. I don't know how you didn't hear."

Sala said, "Home to her village?"

"No." The big man looked at Sala as if he might be simple. "Weren't you listening? It's not safe in the farms or the villages anymore. She's in Jericho—not far from here, I have heard. Men have been hanging around her house hoping to see her but she hasn't come outside."

Sala stood up. "I am going out," he said to his father.

"No, you are not," Lord Nahshon replied, standing as well and putting a restraining hand on Sala's arm. "You are in no condition to be walking the streets."

Sala pulled his arm away from his father's grip, gave him a fierce look, turned, and walked out of the room.

Twenty-Three

DESPITE HIS ACHING BODY, SALA RACED THROUGH the narrow streets, almost knocking down a few people as he went by. When he reached Rahab's uncle's house, he stopped, trying to catch his breath. For the first time since he had left the inn, he began to think about what he was going to do once he got here. Obviously he couldn't just knock on the door and ask to see her; her father would never let him in. He finally decided all he could do was wait until Atene or Shemu came out and hope they would help him.

Sala leaned his shoulders against the mud-brick wall and for the first time noticed the large group of men who were gathered on the other side of the street. He remembered what he had heard at breakfast, that lots of men were hanging around hoping to see the woman whose beauty had killed the king.

Sala's hands clenched into fists. Rahab didn't deserve this notoriety. *I wish she wasn't so beautiful. I wish she were just an ordinarily pretty girl. Then she would have never been chosen to be the hierodule and I might have been able to get her away from Jericho before now.*

"You get a better view of the house from over here!" one of the men from across the street called to him. "We can see right in the door when it opens."

Once again fury knotted Sala's stomach, but he didn't answer. They would get tired of waiting and go away, he told himself. It was best to ignore them. He didn't need to call attention to himself by getting into another fight.

The day passed slowly and the crowd on the other side of the street began to thin. When it was almost suppertime, Rahab's door opened and Shemu came out. Sala watched as he strode across the street and began yelling at the men who remained. The last hangers-on melted away and Shemu turned back toward the house, a disgusted look upon his face. When he was almost at the front door, Sala called, "Shemu!"

Shemu's head whipped around. "Sala!" he said in deep surprise. "What are you doing here?"

"I came to see Rahab. I haven't been able to see her since they took her away to be the hierodule, and I must speak with her. Please, Shemu! I love her. I have always loved her. Please help me to see her."

He hadn't thought about what he would say; the words just tumbled out.

Shemu narrowed his eyes. "You have heard what happened?"

"Atene told me how she came to be chosen. Then I heard that the king died before he even saw her. Is it true?"

Shemu's brows lifted at the mention of his wife's name but all he said was, "Yes, it is true."

A great weight lifted from Sala's heart. "I saw her when she was being carried through the streets. I saw her face. How could her family have done that to her? How could you force her to participate in that disgusting rite? Rahab loves me just as I love her. She was devastated! Could you not see that?"

Shemu replied in a level voice, "You do not understand our rites. To be hierodule is a great honor. The king wanted her and my father agreed. There was nothing anyone else could do."

Sala looked closely into Shemu's face. "Did you want her to do it?"

Shemu shrugged. "What I wanted, what Rahab wanted, had nothing to do with it. This was bigger than any of us."

Sala collected his thoughts. There was no point in railing against Shemu—Sala needed him. "I must see her, Shemu. Can you arrange it? Please? I'm begging you. I just want to speak to her."

Shemu looked down at the ground. There was a frown on his face. When finally he looked up, his words surprised Sala. "Rahab says she believes in this God of yours. Atene told me about it. She said that Rahab prayed to your God and that He saved her from the king."

Sala's heart leaped. "Did she really say that?"

"That's what she said to my wife." Shemu rubbed his jaw. "It seems Atene has come to believe in your god as well. You have been busy indeed, Sala."

"Listen to me, Shemu. It would be well if all of your family believed in my God. The Israelite army has never been defeated and it will be coming to Jericho soon. They are on a mission from Elohim, and they will roll over you like a boulder rolls over a colony of ants. No one in Jericho will survive, Shemu. You must get Rahab and the rest of your family away from here!"

Shemu lifted a skeptical eyebrow and pointed a finger at the city wall that rose behind the houses they were standing before. "The Israelites will not get beyond that. Others have tried and failed. The walls of Jericho are impregnable."

"Not for us, not for the people of Elohim," Sala answered. "He has promised the land of Canaan to the Israelites. Do you know that the seas parted for my people when they left the land of Egypt? Then, when the last Israelite was on dry land, the seas came together again, drowning all the Egyptians who were giving chase. For many years Moses and his people wandered in the deserts that lie between Egypt and Canaan, and they never lacked for food. Elohim fed them with manna that fell from the sky. Elohim has promised the land of Canaan to my people and we will take it, Shemu, even if it means destroying everything that stands in our way. It is the wish of Elohim that we do this, for we are His people and He is our God."

Shemu did not reply at once. Then he said, "I understand you believe this, but Jericho is Baal's city. Baal will protect us from your avenging God, Sala."

Sala slammed his hand against the building. "Why won't you believe me? You are endangering all of your lives."

Shemu lifted an eyebrow. "Everyone is fleeing from the countryside *into* Jericho. It is Jericho that is safe, not the countryside where we would be open to attack."

"You're wrong."

Shemu shrugged again.

"Can't I at least see her, Shemu? That's all I want, just to see her. Just to say . . . good-bye."

Shemu said, "She and Atene went up to the roof awhile ago. That is all I can tell you."

He turned and went back into the house.

It took Sala about a minute to figure out how he could get to Rahab. Walking around her uncle's house, he discovered an attached ladder leading up to the roof. Such a ladder was a common addition to many homes; the inside stairs in Rahab's house were unusual.

Measuring with his eye, Sala judged that he could jump from her uncle's roof to Rahab's, which was about ten feet away. The pain from his bruises seemed to have miraculously disappeared.

He climbed the ladder swiftly and then looked to the roof next door. He was startled to see that it was strung with drying flax. For a moment he thought Rahab had left, but then he saw two female figures heading toward the door.

In a moment they would disappear into the house and he

would lose any chance of seeing her. He took a deep breath and called her name as loudly as he dared. She stopped, then swung around. When she saw him standing on the edge of the neighboring roof, her mouth opened in surprise.

The woman who was with Rahab said something and they both hurried to the edge of the roof. They stopped and stared at him across the divide that separated them. Rahab said, "Sala! What are you doing here?"

She looked the same. He felt some of the knot in his stomach begin to dissolve. "I have to see you. Stand back, I'm going to jump across."

Atene, whom he had recognized, said, "Don't be a fool, Sala. You'll fall and kill yourself."

Rahab said, "It's not that far. I could jump it myself if I wanted to."

Sala grinned. That was his Rahab. He waved the women back from the edge, got a running start, and landed on Rahab's roof. His momentum knocked him to his knees but he jumped right up.

She ran to him, her eyes widening when she saw the bruises on his face. "What happened? Are you all right?"

"I'm fine."

He devoured her with his eyes. Then he took her face into his two bruised and swollen hands and said, "I had to see you. I had to tell you how much I love you."

Her large brown eyes looked up into his. He saw them fill with tears. "Don't cry, my love," he said. "Please don't cry."

Her tears were flowing freely. "I can't help it. I'm so happy."

Atene's voice caught Rahab's attention and she turned away from Sala, the tears still glistening on her cheeks.

Atene said, "I'll wait just inside the stairs so I can warn you if anyone is coming up. If you hear me knock, hide Sala under the flax."

Since the flax was spread on wooden frames about two feet off the ground, this was an excellent suggestion. Rahab said with heartfelt gratitude, "Thank you, Atene."

As soon as the door had closed behind her sister-in-law, Rahab turned back to Sala. He said, "I saw you when they were carrying you through the streets. I thought my heart would break."

She looked up into his intelligent, fine-boned face. One of his eyes was swollen half shut, but the other eye was hard and concentrated as he looked intently at her. She could feel that look in her stomach.

"My heart was breaking too," she breathed.

He reached out and pulled her into his arms. "I thought I had lost you, Rahab. I thought I had lost . . ."

She buried her face in his shoulder, feeling the smooth linen of his tunic under her cheek. She inhaled the scent of him the way a drowning person takes a first breath of air after being pulled to the surface. "I love you too."

She felt his hand twining into her hair, pulling her head back so that her face was tipped up to his. He bent his head and kissed her.

The time, the place, everything that had happened to her, it all dropped away at the touch of his lips. Rahab clung to him fiercely, caught up in an emotion she had never felt before. In the stillness around her, the world coalesced into just this one moment, just this one man.

Then he lifted his head and buried his lips in her hair. "I love you so much, Rahab. So much."

"I have always loved you, Sala. You have always been my savior. You saved me from the slavers and you saved me again when you taught me about Elohim. I prayed to Him, you know. At first I didn't think He had heard me, but He did! He saved me. He made the king die right there in the bed, Sala, before he could do anything to hurt me. It was a miracle."

Sala held her away from him so he could look into her face. His black brows were sharply knit. "In the bed? I thought he died before he ever came into your room."

"That is what they want me to say. You must never tell this to anyone, Sala. I had to promise I would never say anything before they would let me go. But he did come into my room. He was lying in the bed when he died. I was frightened when first it happened, but now I understand. It was Elohim. He heard my prayers and He helped me. He saved me from being degraded, Sala. I . . . I know how you feel about that."

"You could never be degraded in my eyes," he said fiercely.

"Well, in your father's eyes then."

His good eye darkened. "I don't know what my father will think, Rahab."

"What do *you* think?"

He ran a finger along her cheekbone. "I don't know exactly, but I think Elohim wants something from you. I think He has a plan for you, Rahab. He put you into the hands of the slavers and He put you into the hands of someone who would teach you the truth about Him. Now He has saved you from the dissolute rites of a false god. You are important to Him, Rahab. You must just wait and see what it is He wants you to do. Wait and listen."

Rahab shivered.

"It's hard to think I could be so important. I am only a girl, Sala." She smiled up at him. "A girl who loves you very much."

A muscle along his jaw jumped. "I should never have kissed you. I took advantage of you. I'm sorry, Rahab. I wasn't thinking . . ."

Rahab didn't like the look on his face. "If we are to marry, then kissing me isn't wrong."

"Marriage." His voice sounded choked. "I don't think that will happen. My father—"

She stared at him. "I would go against my father for you!"

"You don't understand. If there were other sons, then maybe . . . I don't know. All I know is that my father would never allow me to mix my blood with the blood of a Canaanite woman. He just wouldn't."

Rahab couldn't believe what she was hearing. After all he had said about loving her . . .

"You *do* still think I would defile you."

"No! I would never think that. You would honor me by marrying me. But that is not how my father would see it, Rahab."

Rahab wanted to scream at him that his father didn't matter, that the only thing that mattered was their love. *How can he be so blind? So stupid?*

He said, "There is something more I must tell you."

"I don't think I want to hear anything more from you, Sala."

"You have to hear this." He took a step away from her, distancing himself. "My father and I are not here as merchants. We are here to gather information for Joshua, the leader of the Israelites. The battle for Jericho will begin as soon as the spring flood in the Jordan subsides, and our job is to learn everything we can about the defensive weaknesses of the city."

Rahab stared at him in horror. "You are *spies*? You are here to betray Jericho into the hands of the Israelites?"

"No." His voice was quiet, steady. "You can only betray what you have sworn allegiance to. I have never sworn allegiance to this place, or to any of the false gods who supposedly protect it. My allegiance is to the God of Israel, and He has told us that this land is ours. This is our ancestral home, and I believe with all my heart that we are destined to regain it for ourselves and for Elohim. If you believe in Elohim, Rahab, as you say you do, then you must be for the Israelites and against the false worshippers in Jericho."

She had never seen Sala like this. His voice was calm but his eyes burned with dedication.

"You are either with us or against us, Rahab," he said. "And I know you are not against us. Elohim has chosen you. You belong to Him now."

Rahab felt as if she were being torn in two. "What do you want me to do?" she asked in confusion.

"It is as I said before. You must wait and listen."

"Is there really going to be a battle?"

"Yes."

"Will we all die?"

"Not you! I have been afraid for you since first I knew you were in the city, but now . . . now I think we are all in Elohim's hands. We must do what we are called to do."

If Sala is right, and I am called to do something important for Elohim, then Lord Nahshon won't be able to object to our marriage.

Rahab knew then and there that she was not going to let Sala go without a fight.

She said, "The Israelites will win this battle, Sala. Baal and Asherah are nothing but lies. It is Elohim who is truly God."

He looked at her with such longing in his eyes that she reached up, slid her arms around his neck, and raised her face. He bent from his greater height and kissed her gently, a kiss of farewell. Then he kissed her again, this time not gently at all.

Atene's voice interrupted them. "Rahab, Mother is coming up the stairs. Sala, you just have enough time to jump back to the other roof."

Sala put her away from him, his hands hard on her shoulders. He said, "I love you. Whatever happens, I will always love you."

"I love you too."

He turned, and with a running start, jumped back to the other roof.

PART THREE

The Walls
of Jericho

Twenty-Four

THE VILLAGE OF SHITTIM, WHERE THE ISRAELITES WERE camped, lay some ten miles east of the Jordan, almost directly opposite Jericho on the western side of the river. This meant that in order to reach Jericho, Joshua, the Israelite commander, was going to have to move his army, their families, and their provisions across the river. His problem was that the usually tranquil, meandering Jordan was a raging torrent in the spring, fed as it was by melting snow from the northern mountains. But spring was the time of year when the Israelites had made their escape from Egypt, and Joshua was determined to attack Jericho soon after his people had celebrated their feast of Passover, which commemorated that miraculous feat.

When Isaac and Gideon, the two men Joshua had sent to once more check the level of the river, returned to camp, they found their leader standing alone, his eyes turned westward, toward Jericho. It was late in the afternoon and the sun was hanging low above the horizon, silhouetting Joshua's figure against the red sky. The scouts hesitated, wondering if they should disturb his solitude. His lined face was set like stone and he was so still that Isaac thought he almost looked like a pagan statue. Finally Gideon took a few steps forward and murmured his leader's name. Joshua turned to greet them and ask for their report.

"The river is still in full spate," Isaac said. "We might get the army across, but not the women, children, and animals."

As one, the three men turned to regard the camp spread out before them. They had been at Shittim for some time, and the women had made things comfortable. Tents covered the flat landscape and the smells of cooking wafted their way on the breeze. There were no men in sight; Joshua had sent them off under their commanders to practice with arms and to build up their strength for the coming fight. The Israelite army had never yet lost a battle, and their reputation as a fierce and ruthless fighting force had been honestly earned.

Joshua, who was not a big man, commanded with his powerful personality and burning dark eyes. He said now to the two men, "Do not doubt. If we are strong and courageous and act always in accordance with the laws Moses gave to us, we shall take possession of the land Yahweh has promised to our people. Now listen closely, for this is what I want you to do. Tomorrow you will cross the Jordan and enter into the city of Jericho. We already have two men in place within the city, and they will be looking for you. They have spied out the strengths and weaknesses of the city, and you are to receive this information from them and return to me. Do you understand?"

The two men bowed their heads in acknowledgement. Gideon said, "All that you have commanded us we will do, and wherever you send us we will go. Just as we obeyed Moses in all things, so we will obey you."

Briefly, Joshua laid a hand on Gideon's sleeve. Then he said, "The man you are looking for is called Nahshon and he is in disguise as a Canaanite trader from Gaza. He is lodging in Jericho with his son, Sala. Every morning you may find them at a wine shop on the main road just before the walls that lead into the Upper City. It has a sign outside displaying an olive tree. When you go there you must wear a scarlet cord on your belt. That is how they will know you. Once you receive their information, bring it back to me."

Gideon and Isaac traded a look at this mention of spies already in place. This was the first they had heard of such a thing. Gideon said, "We will follow your instructions, Joshua. But what if we can't find this wine shop? Are you sure it exists?"

"Nahshon knew about it from a friend of his who had been inside the city. Yahweh will guide you, Gideon. You will find this place."

Both men nodded solemnly. Ever since the God they had called Elohim, Creator, had revealed His true name to Moses, the Israelites had no longer used the name Elohim. They said *Yahweh*, a word that in Hebrew meant *I AM*. Yahweh had told Moses that He was: *The Lord, the God of your ancestors, the God of Abraham, the God of Isaac, and the God of Jacob. This is My name forever and this is My title for all generations.* Ever since that revelation to Moses, the Israelites had called their God *Yahweh*.

Joshua said to Gideon and Isaac, "If it is possible, bring Nahshon and his son back with you; it will not be safe for them inside the city. When we take Jericho, we will leave nothing standing that breathes within. We do the will of Yahweh, who wants His people to have this precious land. For this He took us out of Egypt, and for this must we continue to strive."

"May Yahweh be with you, Joshua," the men responded. "We will do as you have asked."

The following day, just as the sun was rising, Isaac and Gideon left Shittim to ford the flooding river Jordan and begin the trek to Jericho.

In the days after the New Year festival, more and more people from the surrounding countryside began to pour into the city. The Lower City, where most of the refugees were living, was full to bursting, but the wealthy merchants and nobles in the Upper City had refused to open their courtyards to the farmhands and shepherds who made up most of the new population. King Tamur realized that some solution to the overcrowding had to be found, and this was one of the reasons he had called the meeting of his council.

The other reason was connected to the first but was potentially even more dangerous. The refugees were full of horror stories about the Israelites and the death and destruction they had sown through all the southern kingdoms. Even behind the huge walls of Jericho their stories were igniting fear among the residents. The unthinkable question was being asked: was it possible that these warlike Israelites might batter down the thickest and highest walls of any city in the land?

The king and the council, which was made up of a mixture of his followers and his father's old advisors, were confident the walls could not be breached.

"Jericho can hold out under a year-long siege if we have to," Tamur said as the group met in the king's apartment. "That is not our immediate problem. The immediate problem is the doubts that are going round the city because of these new people. However, first I wish to discuss the housing problem."

The older men, the ones who owned the big houses in the Upper City, looked at each other then back to the king, wary expressions on their faces.

Tamur went on, "I am going to command that tents be set up in every park and open space in the Upper City." He flicked a glance at one of the lords, who had moved his hand in seeming protest. "I do not want to hear any complaints from the nobles about their space being commandeered. We cannot turn these people away, so we must have a place for them to shelter. The city has plenty of water and plenty of grain. We have soldiers to man the walls if the enemy should be foolish enough to rush us. Nor can the Israelites hope to win if they lay siege. Their provisions will give out before ours do."

Hearty agreement sounded from the men of the council.

"Good," said Tamur. "Now, to this other issue. I have been told that fear is spreading around the city like wildfire. Is this the case?"

Silence fell, then Farut, the youngest, spoke up. "I think it is a serious problem, my lord. Frightened people do dangerous things."

Lord Arazu said, "I have another concern. Suppose this talk is being spread deliberately?"

Tamur nodded, as if he had already had the same idea.

The high priest asked, "Do you mean the Israelites might have agents in the city whose job it is to spread unrest?"

"That could easily be so," said the military commander, Akiz. "With the numbers of people pouring into the city, it would not be hard for spies to hide among the crowds."

Tamur nodded again.

Arazu said, "My lord, I think we should find out exactly who these people are who are spreading the frightening tales about the Israelites."

Tamur spoke crisply, "I agree, Lord Arazu, and I have ordered some men from the guard to dress in ordinary clothes so they can mix with the populace. These rumors are coming from the Lower City, and your fear that spies might be among us is a thought I have had myself."

"Of course it's coming from the Lower City," Lord Edri muttered. His rodent's face was clenched with anger. "The riffraff are the only ones stupid enough to believe our walls can be breached."

"We must watch the gate closely, my lord," one of the younger men said. "Spies might already be here, but we do not want any more coming in."

Akiz said, "That is being taken care of."

"Very well, then," the king said, standing up. "We will begin setting up the tents right away. And I do not want to hear any complaints from the nobility about 'riffraff' in the Upper City. I will leave you your houses, but the parks will have tents in them."

Lord Arazu bowed his head. "Yes, my lord."

The council broke up, leaving the new young king satisfied that he had the city under control.

Twenty-Five

LORD NAHSHON HAD POUNCED ON SALA WHEN HE
returned to the inn after his visit with Rahab.

"Come upstairs," he said, then closed his hand around his
son's arm as if he was taking no chances of Sala running away
again. Once they were in their small room, Lord Nahshon dropped
Sala's arm and the two men faced each other.

"So, did you manage to see her?" Nahshon demanded. He
was doing his best to control his anger.

"Yes, Father, I did see her and she told me exactly what happened on the night of the festival. It's a bit different from the
official story being circulated around the city."

As Sala began to recount the events of Rahab's interrupted
sacred marriage, Nahshon listened with only part of his mind.
The other part was focused on his son and not on his words.

Sala had changed since they came to Jericho. Lord Nahshon
had noticed changes before, but now they struck him forcefully.
His son was no longer a boy. He didn't even look like a boy anymore. His face had thinned and the fine bone structure was more
evident than it had been in the fullness of the younger face. Sala
had never had an awkward moment, even as a youngster, but
that childish grace had turned into lithe male strength. Above
all, the change was in his eyes. He looked upon his father with
respect, but the adoration was gone. Sala was his own man now.

Part of Nahshon felt proud that his son had grown into a man he could admire, but part of him grieved for the boy that was gone.

"Rahab prayed to Elohim," Sala was saying, and Nahshon's full attention abruptly focused on his son's words.

"What do you mean, she prayed to Elohim?"

"I mean that she turned away from her false gods and called to Elohim to help her. And Elohim heard her, Father. Just think: the king dropped dead right there in the bed, before he could do her any harm! Is that not a sign that Rahab has found favor in Elohim's eyes?"

Nahshon turned away from this suddenly mature Sala and went to stand at the tiny window that had been cut through the wall to provide some air to the room. He was quiet for a long time, thinking about what Sala had said. He knew his son was infatuated with this Canaanite girl, and it disgusted him. Nahshon had begun to think of Rahab as the enemy, someone he had to fight for the soul of his son.

He turned and said, "How did a pagan girl like Rahab come to know of Elohim?"

"I told her about Him. Even when we were small and she was staying with us in Ramac, she was curious about my beliefs. Rahab is not like other women, Father. She is interested in things beyond housework. She is smart. And she is brave too. You saw that for yourself. How many other girls would have been able to get away from those slavers?"

"She is beautiful," Lord Nahshon said coldly. "A woman who looks like that can make a man believe almost anything."

Sala's eyes flashed. "She was not lying to me. She prayed to Elohim and the king died before he could harm her! How much proof do you need, Father, that she is special to Elohim?"

"How do you know he didn't harm her? You have only her word."

Sala's cheeks flushed red with anger. "The priestess at the shrine examined her. If the act had been consummated, then the prince would not have had to make a second sacred marriage. It would have already been accomplished. But Rahab is pure. You have only to look into her eyes to know that!"

Lord Nahshon did not want to alienate Sala, so he tried for a mild voice. "Perhaps you are right. Perhaps Elohim does have a use for this girl."

Sala's look was intense. "I'm certain of it, Father. Elohim has some plan that is as yet unclear to us. But it will unveil itself in time, and we must be ready."

Nahshon began to pace around the tiny space. The less said about Rahab the better, he thought. He changed the subject. "I am expecting to hear from Joshua at any time now. People are still pouring in to the city, which makes a perfect opportunity for spies to slip in unnoticed. We should start spending the whole day at the wine bar, not just the mornings. We must be there when they come looking for us. If two men who do not speak Canaanite are caught, the king will immediately assume they are Israelite spies and execute them. We cannot allow that to happen."

"Language *is* going to be a problem," Sala said. "We can't speak to them in the wine bar if we're going to be speaking Hebrew—we'll have to bring them here."

Lord Nahshon was happy his son's mind seemed to have swung away from that girl. "Yes, I suppose we will. There are so many people crammed into the inn right now that they won't even be noticed."

Sala's brows drew together. "The biggest problem is how to get them out of the city once they are in. There may still be many people coming in, but few are going out."

"There is still some traffic going out, though. Men are

leaving to bring in more provisions from their farms while they can. They will just have to be careful."

They both were quiet, thinking about this. Then Sala said, "Joshua needs to act soon. If he waits too long, the scouts *will* have trouble. Tamur is more astute than his father. He will be on the lookout for spies."

"True."

"Father, if they don't come, then I think I should try to get out of the city myself and go to the Israelite camp. Joshua needs to know that the north wall is the place to attack. It's definitely the most vulnerable spot in the city."

Lord Nahshon's heart stopped at the thought of risking his only son. "Don't be a fool, Sala. You have no experience traveling under cover. You don't even know exactly where the Israelite camp is! We will do as we arranged and wait for Joshua's men."

Sala didn't reply, but Nahshon didn't like the stubborn look in his son's eyes. He had been willing to let Sala come to Jericho with him because he burned to be part of the Israelite conquest, and he had also thought the mission would be safe. His son was everything to him—the whole future of the family lay in Sala's hands. Nothing must happen to him.

"They will come," Nahshon repeated firmly. "Joshua is being led to Jericho by Elohim, just as Moses was led through the desert. We must be patient and keep watch."

Sala lowered his eyes. "Yes, Father."

"The gates have been closed for the night, but tomorrow we must start to spend the whole day in the wine bar. We can take turns to give each other a rest."

Sala nodded agreement. "We are to recognize them by a red cord that will be hanging from their belt, am I right?"

"That is the plan." Lord Nahshon put his hand on his son's

arm. "Come," he said. "Let us go now and have some supper before the courtyard gets too crowded."

As the days went by, Mepu still would not allow Rahab to leave the house. "You cannot show yourself to those lecherous men who hang about wanting a look at you. It is not modest. We'll have enough trouble finding you a husband after this misfortune with the sacred marriage; you must not do anything to make things worse."

Then, on a particularly warm and sunny day, the rest of Rahab's brothers, their wives, and their children showed up at the house seeking refuge from the Israelite army. Mepu was relieved that all his family would now be safe, but there was no doubt the new arrivals put stress upon the household. At night sleeping mats were strewn all over the house, even in the kitchen. The children, who were accustomed to being outdoors with space to play in, were cranky. The house was hot and stuffy and Rahab began to feel she would go mad if she didn't get outside for a while, but Mepu held firm.

Atene and Rahab were sharing their room with two other sisters-in-law and their four children. At night the entire floor was covered with sleeping mats. During the day she and Atene fled to the roof in the pretense of working on the flax. Mepu wanted Kata to take the flax down so there would be room on the roof for sleeping mats, but Kata refused. The flax would come down soon enough, she said; it was almost ready to be stripped and combed into fibers. They would be happy to have the ability to make clothes if they were forced to remain in this horrible city for a long time.

Mepu, who recognized the burden all of these extra people

had placed upon his wife, decided to bide his time and not overrule her.

Mepu's brother's house next door was also overflowing with family from the countryside. The whole of Jericho had become a rabbit warren with people living in every possible nook and cranny.

In the midst of all the babble and confusion, Shemu found himself thinking more and more about the two Israelite merchants who had come at such a propitious time to buy merchandise from Jericho farmers. The rumors about spies in the city were all over the place, and Shemu began to wonder if in fact Lord Nahshon and Sala might be the very ones who were the source of the rumors that had the city so frightened.

One day Shemu decided to seek them out at the Sign of the Olive.

The wine bar was packed when Shemu entered. All of the public places in the city were packed these days. There were no more homeless people since the king had ordered tents erected in every possible open place, but during the day the men all crammed into the wine bars to get away from the press of women and children.

Shemu had the opposite problem. Instead of wanting to get away from his wife, he wanted to be with her—alone. He missed her desperately. All he could manage these days was to squeeze her hand whenever they met in the midst of the crowd. They had lost their bedroom when the rest of the family arrived, and he didn't know when they would be able to get it back. Shemu's temper had not been pleasant of late.

When he walked into the wine bar he quickly spied Nahshon and Sala standing at a table in the corner. As he approached them, he evaluated their appearance, trying to see if anything about them might give them away as Israelites.

Normally, there was virtually nothing that would distinguish an Israelite from a Canaanite. Both people were dark haired and dark eyed, with the skin of men who live under a hot sun. Their languages were different, but there was enough commonality for each to be able to have some understanding of the other's words. The great divide between the two was not race, it was religion, and that was an uncrossable chasm.

Shemu pushed his way through the crowd until he reached Nahshon and Sala. Sala spied him first and gave him a friendly smile. "Shemu. How good to see you. How is everyone in your family?"

"Everyone is well," Shemu replied. "And you? Frankly, I'm surprised you're still here. Surely you don't want to be caught in the city while your own people are attacking us."

He looked carefully to catch a reaction to this comment, but neither Nahshon nor Sala changed expression.

Nahshon said genially, "We have just been discussing that very thing, my friend. I had hoped to conclude my business before any warlike activity interrupted it, but it seems I may not be able to do that."

"I doubt anyone is worrying about commerce right now," Shemu said.

Nahshon sighed. "Unfortunately, that is true."

Shemu narrowed his eyes. "I have been wondering if you might not be here for some other purpose."

"What other purpose could you mean?" Sala's eyes were puzzled but still friendly.

Shemu thought he had no reason to seek favor from these men, so he said bluntly, "You could be Israelite spies."

Lord Nahshon scowled. "What kind of talk is this?"

Sala only lifted his brows and said, "Ah."

Silence fell as the three men studied each other. Then Shemu said, "The rumors around town say that the Israelites are merciless in conquest."

Nahshon said, "From what I have heard, that has been the case. But surely you don't really think that any army, however merciless, can breach these walls?"

"What do you think?" Shemu shot back.

It was Sala who answered. "I will be frank with you, Shemu. My father and I have certainly thought about leaving Jericho. The reason we have not done so is our fear that, once away from the safety of these walls, we will be mistaken for Canaanites and killed." He shrugged. "There is little outwardly to distinguish us, and we would be in as much danger as you if we were spotted. As you say, the Israelites don't wait to ask questions. Their mission is to destroy whatever lies in their path. So we have decided"—here he glanced at his father—"that we will be safer inside Jericho than outside."

Shemu had always liked Sala, and no one could look more sincere than he did just now. But Shemu was not sure.

"I wouldn't give you up, you know," Shemu said. "You saved my sister from a life of slavery. But if you *are* against us, I strongly suggest you leave."

"I understand what you are saying, Shemu," Sala said softly. "But we will be all right staying here."

"Good." Shemu stood up. "I must be going home. We have my brothers and their families with us now. All of the villages and farms have emptied out for fear of the Israelites."

"They are safer here than out in the open, that is for certain," Sala returned.

As Shemu walked out of the wine bar he could feel the gazes of the two Israelites on his back until he passed through the door.

Twenty-Six

WHEN SHEMU RETURNED TO THE HOUSE, ATENE WAS waiting for him. When she asked if he had ever encountered Sala and Lord Nahshon when he was walking through the city, Shemu narrowed his eyes. "Rahab told you to ask me that, didn't she?"

"We are both interested," Atene answered with as much dignity as she could muster. "After all, they saved Rahab from a life of slavery."

Shemu searched her face. Then he sighed. "I've seen them, yes. And it disturbs me that they are still in Jericho. Has it ever occurred to you and Rahab that they might be here as agents of the Israelites? They may even be the source of the rumors that are terrifying the city."

Atene was shocked by such a suggestion. "That can't be true." But despite her denial, a seed of doubt was sown and she resolved to tell Rahab what Shemu had said.

The two girls got together later in the day, on the roof, the only place where they could sometimes snatch a few moments of privacy in the crowded house. Once they realized they had the place to themselves, they went to sit in the small patch of shade cast by the wall behind them, their arms clasped around their drawn-up knees.

When Rahab heard Atene's words, she looked away. Shemu

had got it right, of course. Sala and his father *were* here to spy for the Israelite army. But Rahab could not tell Atene this. Atene might tell Shemu, and that could put Sala in danger.

Rahab rested her chin on her knees, closed her eyes, and wished she were a girl again, with nothing to worry about. Then she inhaled deeply and scolded herself for being such a baby. She was part of this intrigue, whether she liked it or not, and she had to protect Sala. She turned her face to Atene and said, "It's not true. They're merchants, not spies. Shemu is imagining problems where there are none."

"I'm not so sure Shemu is wrong," Atene returned. "I've been thinking about it all day, Rahab. Sala's family makes their living from the sea. They ship the agricultural products their customers bring to Ramac. As you saw yourself when you lived with them, they are wealthy. What reason would these sea merchants have to travel to Jericho to seek out farm produce when ample merchandise has always flowed into their port from the countryside surrounding Ramac?"

Rahab looked into Atene's clear, light-brown eyes. *I have to trust her. She's guessed too much. I can't have her saying such things to Shemu and my father. She will only make them more suspicious than they already are.*

Rahab said softly, "Atene, do you remember how we prayed to Elohim?"

"Yes, of course I do."

"Elohim saved me from the king. I know He did."

"I believe He did, Rahab. I truly do."

Atene's eyes had darkened and her hands moved to gently cup her stomach. She said, "It's too soon to be sure, but I think I am with child, Rahab. I have never been late before." A smile trembled on her lips. "I think Elohim listened to my prayer and granted my desire."

"Oh, Atene." Rahab reached out and the two women hugged. Rahab could feel the dampness on her cheek from Atene's tears.

"But what should we do?" Atene said when they had separated and she had wiped away her tears. "Everyone says the Israelites are merciless, that they will kill everyone in the city. If we are here—"

"Atene. The Israelites are the people of Elohim, and if Elohim wants the Israelites to take Jericho, then there will be no way we can stop them."

"If what you say is true, we need to get away. My baby . . ."

Rahab reached out and took her hand. "Elohim gave you this child, Atene. That means He cares for you—and it means that your child is special. You will be safe, my sister. I feel that very strongly. You and your baby will be safe. Elohim will protect the people who worship Him."

Atene said, "Shemu told me something he had heard in the city. He said that when the Israelites left Egypt, the sea separated before them so they could pass."

"It is a true story. Sala told me about it." Rahab tightened her grasp on Atene's fingers. "Sala will take care of us. I think Elohim has placed our whole family here, under one roof, Atene, just so that Sala can take care of us."

Atene's hand returned Rahab's grip. "I pray you are right, Rahab."

"We both must pray. We must pray to Elohim for protection," Rahab said.

The two girls sat quietly, their hands joined, until one of the children came up to the roof to tell them that Kata needed them downstairs.

Tamur, king of Jericho, had posted scouts at the Jordan ford with instructions that they were to report back to him as soon as the Israelites made a move to cross the river. In the meanwhile, he had kept the gates of the city open during the day as usual, to demonstrate to the city's population that life was going on as normally as possible.

People were still trickling in from the countryside, and Isaac and Gideon were able to enter the city in the morning with a band of shepherds who had deserted their sheep to seek shelter for themselves, just as their master had left them behind when he fled to Jericho many days before.

The two Israelites made their way along the main street of the Lower City, taking care not to speak to each other for fear of being overheard. They spoke and understood some Canaanite, but their accents would give them away as foreigners almost instantly.

Both men kept their eyes raised to make certain they wouldn't miss the sign with the olive tree. They were almost to the wall that separated the Lower from the Upper City when they saw what they were looking for. Sharing a relieved glance, they had the same silent thought. *Please, Elohim, let our men be inside.*

They walked into the bar, which was so filled that the customers had spilled out onto the street. Both Israelites had dressed in the garb of poor men, with sandals that were merely soles held on by rope ties and tunics that were worn and patched. The only unusual thing about them was the red cord that hung a little ways out of Gideon's belt pocket.

The owner of this particular wine bar prided himself on catering to the more upper class men who lived in the Lower City—merchants and the wealthier shopkeepers. The two Israelites in their shepherd's garb stood out immediately as not belonging. They realized this but did not know what else to do. This was their designated meeting spot.

It was Sala who spotted them first. He reached a hand to grasp his father's wrist and gestured toward the door with his chin. "What do you think?"

Lord Nahshon looked and put down his wine glass. "I think I had better get them out of here as quickly as possible."

"I agree. You go and I'll stay to make sure no one follows."

Lord Nahshon threaded his way through the crowd to the ragged strangers who were still standing uncomfortably in the entrance.

"You don't belong in here," Lord Nahshon said in a disgusted voice that he raised to make sure his words were heard. "This is a wine shop that caters to gentlemen, not to farm workers. You had better come with me and I will show you where you can mix with your own kind."

The spies nodded, without replying, and, looking as humble and embarrassed as it was possible for an Israelite man to look, they followed Nahshon back out into the street.

Sala remained behind to take a reading of the men who had witnessed this little scene. He prayed no one would find it strange that his father had helped the downtrodden strangers.

"Your father did those shepherds a favor," one of the men at the next table said to him. "If they had tried to come in here and order something, they would have been kicked out."

Sala offered his most charming smile. "With the mood the city is in, the authorities are bound to come down hard on anyone involved in a fight. It was best that they be removed from here before something unfortunate happened."

Around the shop came grunts of agreement.

Sala shrugged. "I suppose I should go along and see where my father is dumping them."

"Good idea. You don't need your father being harassed because he is in company with such people."

Sala pushed his way through to the street and then started off in pursuit of Lord Nahshon. He caught up with the trio quickly and the four men proceeded as casually as they could in the direction of the inn where Sala and Nahshon were staying. No one spoke.

They were stopped just before they turned off the main street by the guard who had hit Sala with his sword on the night of the New Year festival.

"So," the guard said genially, addressing Sala. "I see you have sobered up, my friend."

Sala stared at the guard, his heart beginning to race. He lifted his hands in perplexity. "I'm sorry, I don't know what you mean."

The guard's dark, big-boned face turned to Nahshon. "He doesn't recognize me. Too drunk at the time, eh?"

Sala's father, who evidently did recognize the guard, smiled. "The young men of today can't hold their drink the way the older generation can."

"True, true." The guard looked back at Sala. "I recommend you stay away from the wine, young man. Next time you make trouble you may get more than just a smack on the head."

By now Sala had realized who the guard was and he managed a wry smile. "I am sorry, Officer. You taught me my lesson. I will watch the number of cups I drink at the next festival. My head the next morning was punishment enough."

The guard, who was not an officer, was pleased by Sala addressing him as such. He glanced at the two spies and raised his eyes. "What are you doing with these dirty peasants?"

"Removing them from the Sign of the Olive," Nahshon said. "They came into the city today and don't yet know their place."

The guard looked disgusted. "All the riffraff of the countryside is descending upon us these days."

The two Israelites stood silent, their eyes on the ground.

The guard scowled at them. "Don't you talk?"

Gideon scraped his scandals on the pavement. "We were afraid," he mumbled.

"Of the Israelites," Isaac added, mumbling even more thickly.

"Stupid peasants," the guard said. "They can't even speak properly."

All during this conversation Sala had maintained a slightly hangdog expression even though his heart was slamming so hard he was afraid the guard would hear it. When the Canaanite finally moved off, the four men continued their walk down the street toward the inn.

"Don't rush," Lord Nahshon said in Hebrew, his voice pitched low. "We don't want to call attention to ourselves."

The two spies nodded and kept their heads bent. It seemed an eternity to Sala before they reached the inn, but finally they arrived. Sala blew out a long breath of relief as the old mud-brick building finally came into sight.

Twenty-Seven

THE INN WAS HOUSING MORE PEOPLE THAN IT COULD comfortably hold and, since it was the time of the midday meal, the courtyard benches were filled with customers eating while the front room was packed with more people waiting for their turn at the food. The weather had turned unusually hot and the indoor rooms were stifling.

Lord Nahshon sent Isaac and Gideon up to their room first. As he explained to Sala as they watched the spies go inside, he didn't want anyone to be able to make a connection between them and the shabby newcomers.

The heat was even worse on the second floor when Sala and Nahshon entered their tiny room where the two Israelites awaited them. Sala unrolled the sleeping mats and he and his father sat on one while Gideon and Isaac sat facing them on the other. The men spoke Hebrew in low voices, with Lord Nahshon doing most of the talking.

The information he thought would be most useful for the Israelite army was the vulnerability of the city's north side. If Joshua could get his men over the stone revetment, the single mud brick wall that topped it would fall easily. To demonstrate, Lord Nahshon took the two men to the window and showed them what he meant.

Isaac and Gideon agreed that the wall could be easily breached and that this information would be helpful to Joshua.

"If he does attack on the north he still has to get over the revetment wall," Nahshon warned. "Those boulders are a powerful deterrent. Don't forget to tell him about that."

"We won't," Gideon said. He wiped the sweat off his forehead with the back of his hand. "What about the temper of the city. Will they put up a strong defense?"

Nahshon nodded to Sala that he should speak. He said, "Rumors are flying around the city about the brutality of the Israelite army. To be blunt, many of the people here are simply terrified."

"That is always helpful," said Gideon.

"What about Jericho's military?" Isaac asked. "How resolute are they?"

It was Lord Nahshon's turn to speak. "They seem strong enough. The commander is a tough old soldier, the sort who can be counted on to keep his troops in line. But if the common people panic, they may force the gate open so that they can escape. That would make it nice and easy for Joshua."

Gideon said, "You have done good work here, Nahshon. You too, Sala. Joshua will be pleased."

"When do you think he will attack?" Sala asked.

Isaac lifted his shoulders. "The river is in full spate right now. Gideon and I had to fight to get across. I think we'll probably have to wait until the waters subside enough for the women, children, and supplies to cross over."

Gideon added, "And Joshua will want to celebrate Passover first. We have celebrated this feast ever since we escaped from Egypt, and it is not something any of us would want to omit. Especially now, when we need the blessing of Yahweh so badly."

"Passover?" Lord Nahshon and Sala said at the same time.

"What is Passover?" Nahshon asked.

"Who is Yahweh?" Sala asked at almost the same moment.

At first the two Israelites looked surprised that their companions did not know, but then Isaac said, "I'm sorry. We must try to remember that the Israelites who have always lived here and were not part of the escape from Egypt would not know about Passover."

And so the two scouts explained how Yahweh had sent plagues upon the Egyptians to force Pharaoh to let the Israelites leave. Gideon said, "The last plague occurred when the Angel of Death walked through the city and killed the firstborn of all the Egyptians living there. But the angel passed over those houses belonging to us. Moses had told us to mark our doors with the blood of a lamb and that is how we identified ourselves to the angel. This was why Pharaoh finally allowed us to leave. Then Yahweh instructed us that we must celebrate a holy day every year to commemorate the pass-over of the Angel of Death. This is so we shall always remember what He has done for us."

Sala felt chills run up and down his spine as he listened to this story. How blessed he was to belong to this people, he thought. Truly they were the Chosen ones of—

"Why do you call the Lord *Yahweh*? We have always known Him as Elohim, the Creator who has no name."

Gideon said, "He revealed His name to Moses, our great leader, while we were in the desert. Moses told us that this was His name, His title for all the generations who follow us. Now our Lord has a name, Sala. He is not Elohim any longer, He is Yahweh."

"It means *I am*," Nahshon said slowly, giving the Hebrew translation.

"Yes," said Gideon. "To us Yahweh is all that we need Him to be. He *is* our deliverer. He *is* our strength. He *is* our wisdom. He is our God and we are His people. That is what His name tells us."

"With Yahweh's help, we will conquer Jericho." Sala spoke with all the confidence in his heart. "We will conquer this country of Canaan. If Yahweh is with us, we cannot fail."

There was a moment of solemn silence as the four men contemplated these words.

Then Lord Nahshon said to Gideon, "We must return to more practical matters. You were able to get into the city with no trouble, but it is not going to be as easy for you to get out."

"Why can't we just blend into a group of Canaanites, as we did coming in?" Gideon said.

"That is the only thing you *can* do, but you must be careful. We still have some farmers going out to tend to their lands, but they leave early in the morning so that they will be able to get back in before the gate is closed at dusk. It's too late for you to try to leave the city now; there will be no parties for you to merge with."

Isaac shrugged. "Then we'll wait and leave in the morning. Can we remain here?"

"You will have to."

A loud knock sounded on their door.

The four men stiffened in fear.

"Yes?" Lord Nahshon called. "What do you want?"

The innkeeper's wife answered in the distinctive accent of Moab. "Two shepherds were seen climbing the stairs a short while ago. Do you know anything about them?"

"Shepherds?" Nahshon managed to sound insulted. "What would I know of shepherds, madam? My son and I are just changing our garments to go and dine in the city. I can assure you we know nothing of shepherds."

"I didn't think so, sir," the woman assured him. "I had to check everyone. Surely you can understand that?"

"Of course," Nahshon returned, sounding slightly placated.

"I will leave you then to your dressing."

The four men in the room stood perfectly still and listened to the sound of her feet as she walked down the short hallway.

When the steps were no longer audible, Sala said, "If you've been seen, then you can't remain here. There is a good chance that guards may be sent to search the inn. As I said, the city is frightened. Even the suggestion that a spy might have been here will bring action."

Gideon said, "If you can lend us some clothes, we will pretend to be friends of yours."

Lord Nahshon shook his head. "Even if you change your clothes, someone may recognize your faces. Plus they will ask you questions and your lack of the language will give you away. This is too important a matter to takes risks with. Joshua needs this information."

Isaac said, "Do you know of anywhere else we could stay tonight?"

Lord Nahshon's brow furrowed as he tried to think of someone he could trust with these men. Then Sala said, "They could stay at Rahab's house, Father."

Lord Nahshon stared. "Rahab's house? Are you mad? Why would we send them there?"

"I saw one of her cousins who lives in the house next to her in town yesterday. He doesn't know who I am but I managed to get into conversation with him." What Sala didn't say was that he was so desperate for news of Rahab that he had stalked everyone who left Mepu's brother's house until he finally managed to connect with this particular cousin.

"Hasis—that is his name—told me today is his father's birthday and they are having a big celebration at his house. Rahab's family will be there as well. That means her house will be empty. No one will ever think to search for them there."

Lord Nahshon said with audible irony, "The family will

surely return to the house after the party. Don't you think they may be surprised to find two strange men waiting for them?"

Sala leaned forward. "Listen, Father, half the roof of Rahab's house is covered with drying flax. It would be easy for a man to crawl under it and hide. If I can get them in the house before the party is over, no one need ever know that Isaac and Gideon are there."

Lord Nahshon's eyes narrowed. "And just how do you know the roof is covered with flax?"

"I saw it there," Sala replied.

Lord Nahshon's eyes narrowed even further. "All right, we'll discuss that later. Suppose we do as you suggest, and suppose Gideon and Isaac spend the night safely on the roof. Have you thought of how they are to get *out* of the house, Sala? They need to leave tomorrow morning, when the gate opens. How are they to manage that?"

"Rahab will help us," Sala said.

The spies had been following this back and forth conversation and now Isaac said, "Who is this Rahab?"

Sala answered, "She is a Canaanite woman who has renounced her false gods and learned to worship Elohim . . . um, Yahweh. I know she will help us."

"She won't be able to," Lord Nahshon said. "Even if she wanted to—which I doubt—she won't be able to do anything."

"She is a resourceful girl. She will think of something." Sala's voice was firm and confident.

Gideon said, "Clearly we need a place where we can hide overnight and, unless you have another idea, Nahshon, this Rahab's house seems like our only possibility. We will find some way of getting to the city gates in the morning. Yahweh will help us."

Since Lord Nahshon had no other suggestion, the men

decided to follow Sala's plan. Both of the spies were shorter than Sala and his father, but they did the best they could by using their belts to hold their borrowed tunics off the floor. Gideon took the scarlet cord that had been their identification and tucked it into his belt, saying that Joshua had given it to him and he wanted to keep it.

The strategy they decided upon was simple. Sala would take the spies to Rahab's house, where they would walk boldly inside and go right to the roof.

Sala told them, "If you look confident, anyone who sees you will think you are just part of the party next door and are going into the house to get something. Then I will go next door, find Rahab, and tell her what we are doing. She will help us. She is one of us now."

Lord Nahshon was clearly unhappy with the plan. "I pray you are right, my son. A great deal is resting on this young woman's cooperation."

"Rahab will not fail us."

Lord Nahshon went to the door and listened. "It's quiet. Very well, then. The three of you must leave quietly by the inn's side door and I will go into the courtyard to eat. If anyone asks why I am alone I will say that my son is not feeling well."

After asking Yahweh's blessing for the success of their plan, Gideon and Isaac, garbed in new clothes, followed Sala down the stairs, out the side door, and into the street.

The birthday party had been going on for several hours and Mepu's brother's house was filled to overflowing. Life had been so tense and uncomfortable of late that everyone was happy to have a reason to relax and have fun. Since the day was hot, the party spilled out onto the street, where passersby smiled at the celebration and wished they could join in the fun.

At first Rahab had enjoyed herself. It was the first time her father had let her out of the house since her return and it was good to laugh and joke with her cousins. Unfortunately, those men across the street waiting to see her were still there and Mepu wouldn't allow her to leave her uncle's house. He had even made her wear a veil to get from her own house to the one next door. So when the young people and men moved out to the cooler street, she was stuck inside with the older women, who were all eager to learn the details of her fatal night with the king.

Finally she thought of her usual refuge, the roof. Her uncle's roof could only be accessed by a ladder attached to the side of the house, the ladder that Sala had climbed up the one precious time they were together. She didn't think any of her relatives would be on the roof, and it was a perfect place to get away from the nosy women and the heat of the house.

Rahab made a polite excuse and slipped out the side door with none of the women noticing. The two houses were so close together, and the ladder was so set back from the street, that no one saw Rahab as she kilted up her skirts and climbed quickly to the roof.

She breathed a sigh of relief when she found it was indeed empty. It was hot up here, but the wall offered a patch of shade, and best of all, no one was plying her with intimate questions.

Her thoughts moved, inexorably, to Sala. Once he had stood here, on this very roof she stood upon now. She closed her eyes and prayed:

Elohim, when am I going to see Sala again? I love him so much. Please, please soften his father's heart toward me. I will be a good wife, I promise You. I will follow all Your rules and laws, and I will love him with all my heart for as long as I live.

Her sharp ears picked up the sound of a quietly opening door and she opened her eyes. Across the way, on her own roof, two men stepped out of the door. They looked around furtively and, when they saw her staring at them, they turned back, as if to flee.

Then another sound attracted her attention and she walked to the edge of the roof and peered down. A man was climbing quietly up the ladder. Rahab recognized Sala instantly; no one else in the world moved with such easy grace. She looked up again toward the men on her roof and pointed downward. A moment later Sala's head appeared, then his shoulders, and then he was beside her.

"Rahab! I didn't expect you to be here!"

"Who are those men?" She pointed to her roof.

Sala's eyes followed her finger, then he turned back to her. "Has anyone else seen them?"

"No."

"Then Yahweh is surely with us." He motioned to the two men that it was all right and pointed to the flax. Sala and Rahab stood beside each other and watched as the two spies got down on their hands and knees and disappeared from view.

Rahab looked up at Sala and opened her mouth to ask him what was happening. Before she had the chance to speak, however, Sala's mouth came down on hers, and for a long while she couldn't talk or think at all.

Finally he let out a kind of groan and held her away from him. "Rahab." Her name came out in a husky sigh.

Her knees were weak. "Oh, Sala, I've missed you so much. So, so much. I was up here all by myself, and I prayed to Elohim that you would come to me, and you came! It's like a miracle."

He said, his voice beginning to sound more normal, "I have to talk to you."

"About those men on my roof? Who are they?"

He explained who they were and then told her about the problem they presented. "We couldn't let them stay at the inn because they were seen entering and the inn may be searched. And we can't leave them to find a place on their own because they speak little Canaanite. That's why I brought them here. Your cousin Hasis told me about the party and I thought your house would probably be empty because you would all be over there."

Rahab looked over at her roof and saw no sign of the men. "This might not have been the best place to bring them, Sala. My brother Shemu is suspicious of you and your father."

"I could think of no place else. And you are one of us now. You, too, believe in Elohim. He is calling you to help us, Rahab. You are our only hope of keeping Gideon and Isaac safe."

He looks thinner. And older. Perhaps, if I help these Israelite spies, Lord Nahshon will change his mind about me. Perhaps this is Elohim's way of answering my prayer.

She said, "They should be safe for tonight, but they can't remain hidden under the flax for long. How do you plan to get them off the roof and out of the city without anyone knowing?"

"That's our next big problem. We have to get them to the city gates early tomorrow so they can attach themselves to one of the groups who still go out to the countryside." He looked at her anxiously. "Can you think of any way you might be able to sneak them out of the house in the morning?"

Rahab thought deeply and an idea slipped into her mind. "I could tell my father I found these men on the roof and that they are part of that group who hangs about across the street . . ."

She paused.

"And?" he said eagerly.

She nodded. "I think it would work. I will tell my father they hid in the house with the hope of getting a look at me. Papa is so furious with those men that he will take them and throw them right out the front door. Then it will be up to your friends to get to the city gates."

Sala looked doubtful. "Do you think it would work? Wouldn't your father call the guards?"

Rahab was feeling quite pleased with her plan. She smiled and shook her head. "He's already done that, but they come back after the guards disperse them. Papa says the guards are useless."

Sala looked disgusted. "I can't believe those vermin are still hanging around here."

Rahab shrugged. "I don't think they're so anxious to see me, really. I think they're just bored, and hanging around my house is something to do. Boredom is a big problem these days. We have too many people in the city who have nothing to occupy them."

He gazed down at her, his eyes bright. "You're a wonderful girl, Rahab. You're one of the smartest people I know."

She was delighted. "Do you really think I'm smart?"

"Not just smart, brilliant."

"If I help you with this, do you think your father might let you marry me?"

There was a white line around Sala's mouth. "I think he might. I believe you are an agent of Yahweh, Rahab, and I think my father will come to believe that too."

Her eyes opened wide in confusion. "Yahweh? Who is Yahweh?"

"Isaac told my father and me that Elohim revealed His true name to Moses while the Israelites were in the desert. His name is Yahweh, Rahab. In Hebrew the word means *I am*. Yahweh is to His people everything we need Him to be, and because we are following His plan, we will triumph. Joshua will take Jericho for Yahweh and His people, and when he does, you and I will be able to marry."

He reached out and took her into his arms. Rahab slid her arms around his waist and rested her cheek against his shoulder. His lips touched her hair. He said, "I think Yahweh always meant for us to be together—that is why He arranged it that I should be the one to rescue you from the slavers, that I should be the one to bring you to Him. I truly believe that."

Rahab rubbed her cheek against the linen of his tunic and inhaled his scent. "I believe it too, Sala. I believe Yahweh is with me. I feel it in my heart."

"Look up," he whispered.

She raised her face and he kissed her. Her head fell back under the force of the kiss and he put his hand behind her head. Her arms tightened around his waist.

Someone shouted loudly at the front of the house and they jumped apart. "Just as well," Sala said, breathing hard. "You go to my head like wine and I lose all sense of what is right."

Rahab understood what he meant. Her knees were weak and she felt a little dizzy. She wanted his arms around her again to hold her up.

"I must go," he said. "I'll be a little way down the street in the morning, to take the men to the gate when your father throws them out. If something should go wrong and you need me, I'll be close by."

"All right."

He gave her a crooked smile. "I can't kiss you again or I'll never leave."

Her return smile was tremulous.

He turned and began to climb down the ladder. Neither one of them said good-bye.

Twenty-Eight

THE FOLLOWING MORNING KING TAMUR WAS APPROACHED by his friend and closest counselor, Farut, while he was down at the stable behind the palace, looking at one of his chariot horses that had come up lame. The chariot horses were Tamur's pride and joy, and he still took them out most days for a run. He dreaded to think of what it would be like trying to keep them exercised during a siege.

His face was flushed from bending over when he turned to face Farut. "What is it?" His voice was testy. He didn't like being interrupted when he was with his horses.

"I am sorry to interrupt you, my lord, but some information has come to my attention that I think you should hear about immediately."

"And what is that?"

"It's been reported that two possible Israelite spies have been spotted in the city. Apparently they came in yesterday with a group of shepherds. The two were spotted in the Sign of the Olive wine bar, and one of the patrons, a merchant from Gaza, escorted them out because they were so clearly out of place. A guard stopped and spoke to the men as they were going down the street, but he let them pass because he knew the merchant. The next we heard of them was that they were seen at one of the inns in the Lower City."

"How do we know these men were spies?"

"The guard said that they did not speak our language very well. In fact, they hardly spoke at all. Unfortunately, this didn't seem to give him a clue that something might be amiss."

"Who was this merchant? Bring him in. It sounds as if he might be a spy as well."

"I am having him brought in, my lord. But meanwhile, we must trace these so-called shepherds."

"I want every available man combing the city for them. Try every inn, every wine bar, every shop. They must be hiding somewhere."

"Yes, my lord. I will pass the order immediately."

Lord Nahshon was having breakfast alone, Sala having gone to watch for Gideon and Isaac, when two palace guards came into the inn and asked him if he was the man who had taken the Israelite spies away from the Sign of the Olive the previous day.

"Spies?" Nahshon looked at them in bewilderment. "What spies? What are you talking about?"

"Are you the man who took away those so-called shepherds?" One of the guards leaned his face close to Nahshon's in a distinctly threatening manner.

"I removed two peasant men from a wine bar yesterday, yes. If they were spies I had no idea. They were just out of place in that particular company and I did everyone a favor by removing them."

"Come with us," the guard said. "Some people at the palace want to talk to you."

Word raced around the town like wildfire. Two spies were loose in Jericho. They had come into the city with a group of shepherds yesterday and were in hiding somewhere. All good citizens were to keep watch for them. Anything out of the ordinary was to be reported at once to the military.

When Sala heard this, he knew Gideon and Isaac could not possibly try to leave the city by the gate. Everyone going through would be thoroughly questioned—if they did not close the gate altogether.

He had to let Rahab know.

He did the only thing he could: he walked up to her house, opened the door, and stepped inside. He was surprised to find the front room empty but didn't stop to wonder where all the family had gone. Instead he started toward the stairs. He put his foot on the first step, looked up, and saw Shemu coming down.

"What are *you* doing here?" Shemu asked as he continued to descend.

Sala remembered Rahab's warning that Shemu suspected him of being a spy, but there was no time to invent another story. He would have to tell the truth. "I have a problem, Shemu. Can we go somewhere where we can speak privately?"

Light steps sounded on the stairs and Rahab, followed by Atene, came into view. Rahab's eyes were huge as she looked down at Sala. "Is something wrong?"

Shemu's eyes flicked from Sala's face to Rahab's, then back to Sala's. "Come with me up to the roof," he said. "We can be private there."

He pushed past Rahab and Atene and told them to stay below. The two girls ignored him and followed Sala up to the roof.

The first thing Sala did was look to make sure Isaac and Gideon were hidden. The flax looked undisturbed and the rest of the roof was empty. He began to breathe easier.

"Now," Shemu said, crossing his arms and leaning his back against the mud brick wall, "tell me what is going on here."

The group of men who had made a habit out of standing across from Rahab's house were talking about the rumor of spies being seen in the city when they saw Sala push open Rahab's door and go in.

"Didn't we see some men just walk into that house yesterday?" said the heavyset man who was the group's leader.

One of the men, who had been chewing on a piece of wood he used as a tooth pick, said, "We did."

"And we didn't see them come out, did we?"

"No, we didn't."

"And now this young man, who looks as if he is in a great hurry, does the same thing. I find that odd."

Murmurs of agreement came from the other men.

The heavyset man continued, "No one has gone into that house except the family who lives there for as long as we've been watching. Who are these strangers?"

One of the other men swallowed a date he had been eating and said, "Do you think this might have something to do with those spies the guards are looking for?"

"Hmm," the heavy man said pensively.

"But why would Israelite spies go into Rahab's house?" someone else asked. "They are good Canaanite people. They would never harbor a spy."

The fat man had had time to think. "The family may not know someone is hiding there. Remember, the house was empty when we saw the two men go in yesterday. Perhaps the spies are hiding somewhere inside without the family's knowledge."

"They might have slipped out during the night when every-one was asleep," the man with the stick said.

All of the men continued to squint through the morning sun at the house across the street. Then the heavyset man said, "If we reported to the guards that we saw two mysterious men slip into Rahab's house yesterday when it was empty, they will be sure to investigate. To do that properly, they will have to get all of the family out of the house so they can search it. If they do that, then we might get our chance to see Rahab."

"Aaahhhh." It was a general murmur of approval.

A thin man said, "It will look well for us, too, if we show that we are on the alert for the spies. Even if they find nothing in the house, the guards will appreciate our trying to help."

"A true word," said the man who was now chewing on a second date.

"It certainly can't do us any harm."

Unsaid, but recognized by all, was the fact that the excite-ment of a search would provide a good morning's entertainment for them.

"I'll go to find a guard," volunteered the man chewing on the stick. Everyone agreed.

Having convinced themselves of the worthiness of their inten-tions, he set off while the rest of the men kept their eyes trained on Rahab's door in case they saw the strangers come out.

Up on the roof Shemu turned to Sala and demanded again, "What are you doing here? What made you walk into this house as if you belonged here?"

Sala looked at Rahab. "I think you had better tell him."

"Yes." Rahab turned to her brother, her face grave. "The first thing you must know, Shemu, is that I have become an Israelite. I no longer follow the false gods of Canaan, I worship the One True God, the God of the Israelites."

Shemu swung around to face Sala, his hands balled up into fists. "You have been filling her ears with your nonsense, and it will stop. Do you hear me? It will stop right now."

Sala stared back, his face expressionless.

Shemu felt Atene's hand on his sleeve. She looked up at him and said in the gentle voice that he loved, "I, too, have become an Israelite, my husband. I also have renounced the gods of Canaan to follow Elohim."

Shemu said in disbelief, "You told me once that you had prayed to this god, and I said nothing. But you cannot renounce your *own* gods, Atene. That means you are renouncing your own people!"

She was standing straight, looking at him with clear, steady eyes. "I prayed to Elohim for a baby, Shemu."

Shemu's heart clenched with pain. He knew how much she longed for a child and now that longing had driven her to pray to a false god. "Atene, it is not—"

"Hear me, my husband." She closed her hand around his sleeve. "Elohim listened to me. I am with child."

Shemu's mouth dropped open.

She smiled at his astonishment. "It's true. I'm late with my flow and I'm never late—you know that as well as I. Elohim has given us a child, Shemu. He is the true God. I prayed to Lady Asherah for years and nothing happened. But now"—her whole face lit with joy—"we are going to have a baby!"

He reached out and took her into his arms. Over her head he stared at Sala and the message in his eyes was clear. *If this isn't true, if Atene is disappointed, I will kill you with my own hands.*

He heard Rahab say, "It's true, Shemu. When I was made the

hierodule I prayed to Elohim to save me, and He did. The king died in the bed before he could do anything to me. He just died, Shemu! Elohim did that to save me. I know He did."

This was all becoming a bit much for Shemu to take in. His wife and his sister secret Israelites? He went back to the one question he hadn't gotten an answer to. "So what is Sala doing here?"

Atene, who didn't know the answer, turned in Shemu's arms so she could see Rahab. Rahab said to Sala, "We have to tell him."

Sala looked grim. Shemu's arms dropped away from his wife and he faced Sala. "If this has anything to do with my wife or my sister, then you had better tell me. Are you and your father Israelite spies, Sala? Is that what this is all about?"

It was Rahab who answered his question. "It's not Sala who is the spy, Shemu, but—"

Suddenly Shemu knew. He had been out earlier and heard all the rumors about the spies. "Those spies everyone is looking for. That is what you are here about, isn't it?"

"Yes," Sala said.

"You know where they are?"

Sala looked at Rahab.

Rahab said, "They are right here on this roof, Shemu. Hiding under the flax."

Shemu felt the color drain from his face. "Here? Now?"

"Yes."

He looked at his sister. "How did this happen?"

"They slipped in yesterday while everyone was over at Uncle Ilim's. Sala found me and told me about it and I said they could stay the night. They are supposed to leave this morning—"

Sala cut in, "But now they can't. Somehow word got out about them and the guards are looking for them. The gates have been closed for the day."

"I didn't know that," Rahab said. She pursed her lips. "Well,

I suppose they will just have to remain here until the gate opens again."

"Absolutely not!" Shemu said. "I don't care what happens to them. I want them out of this house now."

The door from the stairway opened and Shemu's brother Mattan stepped onto the roof. "Here you are. We've been looking for the three of you. You won't believe this, but four guards have come to the door and said they had a report that the Israelite spies had entered this house yesterday. They want us all to leave so they can search."

Sala looked at Shemu and said, "It certainly wouldn't look good if spies were found here, would it?"

Shemu gave him a hard look in return. It would look terrible if the spies were found here, as Sala well knew. Shemu had no choice right now but to protect them.

Rahab said to Mattan, "Who could have made such a report?"

"The guards won't say, but Father suspects it is those hyenas who hang around across the street. They will do anything to get a look at you."

"Did Father tell that to the guards?"

"He did, but they said they have to search anyway."

Shemu looked at Sala again. "Very well. I suppose we had better let them do it, then."

"Yes, I think that would be best."

As they headed toward the door, Mattan lowered his voice and said to Shemu, "What is *he* doing here?"

"He came to see me on business," Shemu returned, and the five of them went down the stairs and out onto the street so their house could be searched by the Jericho military guard.

Twenty-Nine

THE MEN ACROSS THE STREET WERE THRILLED WHEN they saw the guards go into Rahab's house. Word had spread quickly and by the time the family came filing out of the house onto the street, an even bigger crowd had gathered. For one delicious moment the hopeful men caught a glimpse of Rahab as she turned her face toward them and gave them a furious glare.

"She's gorgeous!"

"Magnificent!"

"More beautiful than I ever imagined!"

A chorus of ecstasy poured out of their throats. Then Rahab's father hustled her into the house next door and came back out alone, shaking his fist at the gathered group.

The men didn't even care when the guards came out of Rahab's house empty-handed. They had gotten what they were waiting for, a glimpse of the most beautiful woman in Canaan. Something to share with their mates at the wine shop.

One of the guards crossed the street to speak to them as Rahab's family began to return into their house.

Yes, they said, they were certain they had seen two men enter the house yesterday when the family was next door at a party. No, they had not seen them go out.

The guard recrossed the street and spoke to his companions. Then they knocked on the door of Rahab's house once more.

Rahab had been thinking furiously all the time the guards were searching and she had come to the conclusion that the spies would never be able to get away unless the search for them was called off. And the only way to make the search cease was for the guards to think the spies had already escaped. So when the guards came back into the house to ask once again if anyone in the family knew something about the two men who had been reported, Rahab stepped forward.

"I think I know who you must be looking for," she said.

Stunned silence greeted her admission.

She gave the guards an apologetic smile. "My brothers rushed me out of the house so quickly just now that I didn't get a chance to tell you."

"Tell us what, lady?" the largest guard said deferentially.

She gave her father an apologetic glance before she answered. "I came back into our house yesterday during the party. I wanted to get something to show to one of my cousins, and I found two men in my mother's kitchen."

Kata gave a horrified moan.

Mepu cried, "Why did you never tell me this?"

Shemu looked grim.

Rahab said, "I'm sorry, Papa, but I didn't want to worry you." She turned back to the guards. "I was frightened when I saw them and I asked them what they were doing in my family's house. They said they had come in to see if they could find something to eat, that they were hungry."

The big guard asked eagerly, "How did they speak? Did they sound foreign?"

"Yes, they did. They had such thick accents that I could

hardly understand them. But so many strangers are coming into the city these days that I didn't think too much about it."

She gave them a big-eyed, pleading look, an innocent girl who could be easily duped by cunning men.

"You should have left the house immediately and come to tell me," Mepu said angrily.

"But they did me no harm, Papa. I gave them something to eat because they said they were going on a journey and then they left."

"That was wrong of you," Mepu said.

Another big-eyed look from Rahab. "But, Papa, you always say hospitality is sacred."

The big guard said, "Did they say what kind of journey they were going on?"

"They were in a hurry to get out of the city before the gate closed for the night. They didn't say where they were going."

"And you didn't think to ask?" the guard asked with audible exasperation.

Rahab looked down and her voice became even huskier than usual. "I am sorry. I was only trying to be kind. Do you think these may be the men you are looking for?"

"Yes, I do." The large guard turned to the others. "We must report this to the commander immediately. The two of them will be heading for the Jordan. If we pursue them quickly enough we can overtake them."

He turned back to Rahab. "Thank you, lady, you have been very helpful."

Rahab rewarded him with her best smile. "I'm sorry if I did the wrong thing."

The three guards smiled back, one of them even bowed, and they left the house.

Once the door had closed behind them, Mepu rounded on his daughter. "Why didn't you tell me about these men? Don't you realize what could have happened to you, alone in the house with them?"

"Yes, Papa, I did realize," she returned in her normal voice. "I thought the best thing I could do was to give them some food and get rid of them. And I didn't tell you because I knew you would be upset. How could I know they were Israelite spies?"

Shemu said, "Don't scold her, Papa. She did the best she could under the circumstances."

Rahab's other brothers agreed.

"It was those cursed men who put the guards on to us," Mepu shouted. "I am going to demand the guards arrest every one of them! You were the hierodule. You should not be treated like this. I am going to the palace to demand action!"

It took the combined powers of his family to calm him down and convince him that now that the men had had their chance to see Rahab, they would have no more reason to continue their vigil.

While everyone was gathered around Mepu, Shemu said softly to Sala, "Go back up to the roof. I will meet you there."

Sala slipped up the stairs. Rahab watched him go and looked at Shemu. He shook his head.

Rahab had to repeat her story for her family at least a dozen times. Finally she asked if she could go up to her room to rest and Kata agreed, telling everyone to give her some time alone because she had had such a terrible experience.

Rahab went immediately to the roof and found Sala there

by himself. He whirled around at the sound of the door opening and when he saw her, his face lighted up as if the sun had just shone on it.

"You were magnificent!" he said.

She lifted a hand, as if to stop him from touching her. "My whole family is in danger as long as these men remain here. We must be rid of them, Sala."

The radiance faded from Sala's face. "I know. I know. And you have made it much easier for us to do that. Once the guards are out of the city and in pursuit, it will be simple for our men to get out through the gates. No one will be looking for them."

"I wouldn't count on that." It was Shemu, opening the door and coming out onto the roof himself. "They will be stopping and questioning every person who goes out through that gate. They may even keep the gate shut until the pursuers return. Your men won't be able to get out that way, Sala."

Sala looked at Shemu and said, "What do you want me to do?"

"First, I want to know exactly what information you have given these men. What are the results of your own spying?" The last word was pronounced with the utmost contempt.

"Why do you want to know that?"

"I want to know if it is safe for me to turn these men loose or if I will have to kill them."

Rahab gasped in horror.

Sala had gone pale. "I will be honest with you, Shemu. The information my father and I have gathered is slight. The walls of this city are a formidable barrier. My father and I saw that as soon as we arrived. Joshua will lose most of his army if he tries to come against them."

Shemu's lip curled cynically. "If you think I will believe that your message to your leader is that he should turn away from here, you are mistaken. I am not such a fool as that. So let me repeat what I said before: I want to know the message you are sending to this Joshua."

Sala looked at Rahab and then back to Shemu. He nodded. "Very well, I will tell you. The report we are sending is that Joshua should concentrate his attack on the weakest side of the city, which is the north wall. You must know that yourself—you live right next to it. The stone revetment is formidable, but the mud-brick wall on top of it is only one brick thick."

Shemu's lips pressed together so his mouth was one grim line. "And what other information have you gathered?"

Sala laughed ironically. "What else is there to report, Shemu? Jericho is a fortress unequalled anywhere in the land. I do not think it can be taken by an ordinary army."

"But you don't think the Israelites are an ordinary army, do you?"

"No, I don't. We are men guided by the will of Yahweh, the One True God. He has been with my people since the beginning of time, Shemu. He was with our father Abraham, to whom He gave the land of Canaan. Now we have come to take it back. And we will. Jericho, no matter how great its walls, cannot stand against the will of Yahweh."

In spite of himself, Shemu was stirred by Sala's words and by his belief. He tried to shake off the feeling and said, "We have done well enough in Canaan under Baal. We do not need this Yahweh of yours."

Silence fell as the two men measured each other. Then Sala said, "The Israelites will come against Jericho whether or not the spies return. They will come and one of two things will happen. You will be right and Joshua will either give up or wreck his army by throwing it against these walls. Or I will be right and these walls will fall before the will of Yahweh. If that happens, and I believe it will, nothing will be left alive in this city, Shemu. Nothing."

Silence. Then Rahab said, "Shemu, if you are right, it won't matter if we let these men go. And if Sala is right it won't matter either. What will happen will happen whether the spies get to Joshua or not. But to kill them? That makes no sense at all. What would we do with the bodies?"

Shemu let out a long, audible breath. "Ever the practical one. All right, my sister, do you also have a plan for how we can get them away from here?"

"Yes," Rahab said. "I do."

Lord Nahshon had been taken to the military commander's headquarters and the commander had interviewed Nahshon himself. Akiz was a grizzled veteran who had been a supporter of Makamaron, but with the death of the old king his allegiance had switched wholeheartedly to Tamur. He wanted to keep his job and it didn't hurt that his son, Farut, was Tamur's closest friend.

Lord Nahshon steadfastly maintained that his name was Debir and that he was a merchant from Gaza. He knew nothing of Israelite spies. He had only escorted the shepherds out of the Sign of the Olive because they were offensive to the customers. The two men must have followed him to his inn and tried to hide there. The only thing he said that made the commander think he might be telling the truth was his naming Lord Arazu as a reference.

Lord Arazu was sent for and Nahshon was left to sit and worry in the small, windowless, airless room where he had been confined.

While Nahshon was waiting, the guards who had searched Rahab's house arrived to speak to the commander. Once Akiz heard what they had to say, all thoughts of Nahshon vanished from his head. The commander immediately ordered squads of chariots to set off in pursuit of the escaped spies. They were directed to drive as fast as they could to the only viable ford on the Jordan, where Akiz knew the Israelites had to be heading.

The charioteers didn't even wait to make sure their horses had been properly groomed. The chariots were brought round, the horses were harnessed, and the chariot squadron of Jericho's army was galloping down the main street of the city in record time. The gate opened wide for them and they swept out onto the plain, heading east toward the river and the Israelite spies they were certain they would be able to overtake.

Thirty

IT WAS QUIET ON THE ROOF AS SALA AND SHEMU STARED at Rahab in amazement.

"You have a plan? What is it?" Sala asked.

Rahab didn't reply at once. Her experience as hierodule had changed her in some profound and irreversible way. Life no longer looked like a delightful treasure box, open and waiting for her to choose her own happy future. She knew now that terrible things could happen to her. Terrible things could happen to the people she loved. The world wasn't safe and she could no longer depend upon her father to protect her or her family. She must act, and she knew she had a potent bargaining tool to use against these Israelite spies.

She gathered herself and said to Sala, "Tell your friends I will help them to escape, but first they must promise me something."

A flicker of surprise passed over his face, but he answered promptly, "Of course. What is the promise?"

"They must promise me that nothing will happen to my family when the Israelite army takes Jericho. If they want my help, they must promise to keep all of us safe."

Sala looked at her with pain in his warm brown eyes. "Rahab, you know I would never let anything happen to you!"

She believed he meant it, but she was not at all sure he would be able to follow through on his intention. She said somberly,

"You are not the Israelite army, Sala. I must hear it from the lips of these men who have come here on the orders of Joshua. They must tell me themselves that nothing bad will happen to my family."

Sala's eyes held hers for a long moment, then he nodded. "Do you want me to tell them to come out?"

"Yes. Call them out so I may look at them when they answer."

Sala turned toward the large square of spread-out flax, raised his voice slightly, and said in Hebrew, "Gideon, Isaac, come out."

Nothing happened at first, then there was the sound of wood being bumped and the flax trembled. The two spies, wrinkled and dirty, came crawling out from their hiding place. They scrambled to their feet, looking from Sala to Shemu to Rahab then back to Sala.

Sala began to speak to them in Hebrew and Rahab kept her eyes level on the Israelites' faces as she waited for their reply. This was probably the most important moment in her life, this moment now, here on this roof, as she waited for these strange men to pronounce life or death for all the people she held most dear. Rahab understood what was going to happen when the Israelites attacked. Jericho would be destroyed. Decimated. Massacred. That was what Yahweh wanted them to do. They were His chosen ones and they would triumph. Not even the famous walls of Jericho would stand against them.

All these people, Rahab thought with aching sorrow as she waited for Sala to finish his conversation; all these men and women and children. All of them doomed to die. Then, fiercely, *But not my family! Not my father and mother. Not my brothers and sisters-in-law and cousins. Not the people whom I love.*

Before Sala had a chance to deliver Rahab's ultimatum, he had to answer a few urgent questions from Isaac and Gideon. They knew who Rahab was, but they wanted to know about Shemu.

"He is Rahab's brother," Sala assured them. "His wife has become an Israelite along with Rahab."

Gideon met Rahab's level eyes for a moment, then looked away. "How can we be sure this woman isn't merely tricking us? You say she is a follower of Yahweh, but how can this be? She is a Canaanite woman. Her family worships false gods. How can we trust her not to give us away?"

"She has turned her back upon the gods of Canaan," Sala said. "I know this is true."

Gideon's look was skeptical. "Are you sure she has not seduced you, Sala? Many Israelite men have fallen to the wiles of the Canaanite harlots, and this one is beautiful. Can you tell us honestly that you have not succumbed to her charms?"

The blood flushed into Sala's face. "Just because she's beautiful doesn't mean she's a harlot!"

Gideon's lip curled with contempt. "All Canaanite women are harlots. At their festivals they will lie with any man who asks them. Why would a woman who looks like that wish to become an Israelite? Are the rest of her family Israelites also, or is it just her and this sister-in-law you mentioned?"

"The others have not converted. That's why we're keeping you up here in secret. And I do not wish to discuss Rahab with you any longer. She's willing to get you safely away from Jericho if, in return, you promise to save her family from death when Joshua takes the city."

At this point Shemu interrupted. "What are you talking about, Sala? Why are they asking so many questions?"

Sala lifted a hand in a gesture that asked for patience and turned back to the Israelites. "You must decide now. Rahab has promised she will help you get away, but you must first promise her that her family will be safe. She knows we are destined to win this battle. She knows that Yahweh parted the seas for His people to escape from Egypt. She is a believer in Yahweh and His power. So in return for your lives you must promise her the lives of her family. That is the covenant she is offering. What is your answer?"

Isaac turned to Gideon and the two men conferred in low voices. Sala could hear what they said, and when they once more referred to Rahab as a harlot he had to bite his lip to keep from laying violent hands on them. At last the two men turned back to Sala, and Gideon delivered their decision. "Tell the woman these words for our answer: *If you give us our lives, we will give you yours. As long as you keep your word and we get safely back to our camp, we will spare you and all who belong to you when Yahweh gives us this land.*"

Sala translated for Rahab and Shemu.

"Are those their exact words?" Rahab asked.

"Yes."

"Can we trust them?" Shemu asked.

"If you make them swear to it in the name of Yahweh, you can trust them," Sala returned.

"Make them swear then," Rahab said.

Rahab listened to the men, waiting to pick out the name Yahweh. When she heard it, she nodded in satisfaction.

Sala looked back to Rahab. "They want to know how you plan to rescue them."

Shemu muttered, "I would like to know that too."

Rahab stared at the spies as she spoke to Sala. "Tell them they must remain hidden up here until it is full dark. Then Atene will make certain there is no one in our bedroom and I will bring them down from the roof and let them out our window with a rope. Explain that the window is a hole in the wall, and once they touch ground they will be outside the city, on the north side, which is the farthest away from the gates. Once they are outside they must go west, into the Judean hill country and away from the Jordan, so that the pursuers do not run into them. After a few days, when the Jericho military has returned to the city, they will be safe to return to Joshua."

Sala and Shemu both looked at Rahab with admiration. So simple a solution and neither of them had thought of it.

Rahab and Shemu watched as Sala relayed the plan. When he fell silent, one of the spies took a piece of scarlet cord out of his belt pocket and held it out to Rahab. Sala translated his words, "We can only keep to our promise if you make certain that you identify your dwelling place. You must tie this scarlet cord in the window through which you let us down and when the battle begins you must gather all of your family within this house. As long as they stay within they will be safe. We cannot guarantee the security of anyone who goes out into the street."

"I understand," Rahab said as she reached out her hand and took the cord.

Isaac spoke again and Sala translated, "You must keep this promise a secret from the rest of your family. No one must know, otherwise we will consider the promise broken."

"I understand," Rahab repeated.

Shemu put an arm around her shoulders and she looked up into his face. "You have done well, my sister," he said. "I am proud of you."

Rahab managed a wobbly smile and briefly pressed her forehead into her brother's shoulder.

The Israelites had begun to speak again in Hebrew.

"You must come with us, Sala. It is not safe for you to be here any longer. Your father must come as well. Where is he?"

"I left him at the inn."

"Come back before dark and you both can leave with us through the window, as this woman says."

"I will not leave her. I'll ask my father if he wishes to go with you, but I will remain here with Rahab."

Isaac frowned. "Do not be foolish. This woman is acting in her own interests and the interests of her family. This is understandable, but you cannot be certain she will not betray you."

"She would never do that." He glanced at Rahab, whose eyes were fixed on him anxiously.

I will never leave you, my love. You are doing the work of Yahweh, and if my father does not see that, then he is blind. I cannot be loyal to what I know is wrong.

He said firmly to his fellow Israelites, "In our hearts we are betrothed and, once we are free of this place, we will marry."

Gideon scowled. "You cannot do such a thing, my brother. She is not clean. She is old enough to have participated in their filthy rites. She will make you unclean too if you marry her."

Sala said wearily, "When you first said that, Gideon, I wanted to punch you. Now I am just going to say that she is giving you your lives and she deserves better from you than ignorant words about her virtue."

The two men shook their heads in identical gestures of disapproval. Then Gideon said, "We will wait to see what Joshua has to say."

"I do not need to hear anyone else's opinion. But I will ask my father if he wishes to accompany you. I don't want to answer for him."

"Very well."

Sala glanced up at the sky, which was still bright with afternoon light. "I think you had better get back under the flax until Rahab comes for you tonight. Do you still have the water I gave you?"

"Yes, we have enough water."

"I'll make sure you have some more water and food to take with you. You will be out in those hills for a few days at least."

"Thank you, Sala," Gideon said.

"Thank you, my brother," Isaac said.

"It is Rahab whom you should be thanking," was Sala's reply to the two of them.

"We do thank her. You may tell her that for us."

As the men began to crawl back under the shade of the flax, Sala told Rahab they were deeply grateful to her for her help.

Lord Nahshon sat alone in the small barracks room while the commander of Jericho's troops organized the search for the escaped spies. By the time Akiz had done that and had finished reporting to the king, Lord Arazu had arrived at military headquarters.

The first hint Nahshon had of his "friend's" arrival was when a guard opened the door of his tiny, hot, and stuffy prison and took him to a much larger room where he found Akiz and Lord Arazu waiting for him.

"My dear fellow," Arazu said when he saw the merchant he thought was going to make him rich. "I am so sorry for this dreadful confusion. I have just been explaining to the commander here that you are a businessman, not a spy. It was simply your good nature that made you remove those shepherds—or what you all thought of as shepherds—out of the wine bar. The Sign of the Olive is not a place for farm workers."

Arazu's nose quivered as if he had smelled a bad odor.

Both Arazu and the commander were seated, but they allowed Nahshon to continue to stand. The commander said, "It seems that we made a mistake, Debir. Lord Arazu has assured me you could not possibly be a spy. However, I do have one question for you."

"Yes, Commander?" Nahshon was trying to keep his relief from showing.

"If you are only here on business, why have you remained in Jericho when it is so clear that we will soon be under attack from the Israelites?"

Nahshon allowed an ironic smile to tug at the corners of his lips. "Really, Commander, how long do you think that attack is going to last? The Israelites have a large army, I understand, and a large army must be fed. The farmers have stripped most of the produce from their farms and the only good spring lies inside the walls of the city. You have plenty of food and water; they will have little. I do not think it will be long before they move on to look for a less well-defended target. And when they go, Lord Arazu and I will transact our business."

The commander said, "I wish the people in the city had the confidence in us that you have, Debir."

Nahshon shrugged. "They follow whoever was the last person to speak to them. Once they see how it is, they will rally to the defense of their city with pride."

The commander did not look convinced, but he said, "You may go with Lord Arazu, and I am sorry for the inconvenience we have caused you."

Lord Nahshon produced his most gracious smile. "I understand, Commander, and I hope you catch those wretched spies. But what can they have to report, eh? The city walls are unassailable."

The commander's return smile was more natural. "You are right, of course. Good day to you, Debir. I hope your business prospers."

"Thank you, Commander. I hope so too."

It wasn't until he returned home that Nahshon learned that Joshua's spies had escaped and *that* was the real reason he had been let go, not the character witness of Lord Arazu.

Thirty-One

GIDEON AND ISAAC FOLLOWED RAHAB'S INSTRUCTIONS, and after three days of hiding in the hill country, they made their way to the Jordan, passing only a few scattered shepherds with small flocks of sheep. The river was still tumultuous, but they were strong men and they tied themselves together and made it across safely.

Joshua was in his tent when the spies reached the Israelite camp and they hurried to report to him. He greeted them with relief and bade them come in and tell him what they had learned.

Gideon imparted the information they had gathered from Nahshon and Sala.

Joshua was pleased. "Frightened people make easier targets," he said. "But I was worried about you; I expected you to be back sooner. Did something happen that you took so long?"

Gideon looked at Isaac, letting him know it was his turn to take up their story. "We were almost captured, Joshua. We were saved by a woman but we had to make her a promise that we are obligated to keep."

He told Joshua about how they hid on Rahab's roof and how she had smuggled them out of the city by lowering them from her window with a rope.

"I was terrified," Isaac confessed. "Her brother was the one holding the rope and all I could think of was if he let it slip, I was done for."

Gideon added, "I was praying to Yahweh as I dangled in the air over that huge drop."

Isaac said, "But we didn't fall and the woman kept her word. Now we must keep ours. We promised that she and her family would be safe from our attack. Gideon gave her the scarlet cord to hang in her window so that our warriors will know not to enter that house."

Joshua's black eyebrows, which always looked so startling in contrast to his gray hair, lifted with surprise. "How did an Israelite woman come to be in Jericho?"

Gideon said, "She is not an Israelite, she is a Canaanite woman who has rejected her old gods and now believes in Yahweh. That is what Sala told us and it must be true. She saved our lives, after all."

Joshua's brows lifted even higher. "A *Canaanite* woman?"

"Yes, and it looks as if young Sala has fallen in love with her. He is the one who convinced her to change her religion. She is beautiful, but she must have taken part in the rites of Baal; she is beyond the years of childhood."

"She has probably lain with many men," Joshua said. "She is unclean."

"Yes. And her family are still followers of Baal. Her brother helped us because his wife, who has also given her belief to Yahweh, begged him to."

"He also thought it might be a good thing to have us behind him if we should happen to take the city," Gideon added cynically.

"I see," Joshua said. "So you have pledged that the people within the house with the scarlet cord will be safe?"

"Yes. We promised in the name of Yahweh. We had to—we were in her house and at her mercy."

Joshua nodded. "Then we will keep that promise. Whatever the woman may be, she has shown her good faith to us. No harm must come to her or to her family."

The three men had been sitting facing each other and now, as Joshua got to his feet, Gideon and Isaac jumped up as well. He reached out and gave each man an approving slap on the shoulder.

"You have done well, Gideon. You have done well, Isaac. Now I must have the word put around: tomorrow, we will move the entire camp to the shores of the Jordan."

Gideon looked uneasy. "The entire camp? I must warn you, Joshua, that river is barely passable for a strong man. The women and children will not be able to get across yet."

Joshua's mouth remained grave but he smiled with his eyes. "Remember, Gideon. We are the children of Yahweh and He has given all this land into our hands. Did He not hold back the waters of the sea to allow all of us—men, women, and children—to pass out of Egypt? Do not fear, the Israelites will cross the river Jordan and enter into the land of Canaan. Yahweh will open the way."

By the end of the following day, the entire Israelite camp had moved to the banks of the Jordan. Gideon and Isaac stood together on the eastern side with a few of their comrades and looked across to the other bank.

"So there it is at last," one of the men murmured, "Canaan, the land of milk and honey, the land Yahweh has promised to our people since the time of Abraham."

"How did you manage to get across with that current?" another man asked Gideon and Isaac. "It looks impassable to me."

The men stared at the raging torrent that the normally narrow, meandering river became in the spring.

"It wasn't easy," Gideon admitted. "If it was up to me I would say it is impossible to get our whole camp safely across while the water is as high as this. But we must remember that Yahweh Himself has chosen Joshua to lead us. We must believe that if Joshua tells us we can cross the river, then we will do it."

The other men murmured agreement, turned their backs upon the tumultuous river, and went back to their camp. When they arrived at the warriors' section of the spread-out campsite, the first thing they heard was the message from Joshua being cried everywhere.

Tomorrow, when you see the ark of the covenant being carried by the priests, then shall you set forth and follow it. But keep a space between yourselves and the priests as you go. Tonight you must sanctify yourselves, for tomorrow Yahweh will do wonders for His people. Tomorrow we shall enter into the land of Canaan.

Tense silence spread among the warriors as they listened to Joshua's message. There was not a one of them who had not had a look at the raging river, but not a single man uttered a protest.

Shortly after the message had been carried to the farthest limit of the campsite, Joshua ordered a procession of the ark of the covenant around the entire encampment. Carried by the priests, it moved slowly and reverently. The sight of the ark of the covenant was always a profoundly spiritual moment for an Israelite. It was borne aloft so all could see, and was comprised of a long wooden platform upon which reposed a large, beautifully carved wooden chest. This chest was the sacred receptacle that held the tablets Moses had brought down from the mountain when Yahweh had given him the laws that the Israelites must live by. It was the most precious religious symbol of the Israelite people and the sight of it filled them with hope and a determination to do whatever Joshua commanded.

By the time the ark had passed around the entire camp, darkness was falling. The Israelites lay down to rest, readying themselves for the historic moment that would occur the following day, when the wanderers from Egypt finally set foot upon the land that God had given them.

The Israelites rose before the sun to ready themselves to set forth. First in line to cross the river were the priests, bearing once more the sacred ark of the covenant. At a distance behind the priests were grouped many thousands of warriors carrying their weapons of war: spears, axes, slings, bows, arrows, and daggers. Finally, behind the warriors, there came an even larger group of women, children, and baggage animals.

When all the contingents had halted in their proper places, the priests advanced until they stood on the bank of the flooded Jordan. Joshua stood with them, calm, his head tilted slightly as he listened to the loud roar of the water. The priests waited in silence until he said to the ones who were carrying the ark, "Step into the river until the soles of your feet are wet."

Not a single priest hesitated. Looking straight ahead, at the land on the far side of the river, they stepped into the racing water.

Almost instantly a loud rumbling noise rent the air and the earth shook beneath the feet of the gathered Israelites. All heads turned to look upstream, the direction from which the sound had come.

"Wait," Joshua said to the priests.

The four men stood, the precious ark lifted high, and as they waited the racing water began to slow, first to the size of a stream, then to a trickle, and then, amazingly, there was no water at all. They were standing on the riverbed.

"Go forward," Joshua said to the priests. "For as long as you remain standing in the middle of the riverbed, there will be no water and our people may pass."

No one except Joshua and the priests had seen the water cease to flow, so when the warriors finally approached the river and saw the priests standing in the middle of the dry river, they fell to their knees.

"It has happened again," Gideon said to Isaac in wonder, "just as it happened in the days of our parents when they were leaving Egypt. Yahweh has stopped the waters so we may pass."

And pass they did. First the priests who were not holding the ark, then all of the warriors with their weapons, and finally the women, children, and pack animals. By the end of the day, the entire Israelite nation had finally entered the land of Canaan.

After the last donkey had made it across, Joshua ordered Gideon and Isaac to take twelve stones from the riverbed where the ark had stood, so they could place them at their new camp in their new country. They would be a symbol of the twelve tribes of Israel and how Yahweh had shut down the river for them to cross over to the land promised to Abraham's people by their God.

Joshua was not the only leader to think spying on the enemy was a good tactic. Ever since he had become king, Tamur had had spies positioned to report if the Israelites entered into Canaan. The news of the Israelites' getting across the river took only one day to reach the palace.

The king immediately called upon his military commander

and his dearest friend. The three sat together in council late in the afternoon as the sun was staining the sky red in the west.

"We knew it was coming," Akiz said. "We just did not think it would happen so soon."

"Are we ready for a siege?" Tamur asked. "Have all of my orders been carried out?"

"Yes, my lord. The grain supplies are well guarded; there will be no stealing."

The king nodded. "We must make certain the people have confidence in their leaders. They must believe the food supplies are safe. And they must have confidence in our defenses as well."

"We are prepared, my lord. I can begin to station my men at their battle positions immediately if you wish."

"Good," Tamur said. "I will also send a proclamation around the city telling the people that the Israelites have crossed the river and that the city will be ready to repel any attack they might make."

"An excellent idea, my lord." Akiz rose. "I will go now and set the defenses in motion."

The commander left the room and, as the door closed behind him, the two friends looked at each other.

Farut said, "Do not worry, my lord. You have made the right decisions. The Israelites will never break into the city."

The grim look had not lifted from Tamur's face. "What is really worrying me is something else."

"What, my lord?"

"How, in the name of Baal, did the Israelites get across that river?"

Thirty-Two

For over a week after the Israelite spies had escaped, life for Rahab was quiet. No one in the family besides Shemu and Atene knew what had happened under their roof, for which Rahab was immensely grateful.

The men across the street had disappeared. Whether it was because they had finally seen Rahab, or because the guards were more vigilant in dispersing them, they were gone. She was still shackled to the house, however. Her father said that too many people had seen her during the New Year procession, and he feared she would be the subject of gossip and innuendo and the bold stares of knowing men if she went out.

As quiet day succeeded quiet day, Rahab grew progressively more restive. After the life-and-death situation she had just passed through, the conversation of her mother and sisters-in-law seemed tedious and trivial. Her greatest frustration, however, was that she could not see Sala, and she longed for him with all her heart.

Finally she decided to beg Shemu to help her. She knew it wasn't fair to ask him to go against the authority of their father, but she was desperate. She looked for an opportunity to catch him alone, and at last she succeeded.

He was in the small storeroom at the back of the house inspecting a barrel of barley Mepu had just received when Rahab slipped quietly into the room and closed the door behind her.

"I must talk to you, Shemu," she said.

He turned in surprise when he heard her voice. "What is it?"

She threaded her way between the other barrels and looked up at him with pleading eyes. "I want to see Sala. I *need* to see Sala. We love each other, Shemu. How would you feel if you were imprisoned in this house and couldn't see Atene?"

He said gently, "You know Father doesn't want you to go out of the house."

"Of course I know that. I have been a prisoner here ever since I came home from the shrine. It's not fair, Shemu. None of that was my fault, and Papa is punishing me for it."

"He's not trying to punish you, he's trying to protect you, Rahab."

Rahab folded her arms across her chest. "You and I both know, my brother, that it is I who am protecting him." Her eyes held his steadily and her husky voice left no room for him to disagree.

He held her gaze. "*I* know you are not a little girl any longer, Rahab. You are a woman of strength and courage. But Father—"

She said, "I want you to go to see Sala and arrange someplace where we can meet privately."

"Rahab, the city is stuffed with people! There is no private place anywhere."

"What about our roof?"

He shook his head. "With the weather growing warmer, there is always someone up there."

"There must be some way to do this," she cried despairingly.

He thought for a long minute, then said, "Sometimes the best place to hide is out in the open. Suppose I take you to the market, to that jeweler's shop that you and Atene like to look at. I can tell Sala that you will be there at noon. If you pull your headscarf forward over your face, perhaps no one will recognize you. At least you will have a chance to see each other and to talk."

"That would be fine." She smiled as she had not smiled in quite some time. "Just seeing him and talking to him will be something. Thank you, Shemu!"

He looked at her and a return smile tugged at the corners of his mouth. "When you look like that, Rahab, I don't think any man could deny you."

She laughed. "I don't care about other men. I only care about Sala."

"I know he loves you—he told me so. But I don't know what kind of future you can have together, my sister. Will his family accept you, you who have Canaanite blood in your veins? And if they don't, will Sala—a lord among his own people—be content to settle down as a farmer with your family?"

Rahab had spent many night hours thinking about what had happened to her and to Sala during the time they had been together in Jericho, and now she answered her brother: "I believe in Yahweh, Shemu. I believe He saved me from the slavers. I believe He saved me from the king. I think He always wanted Sala and me to be together. Sala says Yahweh has a mission for us. We don't know exactly what it is, but we must be alert and listen for His voice. Yahweh will make things right for us if we do as He wishes."

"You really do believe in this Yahweh, Rahab."

"I do. And I think perhaps He has a mission for you as well."

Shemu looked down at the barrel of barley he had been inspecting, then back up to Rahab. "Perhaps you are right," he said softly. "Atene has told me about the Israelite Abraham, how Yahweh gave him and his wife a child in their old age. Perhaps it is not a coincidence that Atene conceived only after she prayed to Him. I would like to know more about Him, and I know she would too."

Rahab's heart flooded with joy. "I am so glad, my brother, that you feel this way! I want to know more too."

He bent and kissed her on the forehead.

Voices sounded outside the storeroom door.

Rahab said urgently, "You must go to find Sala now, before someone sees you and wants to go with you."

"All right." He patted her on the shoulder, and she watched as he made his way through the barrels and out the storeroom door.

Sala couldn't believe his luck when Shemu walked into the front room of the inn just as Sala was going out. The two men stopped and said each other's names in surprise. Then they both spoke at once.

Shemu said, "I have been looking for you."

Sala said, "How is Rahab? Is she all right? Did anyone else in the family find out about the spies?"

They grinned sheepishly and Sala said, "Let's go for a walk."

Shemu spoke first, answering Sala's question. "Everything went smoothly. I held the rope while Rahab watched the door for me. We had them on their way in no time. But my father has been protective of her, not letting her out of the house, and she sent me here to see if I could arrange a meeting between you."

Relief flooded through Sala at this and he grinned broadly. "That is wonderful news. I have been so anxious to see her, but I haven't been able to think of a way to get word to her."

"If you will go to the jeweler's shop in the market, the one across from the tool shop, I will have her there at noontime."

Sala couldn't hide his disappointment. "In the middle of the marketplace? Can't we meet on your roof again?"

"No, too many people are using it now. Besides . . ." Shemu

gave him a calculating look. "I'm not sure if I want my sister to be alone with you."

Sala couldn't hide his disappointment. He didn't just want to talk to Rahab. He wanted to feel her in his arms, he wanted to—

He sighed. "Perhaps you are right."

"I heard that your father was arrested. How did that happen?"

"It was because Gideon and Isaac were seen at the inn, and my father had taken them away from the wine shop. Someone reported him to the guards as an Israelite spy himself. He was taken to military quarters for questioning. Fortunately, Rahab's tale that the spies had been in her house and had left the day before helped to convince the commander that my father wasn't involved with them. They ended up letting him go. But it was an unpleasant experience, and he owes Rahab for saving him as well as saving Gideon and Isaac."

"Good. I'm glad he realizes that."

Sala stopped walking for a moment and put his hand on Shemu's arm. "Thank you for doing this for us. And thank you for your help in saving my people from discovery."

Shemu nodded and the two men continued to walk on, each concerned with their own thoughts. Finally Shemu said in a low voice, "I must confess I am curious about this God of yours. After four years of marriage Atene is finally with child, and it didn't happen until she prayed to Yahweh."

Sala slapped Shemu on the shoulder in congratulations. "That is wonderful news. I am happy for you both and I am also happy you want to learn about Yahweh. He has touched you and Atene, I think. He wants you to come to Him."

Shemu shrugged uncomfortably and Sala did not pursue the topic. When they reached the main road, Sala said, "I think I will go along to the market now. Can you go to fetch Rahab?"

"I will," Shemu said.

The two men parted and Sala stood watching Rahab's brother stride away, every part of him, body and soul, reverberating with happiness that soon he would see her.

Every minute seemed like an hour to Rahab as she awaited Shemu's return. When he finally came up to the roof where she was sewing with some of her sisters-in-law, she flew to him.

"Get your headscarf," he said as she followed him down the stairs. "We're going right now."

Another one of her sisters-in-law was in their bedroom suckling her baby when Rahab came in. "Where are you going?" she asked when Rahab grabbed her most concealing headscarf.

"Just outdoors for a bit," Rahab called back as she descended the stairs to where Shemu awaited her.

Kata was in the front room, folding clothes with the help of a few of her granddaughters. She looked up sharply as Shemu and Rahab came through on their way to the door.

"Where are you going?" she asked in bewilderment.

"I'm taking Rahab out for some air, Mother. She's been cooped up in the house for too long."

"But your father—!"

"Don't worry, Mama," Rahab said, "I'm in disguise."

She pulled the headscarf so far forward that it almost covered her eyes and followed Shemu out the door before Kata could reply.

Rahab didn't say anything as she walked closely behind Shemu on their way to the market. She was happy about seeing Sala, unhappy they could not be alone, and worried about what he might have to tell her of the Israelite attack.

Deep in her heart, Rahab was conflicted about the coming

confrontation between the Israelites and the people of Jericho. It was hard for her to imagine what such a battle might be like. She believed what Sala had told her about Yahweh's desire for the Israelites to return to Canaan after their long captivity in Egypt. She believed they were His people, and she wanted to be one of them.

But when she thought of all the people who were packed into Jericho. All of the men and women and children . . . how could it be possible they all would die? It was an idea her mind struggled to understand but could not encompass.

All of these thoughts disappeared the moment she saw Sala. He was hard to miss, he was so much taller than most of the men around him. He spied her almost as soon as she saw him and, even though she was almost covered by the headscarf, his face lit up with a blinding smile.

He was in front of the jeweler's shop and, aside from the grin, he made no move toward her. She continued to follow closely behind Shemu.

When they had reached the shop, Shemu acted surprised. "Arut! What are you doing here?"

Sala said, "Just passing the time until I have to meet a friend. How are you, Shemu?"

"Very well. I've come to pick out a piece of jewelry for my wife and I've brought my sister with me to help me choose."

"Good idea," Sala said, nodding toward Rahab's partially covered face.

Shemu said, "I also have to pick up something for my father in the tool maker's shop. Can my sister stay with you while I go in? She has no interest in tools."

"Of course," Sala said with grave courtesy.

"I won't be long." Shemu gave a warning look at Sala, then ducked across the street.

"Let us move into the shade over there," Sala said.

Rahab nodded, not trusting herself to speak.

They walked over to the small patch of shade provided by the overlapping awning of one of the stalls and stopped, facing each other.

Sala's expression was as intense as his voice. "I have missed you so much, Rahab. And I've been worried about you."

"I've missed you too," she answered.

He looked around. "Can't you at least push that headscarf up so I can see your eyes?"

She did as he asked.

He gave her a crooked smile. "When I'm away from you, I think that you can't possibly be as wonderful as I remember, and then when I see you again I discover that my memory was dim compared to the reality."

Rahab smiled back at him. "I feel the same way about you."

He laughed at this, then pressed his lips together. "I wish we could be alone!"

"I wish it too," she said, a tremble in her voice.

He inhaled deeply, as if to steady himself. Before he could speak, however, there was a rush of movement by the crowd and a rising rumble of excitement. Rahab and Sala looked in the direction in which the crowd had begun to move and Sala asked someone what was happening.

"There is a proclamation from the king," came the answer. "And there is a unit of guards marching down the main street!"

Sala put his arm around Rahab's shoulder, to keep her from being pushed by the now thrusting crowd. To his relief he saw Shemu come out of the shop across the way. Shemu fought his way to them and took Rahab away from Sala and into his own protective embrace. He said, "Someone came into the shop and said there was a proclamation from the king."

"That's what we heard," Sala returned.

The two men looked at each other across Rahab's head. Then Shemu said, "You go and find out what the proclamation is about. I will take Rahab into the jewelry store to keep her safe."

Sala nodded and slid gracefully into the moving mass of people while Shemu guided Rahab into the shop to wait.

They remained inside until Sala came back some twenty minutes later with a report. "I missed the proclamation but I heard about it from some people who were there. The Israelites have crossed the Jordan and are encamped five miles south of Jericho. The king has ordered the military to take their battle stations on the wall and he urges the city not to panic. He says Jericho is the best protected city in all of Canaan and it will never fall."

Shemu looked stunned. "They crossed the river? But it's still in full flood!"

"Nothing is impossible for Yahweh," Sala replied soberly. "Did you not know that He parted the sea for us when we escaped from Egypt? Jericho is doomed. Shemu, it is vital that you make certain your family knows what to do when the attack comes. They will be protected but they must be inside your house."

Rahab said urgently, "Shemu, I want Sala and his father to come stay with us. They are Israelites and we will be safer if we have them there to vouch for us."

Shemu gave Sala a grim look.

Rahab put a hand on his arm and said his name.

Shemu shrugged. "All right. You had better come."

"How will you explain our presence to your father?" Sala asked. "He does not know about your bargain with Gideon and Isaac. Or does he?"

"He knows nothing," Shemu replied. "I will tell him you have volunteered to vouch for us if our family is endangered, that you have some power with the Israelite leader."

"I will speak to my father and see if I can get him to agree to move in with your family."

The two men looked at each other for a long time. Then, "That will be best," said Shemu.

Thirty-Three

IT WAS A WEEK BEFORE THE GUARDS ON THE WALLS OF
Jericho spied the first of the Israelites coming from the southeast.
For an entire day the grim-faced guards watched as thousands
of men, women, and children, along with their animals and
supplies, made camp no more than a mile away from the city
gates. Since civilians were not allowed on the walls, the people
of the city had to rely upon the information that trickled down
from the guards when they changed watches. The size of the
enemy grew larger with each retelling.

"They say it's a huge army," Mepu informed his family as
they all crowded together in the front room of the house to hear
what he had learned in the city.

"The largest force in the world could not batter down these
walls," one of Rahab's brothers said with staunch bravado.

As if a signal had been given, everyone in the room turned
to look at Nahshon and Sala, who were standing at the back of
the room, arms folded and leaning against the wall. It had taken
Sala some convincing to get his father to move to Rahab's house,
but Nahshon had finally agreed that he owed it to her for saving
the lives of the Israelite spies. Father and son had been sleeping
up on the roof for the last few days.

Sala and Nahshon returned the Canaanite gazes, their faces
expressionless, and the family turned back to Mepu.

He said in answer to his son's expression of confidence, "I suppose we shall find out soon enough how strong our walls are. I doubt these Israelites have come here just to look at us."

One of the smaller children, sensing the tension in the room, began to whimper. His mother picked him up and soothed him with gentle words.

Shemu said, "Sala, what do *you* think will happen?"

Everyone turned once more to look at the man Shemu had singled out.

Sala did not stir from his relaxed pose against the wall. "I cannot tell you how the walls will fall, only that they will. And I urge you to remember that if you and all your family are not inside this house when it happens, we will not be able to protect you." His eyes moved around the room. "Nobody is to leave the immediate area of the house until this is over. Is that clear?"

Rahab's brother, the one who had made the comment about the walls, snorted derisively.

Rahab said sharply, "Don't be a fool, Mattan. We have plenty of food and water in the house. There is no reason for you to venture abroad."

Mattan rounded on her. "You call me a fool? You think these two Israelites will be able to protect us from an entire army? It's the walls that will protect us, my sister, not these"—he waved his hand disdainfully toward Nahshon and Sala—"*merchants.*"

Shemu's "Don't speak to our sister that way," clashed with Sala's hot reply, "No walls in the world will protect you from the will of Yahweh!"

"Yahweh," Mattan muttered and shook his head in disgust.

Mepu said with all the authority of the patriarch, "It is my wish that every member of the family stay close to this house until the confrontation is over. I want to hear no more discussion on this matter."

Silence greeted his pronouncement.

"Good," Mepu said. "All we can do now is wait and see what happens next."

What happened next confounded the entire population of Jericho. The following dawn they were awakened by the cacophony of horns being blown more loudly than anyone believed possible. The sound came from outside the walls and Mepu's immediate conclusion was that the Israelites were attacking. He forbade anyone to leave the house and the men crowded into the upstairs bedroom where the window from which Rahab had lowered the spies would give them a view.

Mepu and Shemu stationed themselves at the window and for a long time had nothing to report. The noise of the horns was obviously coming closer but it wasn't until the first of the lines of Israelite soldiers came around the bend and began to follow the city's north wall that they were able to see anything.

"What—" Mepu put his hand on his son's arm. "What are they doing?"

"Wait," Shemu said.

The room was filled with a silence so tense it seemed almost palpable. Then Shemu said, "The Israelite army seems to be circling the city!"

"Let me see." Mattan crowded Shemu out of the way. "Why are they doing this?" he demanded as he looked out.

As they spoke, the din of the horns grew even louder. Shemu took back his spot from Mattan, and he and his father remained at the window as the noise of the horns grew nearer and nearer. When the blasts had reached a level that was almost deafening, Mepu turned to his son and shouted, "What are they doing now?"

Shemu turned and yelled to Sala, who was out in the hall with Rahab, "Sala, get in here and take a look!"

Everyone made way for Sala and Lord Nahshon, who was right behind his son. The two Israelites exchanged places with Shemu and Mepu and leaned out the window to have a look.

When Sala saw the procession making its way around the walls, his breath caught and a chill ran up and down his spine. Carried by priests, the ark of the covenant was just going past under their window. Seven priests processed before it, blowing on huge ram's horns. In front of the priests, a short distance away, Sala could see a seeming endless phalanx of marching warriors.

He glanced at his father and saw that Lord Nahshon's eyes were bright with unshed tears. They remained where they were, ignoring the questions that were raining on them from behind, until they saw the massed men of the rear guard marching at a distance behind the ark. Then they turned to face the family gathered in the room.

The eeriest thing about the whole procession was the silence. None of the marching men spoke to each other, or even called out a taunt to the guards on the walls. Only the blasts of the horns disturbed the early morning air.

"Well, what is happening?" It was Mepu's voice sounding both irritated and frightened.

Sala looked to his father as the proper person to answer Mepu's question.

Lord Nahshon said with calm certainty, "This procession is a statement by Yahweh that He is the one true God and that the walls of this city will fall before Him."

The family members shuffled their feet and looked at one another with a mixture of fear and disbelief. Then Mepu said, "What is that thing they are carrying?"

Lord Nahshon explained to everyone about the ark of the covenant.

Silence greeted his account of the tablets brought down the mountain by Moses.

Then Mattan swung around to glare at Rahab, who had come into the room in the wake of Sala. "You believe in this god who gives stone tablets to his people? And you had the audacity to call *me* foolish?"

Rahab looked back at her brother, then she let her eyes move slowly from face to face around the room. When she had gathered up everyone's attention, she said, "The tablets contain laws for the people of Yahweh to live by. Does not a God who cares that His people live their lives in goodness sound more real than a god who fights with other gods and expects a woman to sleep with a horrid old king because it is supposed to make the crops grow?" Her voice grew more heated as she said these last words. "The crops will grow because when Yahweh created the world, He put it into their nature that they should grow. I think the Israelites will win because Yahweh wants them to have this land and live their lives in the goodness that He expects of them."

Sala stared at Rahab, his heart glowing with pride. Moses himself could not have answered better, he thought. He glanced at his father and found him regarding Rahab also, and for the first time Sala saw respect in his father's eyes.

Lord Nahshon said, "We must wait and see what will happen next." He touched the scarlet cord hanging in the window. "We have put this here to show our army that this house is not to be touched. Stay within these walls and wait."

The Israelites processed once around the city each day for the next five days, following the exact pattern as on the first day. The rams' head horns were the only sound that came from the mass of warriors, who were parading just far enough from the walls for the guards to be unable to reach them with arrows. Some of the guards wanted to try slingshots, but Akiz, the military commander, forbade it. He, along with the king and his council, thought it would be a better strategy to show no sign that the strange processions had concerned them.

On the night of the sixth day, Sala told Mepu that he should gather the family next door into his house. "The number seven has great significance for my people," he told Rahab's father. "I think whatever is going to happen will happen tomorrow."

Mepu, like most of the citizens in Jericho, had been made increasingly anxious, even frightened, by the silent processions. He agreed and went to tell his brother and his brother's family to pack up some basic belongings and come next door.

Rahab and Sala may have been living in the same house, but over the past week they had had little chance to speak to each other and no chance to be alone. Rahab had found their imposed distance hard, but she comforted herself with the thought that at least she could see his face and know he was safe. For now it was a blessing just to meet his eyes across a crowd of people and see their warmth and know that he loved her.

The only people who got any sleep the night before the seventh day of the processions were the children. There was scarcely room for the adults to stretch out and, even if they could, everyone was in a state of high anxiety. When the first light of dawn stained the sky, the men crowded into the third-floor bedroom and Mepu and Shemu once more took up their stations at the window.

The sound of the rams' horns floated to their ears at the usual time, growing louder and louder as the procession came closer to the north side of the city. As the gathered families waited, the front guard of warriors, the priests, the ark of the covenant, and the rear guard of warriors marched as they had for the past six days—in silence, with only the sound of the horns breaking the quiet of the morning.

Lord Nahshon and Sala had been standing behind Mepu and Shemu as this was happening and, when the last of the Israelite army had passed them by, the two Canaanites turned to confront Sala.

"I thought you said something would happen today," Mepu said. "You have gotten us all into a panic and nothing is different!"

Sala knew he couldn't explain his feeling to Mepu. He couldn't even explain it to himself. He just *knew* that this was the day the Israelites would attack.

"Wait," he said softly to Mepu. "Give it some time."

They waited, listening to the blowing of the horns as the procession marched along the eastern wall toward the gate in the south. On past days the Israelite procession had turned at the gate and proceeded back to its camp, making not a single warlike gesture toward the city.

An hour passed and the men in the room realized that something was indeed different from the previous six days. The sound of the horns had not stopped. In fact, they were coming closer.

Mepu and Shemu looked out the window again and were stunned to see the front guard of Israelite warriors approaching once more.

The Israelites marched around the city twice. Then three times. Then four.

The marching and the silence were terrifying. What was happening? What were they planning to do? What kind of battle plan was this?

No one knew. The king met with his council, and they did not know. The military commander met with his chief officers and they did not know. Finally Akiz decided to post even more men on top of the walls. Something was going to happen this day, and the commander was determined to have his men in position to counter whatever attack the enemy might be planning.

Seven times did the Israelites process around the city, and on the seventh time the parade passed under Mepu's window, Sala removed the scarlet cord from the window and told his father that one of them should stand by the window and wave it while the other should take up a position by the front door.

Lord Nahshon agreed and volunteered to take the post by the door.

"Get away from the window," Sala told Mepu and Shemu. "If men should break into the room, I must be the first one they see."

"All right," Shemu agreed and he put his hand on his father's elbow to lead him away.

"Will you send Rahab to me?" Sala asked. "If Gideon and Isaac are the ones to come into the house, they should see her also."

Shemu hesitated, then nodded. "All right. I'll send her."

They went out the door and Sala could hear Mepu asking, "Who are Gideon and Isaac?"

Rahab had just joined Sala at the window when a terrifying shout issued from the throats of all the Israelites in the procession, a shout so thunderous it seemed to be roaring out of the sky above. Rahab couldn't help herself, she clutched Sala's arm in terror.

It was when the shout was at its loudest that Yahweh made Himself known. The ground under the city began to rumble.

Rahab felt the floor under her feet rock and she saw the walls of the room begin to ripple. Sala grabbed her, flung her to the floor, and covered her body with his.

For as long as she lived, Rahab would never forget what happened next. The noise was louder than the worst thunder she could ever imagine. Then came a cracking noise, as if something huge was shattering. The whole house shook, and then there was a rumbling, sliding sound, and the back wall of the house, the wall which formed the north wall of the city, began to come apart.

Rahab lay on the trembling floor with Sala's protective body over her and prayed to Yahweh to save them and to save her family. She had no doubt that this was the work of Yahweh. He was making the walls of Jericho fall down.

When the rumbling finally slowed then died away, the sound of screaming took its place. The noise was bloodcurdling, the sound of trapped men, women, and children crying out for help.

"I think we can get up now," Sala said in her ear. He lifted himself off her and helped her to her feet. Without speaking, the two of them went to the back wall, which, while cracked, still stood. Sala had the red cord gripped in his hand.

Rahab looked out the still-intact window and saw that the back wall of her house was the only wall still standing. The Israelite army was pouring into the city over the mass of fallen bricks from the destroyed wall. The bricks had actually formed a ramp from the top of the stone revetment to the ground, fatally exposing the city to its enemies.

Sala took the red cord and, leaning out the window, he began to wave it wildly. Rahab grabbed the back of his tunic, to keep him from losing his balance and falling out. He was still waving it when Shemu came pounding into the room.

"It's all right," he said to Sala. "Isaac and Gideon are here. They are going to get us out of the city, so come quickly."

"Has anyone been hurt?" Sala demanded.

"Everyone in the house is safe. But we need to get away as quickly as possible."

Sala put an arm around Rahab, pulling her close to his side. "Are you all right?"

"Yes." She leaned against him briefly, drawing from his strength and courage.

Shemu came over and tilted her chin up so he could look into her eyes. "Thank you," he said. "Thank you, my sister, for saving my wife and my child. Thank you for saving all of us. I think you have indeed been blessed by Yahweh."

He bent and kissed the top of her head.

"Come," Sala said, his arm still around Rahab's shoulders. "It's time for us to go."

Thirty-Four

NO ONE IN RAHAB'S FAMILY, ADULT OR CHILD, WOULD ever forget that escape from Jericho. The crumbling walls had buried most of the people in the Lower City, trapping the living as well as the dead under piles of bricks. Screams of pain and terror reverberated throughout the dust-filled air. The Israelites, who were pouring into the city by the thousands, were cutting down those in the streets who had been fortunate enough to escape the toppling wall. All of the guards who had been posted on the walls were buried, and the remaining Jericho military were hopelessly disorganized and defenseless before the Israelite onslaught.

Sala walked close beside Rahab, both of them holding the hands of children. They climbed over piles of fallen bricks, listening to the frantic cries of the injured and trapped. The Israelites had forced open the gate, which was still standing, and Sala kept watching to make certain that the family group stayed together so they could all get out safely. Isaac and Gideon were walking before them, calling out in Hebrew so the armed Israelite warriors would know who they were. If someone lagged behind, they might not make it.

Sala could still hear the screaming as they emerged out onto the plain and began to follow Gideon and Isaac toward the

Israelite camp a mile away. The two spies took them to a grouping of tents set up at the eastern end of the camp.

Gideon told Sala, "These tents are for your people. You will find food and water in the smallest tent and our women have already baked you some bread. Stay with them, Sala. Isaac and I must get back to Joshua."

Sala thanked him and turned to Rahab, who was standing by his side. They both were still holding the children's hands.

"What did he say?" she asked as Gideon moved off.

"He said these tents are for your family and that there is food and water in the little tent over there. We should start to get everyone settled, I think."

Rahab's face was white and strained, her eyes deeply shadowed. "I can still hear the screaming," she said.

Sala's heart was wrung with pity as he looked down at her. "You can't, really. You just think you can."

She shook her head slightly. "I don't think I'll ever stop hearing it," she said.

The needs of the children helped to keep Rahab from dwelling on the horror of what was happening in Jericho. Her little cousins and nieces and nephews were frightened and tired and thirsty and hungry and all of the families had to decide which tents to take and whom to share them with. In the end the women and children took three of the tents and the men and the older boys shared the last two.

After food and water had been distributed and the children settled in their own places, the sun was setting. Rahab and Atene walked a little distance from the encampment, stopped, and looked toward Jericho. There was a red glow in the sky where the city should be.

"What can that red light be?" Atene said. "It can't be the sunset—Jericho is to the north of us, not the west."

The two girls stared at the city, then Rahab said, "It's fire, Atene. They have set the city on fire."

Atene inhaled sharply. "If you had not saved those two spies, Rahab, we all would have died in there."

"Yes."

They stood in silence, watching as the flames leaped higher into the rapidly darkening sky.

"The walls fell down," Atene said at last, her voice trembling. "The Israelites shouted and the walls just . . . fell."

"Yahweh made them collapse."

"There is no other explanation."

Rahab turned away from the fire-lit sky and asked Atene the question that had been in her mind all day. "I wonder why Yahweh wanted me to be saved?"

Atene slipped an arm around Rahab's shoulders. "There must be a reason why you are important to Him, Rahab. And because you are, all of us have been saved as well. Because you taught me about Him, I am going to have a child."

A child . . . The word resonated in Rahab's mind. *How wonderful to have a child. How wonderful to bring life into the world in the midst of all this suffering and death. My child . . . mine and Sala's . . .*

She closed her eyes and hugged the thought to herself.

Perhaps it is our unborn child who is important to Yahweh. For the first time all day, Rahab's lips tilted in a smile. They weren't even married yet and she was planning the importance of their child!

She put her arm around Atene's waist. "Both of us have been

blessed, and I think Yahweh would like us to tell our family how He saved them. In thanksgiving for their lives, they must become worshippers of Yahweh and put aside the false gods of Canaan. They must all become Israelites."

"They will," Atene said with utter confidence. "They will."

The Israelites did not remain long in their camp south of Jericho. The silver and gold and bronze they had taken from Baal's temple and the homes of the nobles went into the treasury. Following the orders of Joshua, they had not robbed any of the houses in the Lower City or taken any of the food, so they could move quickly since they weren't burdened down with loot.

Jericho had been burned to the ground along with all the people in it.

After the last of the warriors had returned to camp, leaving behind the smoking ruin of what had once been a living city, Sala wandered among them, speaking to some of the ordinary soldiers as they cleaned their weapons. He was surprised to discover that everyone seemed to know who he was and the part he had played in saving the lives of Gideon and Isaac. They told him that before the battle Joshua had given orders to his commanders that Rahab was to be spared. That order had, of course, been passed down to the rank and file.

Sala was pleased that Joshua had protected Rahab, but he was not pleased by Joshua's choice of words. In his orders Joshua had referred to her as "Rahab, the harlot who lives in the city walls." And now all the men in the camp were calling her *Rahab, the harlot*.

In vain did Sala insist Joshua had misunderstood, that he must have heard a garbled version of Rahab's role as hierodule from Gideon and Isaac, that she was a virtuous woman and most definitely *not* a harlot.

Sala could tell by the shared smiles and raised eyebrows that his explanation was not finding fertile ground. The men thought he was trying to protect Rahab's reputation. Sala even brought the subject up in a private meeting he had with Joshua two days after the battle, but Joshua assured him that he didn't care what Rahab had been, that she had acted as an agent of Yahweh and he would gladly welcome her into their midst.

During that conversation Joshua also invited Sala to join his military staff. The invitation had stunned Sala, and he had managed to say something courteous about how honored he was and how he would think about it carefully.

When he left Joshua he went to the tent he shared with his father and, lying stretched out on one of the mats, he did think about it.

He was tempted. To serve under Joshua, the successor to Moses, the commander who would retake Canaan for Yahweh's people, was an awe-inspiring opportunity. But even as he pictured himself leading men into battle, Sala knew he would not accept Joshua's offer. His future lay with Rahab and he would never ask her to live among people who thought she was a harlot. The thought of what the men were saying made his blood boil.

He decided, however, that he might be able to make *some* use of Joshua's invitation to join the army and he remained in the tent, waiting until his father should return.

Sala and Nahshon had been staying in the Israelite camp, not on the outskirts with Rahab's family. He had seen her only briefly but they had not spoken—she always seemed to be surrounded by children. Anyway, he had to speak to his father before he could approach her about what was important to them both. And he thought Joshua had just put a weapon into his hands.

Lord Nahshon came into the tent a few hours later. When he saw Sala, he groaned and lowered himself to his own mat. "I cannot wait to get home to my own bed. I am too old for sleeping on the hard ground. I want my nice, soft mattress."

Sala laughed and sat up cross-legged to face his father. "Home," he said. "It has seemed very far away this last month."

"It certainly has. But we have done good work, my son. By the time Joshua is finished, Canaan will belong to the Israelites, as Yahweh always intended it should."

Sala agreed, took a long drink out of a water skin, then told his father about his conversation with Joshua. He ended with the commander's invitation to him to join the army as part of Joshua's staff.

"I don't believe it's because he thinks I'm so brilliant; I think it's rather that he would like to have an Israelite who has always lived in this country on his staff."

Lord Nahshon pushed himself up on his elbow, his brows drawn together. "What did you answer him?"

"I said I would think about it."

Fear glittered in Nahshon's eyes. "Sala . . . you are my only son. Your responsibility is to me."

Sala just looked back at his father and did not reply.

"It was always expected that you would return home after this mission was finished. Ramac is an Israelite city, one of the few that has remained so since over half our people followed Joseph into Egypt. It is the only Israelite port in Canaan. It's important to the interests of our people that it remain a power on the Great Sea. We need you at home, Sala. Joshua has enough men without you."

Sala said, "Joshua told me he would accept Rahab into our midst as one of us. He said she was an agent of Yahweh."

Lord Nahshon's nostrils flared. "It always comes back to Rahab, doesn't it, Sala?"

Sala said softly, "I cannot go home unless I marry her and bring her with me. I will not leave her behind."

Lord Nahshon lay back down, crossing his arms under his head. There was a long silence. Finally he said, with resignation in his voice, "I have changed my mind about Rahab. She is a remarkable young woman and I think Joshua was right when he said she was an agent of Yahweh." He pushed himself to a sitting position and looked at Sala. "I would be honored to have her as my daughter."

Happiness flooded through all of Sala's body. He wanted to leap to his feet and shout for joy, but he contented himself with saying, "Thank you, Father. Thank you. She will be a good daughter to you, I know she will."

"I hope so," Lord Nahshon replied, and Sala ignored the tiny note of doubt that sounded in his father's voice.

"I'll get one of Joshua's priests to marry us," Sala said, jumping to his feet as if he was going to run out the door and find the priest immediately.

"Sala!"

He turned to look back at his father.

"Come back in here. You must get her father's permission first. And Rahab may not want to be married in a war camp; she might wish to wait until we return to Ramac where the ceremony can be done with all the correct rituals."

Sala didn't think so, but he didn't want to push his father too much. He summoned up his most agreeable voice. "I'll ask Rahab what she wants to do and I'll abide by her decision."

"It will be her father's decision, Sala. Now, what about the rest of her family? What are *they* going to do?"

"Shemu told me that their farm is still intact. Joshua didn't raid south of the river crossing."

"That is excellent news." Sala saw the relief on his father's face and realized Nahshon had been afraid he would be saddled with Rahab's entire family.

Nahshon said, "Come back in here and sit down. We will speak to Mepu tomorrow morning. I have a few ideas that I want to sleep on."

Sala exerted all the self-control he was capable of and agreed.

The following afternoon Rahab and Atene were sitting in the shade cast by their tent watching a group of little girls play with the dolls some of the Israelite women had given them. When they saw Mepu and Shemu coming toward them, they both started to get up.

"Sit, sit," Mepu said, waving them back down as he came up to them. The two men joined them in the shade, careful not to block the women's view of the children.

Mepu got straight to the reason for his visit. "Rahab, Sala's father has asked for you in marriage to his son and I have agreed. He has further asked if Sala may take you to live in Ramac, and I have agreed to that as well. I hope you are comfortable with this arrangement."

Rahab's smile was more blinding than the sun reflecting off the heads of the children. "Oh, Papa, thank you! Of course I am comfortable with your arrangement!"

Mepu smiled back, as did Shemu. Mepu went on, "There is one more thing to decide, and Lord Nahshon has left the choice to me. So I am asking you, do you wish to be married now, by one of Joshua's priests, or do you wish to wait until you get to Ramac."

"Now," Rahab said. "I want to get married now."

Atene laughed.

Rahab turned and gave her friend a tight hug. "Oh, Atene! I am so happy!"

"And I am happy for you, my dear, dear sister." She looked at her husband over Rahab's shoulder. "What are *we* going to do, Shemu? Surely you're not planning to remain with these Israelites?"

Shemu said, "I think we must all be called Israelites now, no matter where we might be. But following an army is no life for a family. We have learned that our farm was not disturbed, so we can return home."

Atene's smile was almost as dazzling as Rahab's. "That will be good."

Rahab looked at her father. "But without Jericho as a market, where will you sell your wine, Papa?"

Mepu was looking younger than he had in months. "Lord Nahshon told us there is a small Israelite community to the south, at Jerusalem. We can sell some wine to them. But even better, Lord Nahshon has offered to take most of our wine and sell it into Egypt." He chuckled. "It seems we will be following my original plan after all."

Shemu grinned. "Lord Nahshon has asked me to supervise all of his wine trade, *and* he will pay me a handsome salary to do so."

Rahab and Atene looked at each other, almost dazed by all this good news.

"We won't be completely separated then," Atene said.

An angry squeal came from the group of children and Rahab looked over to see that two of them had decided they wanted the same doll. She jumped up to smooth the quarrel and soon had the children playing happily again.

Mepu had risen. "So, shall I go and give Lord Nahshon my answer?"

Rahab ran to give her father a hug. "Yes," she said into his ear. "And don't be too long about it!'

He laughed.

It was almost midnight when Rahab slipped out of her tent. Her father and Lord Nahshon had made all the marriage arrangements earlier in the day. There had been no talk of the money and goods that the new husband's father traditionally gave to the father of the bride before a marriage could be finalized. The business arrangement struck earlier between Nahshon and Mepu would suffice; it was going to be profitable for both men and their families.

Nor was there talk of a betrothal. They were not living in normal times and both fathers agreed to bypass the betrothal so the children could marry and leave for Ramac as soon as possible. As soon as possible turned out to be the following day and arrangements were made with one of Joshua's priests.

Rahab was so happy and excited that she couldn't sleep. In the morning she would get her heart's desire; she would marry Sala. She felt a twinge of sorrow when she thought about leaving her family, but it was only a small drop in the great sea of her happiness.

The night was deeply silent; everyone was asleep. She crept out of the tent and walked a little distance from the encampment, shivering in the chill night air. Smoke was still rising from the ruins of Jericho, but Rahab did not look in that direction. Instead she faced east, toward the place where the Great Sea lay, where her new home would be. She looked up into the sky and her breath caught at the magnificent display in the blackness of the overreaching heavens. She felt as if Yahweh was shining each and every one of those brilliant starry lights just for her.

He had been so good to her. He had saved her family from destruction and given them a future. Most of all, He had given her Sala, without whom her life would be like a sky filled with heavy dark clouds and rain. Instead she had the stars.

"Thank You, Yahweh," she whispered into the cool night air. "Thank You for choosing me to be Your servant."

A soft step sounded behind her and she turned to see Sala come up to her side. She smiled up at him. "You couldn't sleep either?"

"No." He put his arm around her and she rested her head on his shoulder.

They stood for a while in silence, their eyes upon the dazzling blanket of stars. Then he bent his head and buried his lips in her hair. "I love you so much. You have been through so many terrible things, Rahab, but now you have me to take care of you. I will make you happy. I promise you that. I will make you happy."

She slid her arm around his waist and turned her body into his. "I know you will, Sala. And I will do my best to make you happy too."

"You make me happy just by existing," he said, his voice muffled by her hair.

She tilted her head to look up at him. "I know one thing that would make me happy."

"And what is that, my love?"

"A ride in a boat."

He laughed, a free, carefree laugh that lifted her heart and made her smile.

He said, "I will buy you your own little sailboat and you can go out whenever you want. And if ever any man questions your freedom, you will say that you are Rahab and you saved the warriors of Israel."

She chuckled. "I will remember that."

"Yahweh has been good to us," he said, his voice suddenly grave.

"I know. Remember how you once told me that I had to listen for Him?"

"Yes."

"That is what we both must do, now and for the rest of our lives. Listen for Him and do His will."

"Yes. We will always do that."

He held her close to him, so close that she could feel the beating of his heart through their clothing. Then with deliberate resolution, he moved away. "Tomorrow night we will be man and wife, but for now I think it's best if we go in."

She stood on tiptoe and kissed him on the cheek. "All right."

He picked up her hand and the two of them walked side by side back to the camp.

A Letter to My Readers

RAHAB AND SALA'S GREAT DESTINY, OF COURSE, WAS TO be among the direct forebears of Jesus. We know this because their names are listed with Christ's ancestors at the beginning of the gospel of Matthew: "Salmon the father of Boaz by Rahab . . ."

The most amazing thing about Matthew's genealogy is that it actually includes the names of women. This was highly unusual for Jewish pedigrees. Luke's genealogy of Christ, which names only men, is far more the norm. The reason for the accustomed absence of female names is that in the Jewish world women had no legal rights. From the time of their birth to the time of their death, they were under the command of a man—be it father, husband, or son. It has always seemed to me a wonderful sign of the changes that Jesus brought into the world that a woman's name should appear in His genealogy.

As those of you who have read the book of Joshua know, Rahab's story takes up about five paragraphs, and out of those five paragraphs I've created a book of 85,000 words. One part of Rahab's story in Joshua that intrigued me was the fact that she was a believer in the Israelite God. How did that come to be? I asked myself, and there was my story.

Clearly I had to look elsewhere to get material for my novel and so I investigated whatever information was available on the period. The areas that I looked into were the religion and archeology of Canaan generally and Jericho specifically.

When Jericho was excavated, no written records were discovered. Our knowledge of the city and its culture comes from the other archeological evidence that has been found there. Over the years there has been controversy among archaeologists about the date that Jericho fell. Kathleen Kenyon, who excavated the site in the 1950s and published a book about it—*Digging Up Jericho*—declared that the city was destroyed about 1550 BC, the end of the Middle Bronze Age. The biblical narrative, however, places Joshua in the early part of the Late Bronze Age, about 1400 BC. Needless to say, this difference caused many difficulties for biblical scholars.

The most recently accepted dating of the demise of Jericho and the earthquake that destroyed the city—about 1400 BC, the early part of the Late Bronze Age—can be found in the work of archeologist Bryant G. Wood.

Although we currently have no written records from Jericho, the city of Ugarit on the eastern Mediterranean had great libraries from which a number of scrolls written in early Canaanite were recovered. It is these scrolls that give us the stories of the god Baal, the goddess Asherah, and the fertility religion they embodied. I used the material from Ugarit as the background for the religion that was probably also practiced in Jericho; the ideas of a sacral kingship and a sacred marriage are drawn from these manuscripts.

The biggest difficulty I had in writing the story of Rahab was the dramatically different worldview of the people I was writing about. Joshua and his army were embarking on what Muslims today call *jihad*—the destruction of everyone and everything that does not conform to their own religious practices and belief. We don't approve of *jihad* today—in fact, we deplore it as being against everything the modern Christian believes to be ethical. How was I to make heroes out of people who thought like this? People who thought nothing of killing every man, woman, child, and animal in a city they conquered?

There really is no satisfactory answer to this problem, so I simply tried to create the world of three thousand years ago in a way that would seem coherent and real. You, the reader, will have to judge whether or not I have been successful.

Joan Wolf
January 2012

Reading Group Guide

1. What can you take from the ancient story of Rahab that will apply to your own life in the modern world?
2. How did you feel about this different way of viewing Rahab? She has been known as a prostitute for so long. Did it ever bother you that a prostitute was listed as one of Jesus's ancestors? Did you think the author was successful in explaining how this reputation might not be true?
3. The instructions of the God of the Old Testament often seem to contradict the teachings of Jesus. Certainly it would be hard to imagine Jesus advocating the murder of entire populations. Can you reconcile the two? And if so, how?
4. What is it that Sala sees in Rahab that makes him love her so much? Was it just her beauty or was there something else?
5. What is it about Sala that is so attractive to Rahab? Is it just the fact that he rescued her from the slavers or is it something more?
6. Rahab and Atene both have their prayers answered by God and this is a vital part of their conversion. Did you find these "miracles" came too quickly to be real? Or did they perhaps

remind you of the miracles that Christ worked that resulted
in the conversion of so many of the people of His time—or
miracles in your own life that have strengthened your faith?

7. Obedience to a father was one of the ethical beliefs of almost
every people throughout the world. In the book, Sala feels
that he can never go against his father's wishes, even if it
means breaking his own heart. Can you see why this duty to
a father might be a good thing? Can you see where it might
cause problems for a family and a society?

8. The friendship between Rahab and Atene grows as the book
progresses and is a great help to Rahab. How important do
you think friendship is to most women? Is it as important as
family relationships and if so, how?

9. Fertility religions were practiced throughout the entire
ancient world. Can you see why they might have been so
prevalent and powerful? What does this say about the importance of revelation?

10. What are some of the essentials of a good marriage? Do you
think that Rahab and Sala have them?

Acknowledgments

THERE ARE TWO PEOPLE TO WHOM I OWE A GREAT deal and whom I would like to acknowledge here. The first is my husband, Joe. He is the reason that I turn in clean manuscripts to my editor. He proofreads everything and very little gets by him—it's that Jesuit education, I'm sure. He is also the reason I usually manage to turn in my books on time. He's very good at giving me *that look* at breakfast and asking when I plan to do my writing for the day. Visions of an afternoon at the barn or the mall disappear very quickly under *that look*.

I also must thank my wonderful agent, Natasha Kern. Not only does she sell my books, but she mothers me through the entire process of dealing with their publication. It such a comfort to know that she is only a phone call away.

Thank you, Joe and Natasha.

You've read it as a
biblical tale of courage.
Experience it anew as a
heart-stirring love story.

About the Author

Author photo by J.C. Carley

JOAN WOLF WAS BORN IN NEW YORK CITY BUT HAS LIVED most of her adult life in Connecticut with her husband, two children, and numerous pets. She's the author of *A Reluctant Queen* and *The Road to Avalon,* lauded as "historical fiction at its finest" by *Publisher's Weekly.*

10-22-12 3